MW01602370

Dr. Prepper

Freaky Florida Investigations, Volume 2

Margaret Lashley

Published by Zazzy Ideas, Inc., 2019.

Copyright

What Readers are Saying about Dr Prepper ...

"*The X-Files has found its funny bone!*"

"*Margaret Lashley does not disappoint with the second installment. The only downside is that the book had to end! I can't wait for number three!*"

"*Full of wacky characters, amazing descriptions, and lots of theories of the unknown, this book makes for a funny mystery.*"

"*WOW...Lashley does it again. Installment #2 in this rare book series is another that one reads with a perma-press smile. The laugh out loud banter between the main characters moves almost as fast as the twists, turns and u-turns of the mystery. The situational descriptions of many of the player's actions and activities are unforgettable. Bobbie's unspoken thoughts...are as humorous as what she says out loud. Whodunit? You will not guess until the shocking moment of reveal.*"

"*If you enjoy sci-fi, drama, mystery, comedy and just a tiny tease of romance, then this is for you!*"

"*Rampant with humorous banter and fun interpersonal relationships over a solidly bizarre mystery and great characterization.*"

"*This is a rollicking ride from the very beginning with laugh-out-loud prose, rednecks, weirdos and Tootsie Pops...oh my!*"

Prologue

L ast week, I got shot in the head.

The doctor said I didn't have brain damage. But the things I did afterward make me question whether I should've gotten a second opinion.

First, I let a complete stranger stay in my Grandma Selma's apartment.

Okay, that's not *so* crazy.

But then I spent a week with that same stranger, rambling around Alachua County chasing after Mothman.

Yes, Mothman.

When I finally realized the guy might be a raving lunatic, I did the only sensible thing I could think of.

I ditched my entire life, climbed into his dumpy RV, and headed off to Plant City to help him save the world from an alien invasion.

You're welcome.

Chapter One

I woke up and smelled the coffee.

I cracked open a crusty eye. What I saw in the dim light sent memories of yesterday slamming into my brain like a saltwater tsunami.

Less than twenty-four hours ago, my cousin Earl Shankles had hit me with a family secret that turned my life into a complete dumpster fire.

My father who'd died six months ago wasn't my father. And my mother had run off with Mr. Applewhite, the postman. According to Earl, 37 years ago, I was Mr. Applewhite's "special delivery."

Funny. I didn't feel special.

So, with no one around to point my bastard-child finger at, I did something that a mere week ago I'd have considered totally irrational.

Insane, even.

I ran off and joined the circus.

To be more specific, I joined a monster-chasing, freak-show of a circus led by a man I'd known for all of six days.

From what he'd told me, Nick Grayson was a private investigator, an amateur entomologist, an alternative healer, and a noted—albeit somewhat disgraced—physicist.

If *any* part of what he claimed was true, his credentials blew mine out of the water.

All I brought to the table was a bachelor's degree in art appreciation, a fairly limited knowledge of antiques, and a fairly *un*limited distrust of ... well, pretty much anything that talked.

But I could shoot a gun better than anyone I knew—including Grayson. I'd pinned my hopes on that being enough to convince him to keep me on as a PI intern.

Otherwise, I was totally screwed.

Last night, after leaving my cousin in charge of running my family's auto repair business, I'd jumped out of my old life and into Grayson's RV.

But I hadn't started my life over with a clean slate. Not even close. I'd climbed aboard toting enough baggage to significantly lower the guy's overall gas mileage.

As I lay curled up on the RV's sofa, I thought about my friend Beth-Ann. The last words she'd said to me blasted through my mind like a hurricane siren.

Are you outta your ever-loving gourd?

Maybe I was.

But it didn't matter. It was *way* too late to turn back now.

From the gentle rocking of the RV, I could tell it was rolling down the highway, full steam ahead. I closed my eyes again.

Screw it, I thought. *Life is for living.*

I was a carpetbagger in search of *carpe diem.*

Woohoo. Let the good times roll ....

Chapter Two

It had been way past midnight when Grayson pulled his vintage RV into the parking lot of a Walmart in Inverness, Florida. I'd woken when he stopped, and watched him pass by me silently on his way to his bedroom in the back of the RV.

Exhausted, I'd immediately fallen asleep again on the couch. When I woke up again, it was still dark.

Coffee was on the stove. Amy Winehouse was on the radio.

I fumbled for my cellphone. It was 7:03 a.m. and we were already rolling again.

Ugh.

I dragged myself to sitting and touched the scab in the middle of my forehead. It was almost healed. Not bad for being the target of a ricochet bullet a little over a week ago. I scratched the itchy stubble growing in where my long auburn locks used to be.

My new hairdo was a memento from the overzealous staff at the hospital in Gainesville. They'd shaved my head all the way to my ears, leaving me with a bald spot not even the most ambitious comb-over could hope to cover.

I scanned the RV's tiny kitchen/living room area for Lucky Red. It was the Redman chewing tobacco ball-cap my cousin Earl had lent me to cover my billiard-ball noggin. I spotted it at the end of the couch, perched atop the head of ET, the extraterrestrial. Or in this case, ET, the world's ugliest lamp.

Good one, Grayson.

I leaned over and snatched the cap off ET's gray plaster skull. Lucky Red was my fallback until I could procure another wig. My last one had

met its fate at the hands of a frisky Mothman. But that's another story
....

I yawned and pulled the cap over my stubble. My body reminded me I was in dire need of a shower and at least a half a gallon of coffee.

Sitting on the couch, I could almost reach the coffee pot on the kitchen.

Almost.

I groaned and made a Herculean attempt, but the pot of life-inducing go-juice remained irritatingly out of reach.

I scowled at the stove.

Why couldn't I have gotten some useful skill out of getting shot between the eyes? Like The Incredibles' stretchy arms, maybe. But no. All I got was the knowledge that I had my twin brother's gonad knocking around in my brain.

And, like all men, he was not being particularly helpful.

I grunted, hauled myself off the couch, and poured myself a jittery mugful of coffee. After gulping half of it down, I refilled my mug and wormed my way up to the RV's cab.

A slim man dressed all in black tipped his vintage fedora at me, giving me a glimpse of his own shaved dome.

He shot me a sideways glance. "Morning, sunshine. Sleep well?"

Grayson's cheery, morning-person tone might as well have been fingernails on a chalkboard.

"Yeah," I said. "Like a balloon animal in a cactus garden."

I flopped into the passenger seat beside Grayson and rubbed my sore neck.

Grayson laughed. "I told you to take the bed."

"Chivalrous of you, but no thanks."

The bedroom in Grayson's RV moonlighted as an electromagnetic monster trap. Call me paranoid, but I wasn't keen on the idea of losing consciousness inside a strange man's small, padded, soundproofed bedroom that had enough locks on the door to restrain Godzilla. I already had enough trust issues, thank you very much.

I blew out a sigh. "What happened to Walmart? I was gonna buy a wig."

Grayson fiddled with the knobs on some electronic contraption mounted to the underside of the dash.

"I wanted to get an early start," Grayson said. "Last night I got an update on that incident in Plant City. And, as you country folks are fond of saying, 'Time's a-wastin.'"

I shot him some serious side-eye. "I've never heard *anybody* say that."

I blew out a breath and took another sip of coffee. "Use that awful country accent one more time and I can't be held responsible for where the contents of my coffee mug fling themselves."

Grayson smirked. "I see you're not a morning person. Duly noted."

I looked out the window and almost smiled. Despite the crick in my neck and the grayish weather, it felt good to see the distance widening between me and my dead-end life back in Point Paradise. I took another slurp of coffee. It was damned good. I'd give Grayson that much.

"What's so interesting in Plant City?" I asked.

Grayson shook his head. "Not so fast, intern. First order of business is to get the boss a refill." He handed me his empty coffee mug.

"Is this part of my P.I. training?"

Grayson shrugged. "Only if you want to *continue* your P.I. training."

I grinned. Grayson was only a few years older than me, but he was already a seasoned private investigator. I was just a P.I. wannabe with a brand-new intern license. I needed two years of on-the-job training to qualify for a full-fledged Class C license. Thanks to Grayson and his traveling investigator show, I only had 103 weeks to go.

I grabbed his coffee mug. "Pinch of salt, right?"

Grayson's eyebrow ticked up. "Gold star, cadet."

I tumbled back to the kitchen, threw a couple of Pop-Tarts in the toaster, and poured us both more coffee. After delivering the mugs to the cup holders on the dashboard, I grabbed the pastries and parked my rear back in the passenger seat.

"Here you go." I handed Grayson a blueberry Pop-Tart.

He raised a suspicious eyebrow. "Already brownnosing, eh?"

I shrugged. "Figured it couldn't hurt. So *now* will you tell me what's going on in Plant City?"

"I got a call from one of my sources."

"Your *sources?*"

Grayson nodded down at the weird-looking equipment installed under the dash. "That's a ham radio. I use it to operate an informal hotline on an obscure channel. People call in with information. If it sounds interesting, I follow up."

I took a bite of Pop-Tart. "What kind of information?"

"You know. Unidentifiable tracks. Weird lights in the sky. Mutilated corpses. That kind of thing."

I sucked the sticky frosting from my front teeth. "Sorry I asked. So what's in it for the informants?"

"*Operatives*," Grayson corrected. He shot me a grin and batted his eyes. "Why, my undying gratitude, of course." He turned back to face the road. "That, and cold, hard cash."

"So, exactly what kind of strange phenomenon are we looking into?"

"A fellow in Plant City overheard an unusual radio transmission two days ago. A guy named Lester Jenkins got on a frequency and starting screaming, 'They're here! They're here!'"

I took a sip of coffee. "Huh. Maybe his in-laws came into town."

Grayson shot me a sideways glance. "A cop found him dead a few hours later."

I smirked. "Like I said, maybe his in-laws—"

"His head covered in some kind of slime," Grayson said.

"Huh. You've obviously never dealt with in-laws, Grayson."

He snorted. "Shut up and eat your Pop-Tart."

My gut gurgled. "Hey, can we stop at the next rest stop?"

"I guess. Why?"

"Let's just say I've got something I want to get rid of."

"If you mean what I think you mean, the toilet works just fine while we're underway."

I frowned. "Thanks. But that's something I'm going to need a bit more time getting used to."

Grayson eyed me. "Claustrophobic?"

I shrugged and stared at the road ahead. "Sure. Let's go with that."

Chapter Three

Downtown Plant City appeared to have been snatched directly from an episode of *Mayberry R.F.D.* Compared to my hometown of Point Paradise, the place looked like Camelot.

Grayson, on the other hand, wasn't quite so impressed. After a quick drive past the main street's quaint little collection of coffee shops, boutiques, antique shops and restaurants, he announced he'd seen enough, and turned the RV onto US 92.

A mile or so down the road, a touristy billboard for Parkesdale Market came into view. I whined like a brat until I convinced Grayson to stop for a "World Famous" strawberry shake.

When he spotted Parksdale's candy-cane striped awnings, he sneered, but grudgingly pulled in. We got the shakes to go, and I was sucking down the last slurp when Grayson stopped the RV on a rural backroad we'd turned onto a few miles back.

"This looks like it," he said.

I eyed him sideways. "Is this a joke?"

Ignoring me, Grayson maneuvered the shabby RV up to a ten-foot-high, chain-link gate spanning a dirt driveway. It appeared to be the only way in and out of a barbed-wire-topped compound encompassing a couple of acres of half-cleared Florida scrubland.

The place looked like a low-rent prison for blue-collar offenders.

"Are you sure this is the right place?" I asked Grayson.

"Yes. Positive."

I was afraid of that.

The compound was situated in the back forty of a rural suburb comprised mostly of similar properties—trailer homes on small clearings tucked in amongst native palmetto bushes and pine trees. Most of the other neighbors, however, hadn't put quite so much time and effort into creating such an impressive *un*welcome mat.

I rolled down the window and stuck my head out for a better view. Partially hidden by trees, overgrown bushes, and an assortment of rusty household appliances, I spotted the outline of an old trailer. Beside it stood a satellite dish big enough to impress NASA engineers.

I crinkled my nose. "Well, at least he's got *something* worth protecting."

Grayson mashed a button on a black metal box beside the gate. A robotic voice crackled from a speaker.

"Identify yourself."

Grayson glanced over at me. Not knowing him that well, I would've sworn he looked just the teensiest bit embarrassed. He tipped his black fedora to no one I could see and said, "Gray Hotline."

I bit my lip as we waited in silence for a reply, seesawing between the desire to burst out laughing and the urge to ditch everything and run for my life.

A voice came over the speaker, deciding my fate.

"Proceed."

The gate clicked open and swung slowly across the dirt driveway with a long, painful *creak*. It came to a stop as it hit the side of a rusted-out refrigerator.

Grayson maneuvered the RV into what I could only describe as the abandoned set of *Sanford and Son—The Final Years.* Our dilapidated RV fit right in.

Grayson cut the ignition.

I nodded toward the junk. "I'm curious, Fred. Does this make me Lamont?"

Grayson groaned. "That joke belongs on the pile with the rest of this garbage. Just keep your head low and follow my lead."

We climbed out of the RV and picked our way through the maze of discarded rubbish clogging the yard. After tripping twice over the same rusted bicycle carcass, I managed to make it with Grayson to the steps of a wooden deck. Attached to it was the yellowed, algae-covered husk of a doublewide trailer.

A poorly hand-painted sign hung on the front door. It read: "The Tooth is Out There."

It was my turn to groan.

Grayson rang the doorbell with the elbow of his jacket.

I shot him a look. "What are you doing?"

He leaned in and whispered, "These people can be a bit obsessive when it comes to fingerprints and DNA."

As my mind ticked off the walking distance between here and the highway, the door cracked open.

Standing in the doorframe was a thin, pasty guy, probably in his late twenties. He sported a long, blond mullet and the kind of muscle tone that only gets chicks at Comic Con conventions.

I smiled to myself. The guy reminded me of Garth on *Wayne's World*. Except this dude was nerdier. His hair was frizzier. And, like the sign on his door foretold, his front teeth were "out there." I'd never seen such a pair of buck teeth.

I'd bet good money he could floss those beauties with his lips closed.

The guy smiled, making me want to double down on my bet.

"It's the mysterious Mister Gray! Welcome!" the Garth lookalike said. He turned to me. "And his beautiful protégé, I presume?" He bowed slightly and made a sweeping gesture with his arm. "Please, come in!"

Grayson handed over a business card as we entered mullet-man's secret lair. One glance around the interior and my mind wrote "bleach" on an imaginary shopping list. Then I scratched that through and wrote "dynamite."

"Thank you for your call," Grayson said.

The young man squinted at Grayson's card through the thick lenses of his black-framed glasses. "Gray Hotline," he read aloud. "Like gray *aliens*, right?" He winked at Grayson.

Grayson gave him a quick nod. "As far as you know."

The man extended a hand. Grayson shook it. "Well, pleased to meet you, Mr. Gray. I'm—"

"No *real* names," Grayson said, cutting him off. "Pandora, assign this new operative a name."

I looked around for a moment for Pandora, then blanched, cleared my throat, and said, "Uh ... Garth Waynesworld."

"First names only," Grayson corrected.

I saluted. "Yes, Commander Beetlejuice."

Grayson winced, but otherwise didn't skip a beat. "Operative Garth," he said, clearing his throat, "for our casework, we'll need to record your entire statement. We will, of course, use a voice-scrambling device to protect your identity."

Garth nodded solemnly. "No prob. That'll be a hundred bucks."

I stifled a smirk. Grayson reached into his jacket and pulled out a crisp C-note. "I heard you have pictures, too."

"Yeah. You can look, but no touch. You want copies, that's extra."

Garth might not have fashion sense, but he's got merchandising down pat.

"Fair enough," Grayson said. "Let's get started."

While Grayson set up to record Garth's statement, I looked around for a place to sit. Given the options, I decided to stand. The two men settled into a pair of old recliners I wouldn't have let a pet rat use for an outhouse.

I leaned against the doorframe between the living room and kitchen and tried to keep disgust—as well as mold and mildew—from congregating on my face.

Suddenly, I heard heavy breathing behind me. My back bowed into a prickly arch. Against all my willing myself not to, I turned and traced the source of the noise.

It was coming from the corner of Garth's kitchen.

I craned my neck, then took a step backward for a peek.

Glaring at me from inside a heavy wire cage was a monstrous black hound. As I locked onto its yellow eyes, the dog erupted into a snarling fit. Then it then let out a long, low, continuous growl that turned my Pop-Tarts and coffee into bubbling sludge.

"I see you've met Tooth."

Garth's voice sounded mere inches to my right, startling me so badly I nearly screamed. I swallowed hard, and plastered on a smile while my heart played a drum solo in my chest.

"Yeah. Nice puppy," I managed.

Garth laughed. "I put him in his cage whenever I'm expecting company. As you can see, he doesn't care for people all that much. But look. I think he likes you."

I stared at the gleaming, inch-long incisors on Cujo Jr. and was thankful for the metal bars between us. I envisioned the dog patrolling Garth's junkyard and the joke finally hit home.

The Tooth is Out There.

Hilarious.

Chapter Four

"And that's when I heard Jenkins hollering, 'They're here! They're here!'" Operative Garth said, and took another swig from a half-gallon plastic bottle of Mountain Dew.

"Just to be clear, we're talking about *Lester* Jenkins," I said. "The guy who was found dead?"

"The dude himself, yeah. Then T-Rex got on the horn and yelled, 'Jenkins! I told you to I.D. yourself!' Haha! He's totally retrograde, man!"

"T-Rex?" Grayson asked.

"Oh. Theodore Rexel. Old army vet. He's got the closest repeater to Jenkins' cabin."

"Repeater?" I asked.

Garth's face suddenly collapsed. He stared at me as if I'd zapped him with a stun gun, then he shifted his flabbergasted gaze to Grayson.

Grayson shrugged apologetically. "She's new."

Garth eyed me up and down, as if I might be a spy, while Grayson explained the terminology. "A repeater's a *tower*, Pandora. It's like an amplifier for ham radio operators. You can bounce your signal off it to gain distance and volume."

"Oh. Right," I said, and laughed. "I forgot."

Garth appeared bored with the tedium of having to deal with a newbie. He let out a huge sigh and addressed Grayson as if he were the only worthy audience member in the room.

"Anyway, like I was saying, Mr. Gray, old man Rexel was ragging on Jenkins to follow protocol and give out his call sign. Rexel's a real stickler for the rules. Throwback from his crew cuts and shiny shoes military days, I guess."

Garth turned to me and spoke slowly, as if addressing a toddler with unpromising potential. "So, Pandora, you're supposed to give your call sign when you ping somebody's repeater. It's common courtesy. But Lester Jenkins never did. And that pissed Rexel off big time."

"Right, thanks." I thought about asking Garth what a call sign was, but I didn't want to piss *him* off big time, either.

Garth gave me a curt nod, pushed his glasses up on his pug nose, and continued his story with Grayson.

"So while Rexel was bitching at Jenkins, I got off the channel and called my brother, Jimmy. He's on the force. He hightailed it out there to Jenkins' cabin. Took photos before any other donut slugs showed up."

Garth turned to me. "A donut slug is—"

I gave him a sharp nod. "I think I got it."

Grayson clapped his hands together. "Excellent, Operative Garth. Now, how about a look at those photos?"

Garth grinned. "You're in for a treat, Mr. Gray." He fired up his laptop, clicked a few buttons on his keypad, and a full-screen view of Lester Jenkins' remains flashed on the display.

I blanched.

Dressed in jeans and a flannel shirt, Lester Jenkins' body was lying face-up in a bed of pine straw. His hair and face were wet with a gooey-looking substance. And something was off with his body. It was too ... *narrow*. And too flat. It was as if he'd somehow *melted* inside his clothes. My nose crinkled in disgust.

"This is interesting," Grayson said, pointing at Jenkins' neck and face. Both were peppered with small, narrow gashes. "Strange pattern for teeth marks. Short. Needle-like. Definitely not a predator with large canines."

Garth nodded, eyes narrowed in contemplation. "I see your point. And what about that slime? My brother said Jenkins' head and neck were covered in it. What kind of being could do that?"

I smirked. "A Chihuahua with a bad cold?"

The two men shot me dirty looks. I shriveled and backtracked. "Sorry. It's just that ... the pictures are so gruesome. I was ... comic relief, anyone?"

I shut my babbling mouth. Grayson turned his attention back to Operative Garth. "Like I said, she's new. So what did your brother think was the cause of death?"

Garth shrugged. "Gettin' his guts squashed out."

Again, Grayson didn't miss a beat. "I mean, *what* did the squashing? Have there been any unusual phenomena noted in the area recently?"

"He could've been stomped by Bigfoot," Garth offered hopefully. "Does that count?"

"Absolutely. So, Operative Garth, do you know if Jenkins was into Ufology?"

"Well, yeah. He was always trying to contact aliens with his ham radio. But he couldn't even pull off an EME. Can you believe it? What a doofin' putz."

I opened my mouth to say something, but Grayson's face read, "Can it." So I did.

Grayson shot Garth an insider's smile. "Couldn't do an EME? What a newb."

Garth's face relaxed, as if Grayson had earned another level of trust. He leaned in closer to Grayson. "When I use EMEs to signal to aliens, I'm careful. Discrete, you know? I use a signal deflector. That way, if I make contact, they can't find me directly. Jenkins wasn't much for following protocol. If that's what he was doing, he could've led them right to him."

"So you actually knew Jenkins?" I asked.

Garth looked up at me as if he'd forgotten I was there. "I've talked to him a couple of times. At Blarney's Bar."

I nodded. "You sure the body in these pics is Lester Jenkins?"

Garth shrugged. "Pretty good likeness, if you ask me. Especially after he'd had a couple shots of Mr. Jack D."

"Who do you think he was referring to when he said, 'they're here,'" I asked.

Garth pushed his glasses up. "Like I said. It could've been animals. Or aliens. Or even trespassers on his property. Jenkins was a hothead. I'm pretty sure he'd shoot at any of them."

"So, how much for copies of the pics?" Grayson asked.

Garth shot him a buck-toothed grin. "Depends, Mr. Gray. How much you willing to pay?"

Chapter Five

"Nice doing business with you, Mr. Gray."

Garth folded the greenbacks, then tucked them safely among the pens stashed in the plastic pocket protector safeguarding his flannel shirt from ink stains. He patted the front of Grayson's RV, then hit a switch on a remote-control device.

The gate on the chain link fence slowly creaked open.

"Contact me any time," Grayson said out the rolled-down window. "You do excellent work, Operative Garth."

Garth's wimpy shoulders straightened. The lenses of his glasses flashed yellow-white in the midday sun, as did his bucktooth grin. He stood at attention and stayed that way until we'd backed down the drive and were pulling away.

I waved at him one last time, then shot Grayson a sideways glance. "You really seemed to make an impression on him. What are you, some kind of nerd superstar?"

Grayson shrugged. "I'm known in certain circles."

"Really? What kind? *Crop* circles?"

"Among others."

I rolled my eyes. "No offense, Grayson, but that guy got my spidey senses tingling."

Grayson's left eyebrow hitched up a notch. "Huh. I didn't picture him as your type."

"Argh!" I whacked Grayson on the bicep with the back of my hand. "That's not what I meant!"

His lip curled. "You hungry?"

I winced. "After *that?* Geez, Grayson! We just saw pictures of a guy smooshed to pudding!"

Grayson licked his lips. "Mmm. *Pudding.*"

I snorted. "Okay. To tell you the truth, I'm starving."

"What say we find us a nice taco stand, Pandora? Then go check out what's swinging with T-Rex?"

I grinned and shook my head. "Oddly enough, that's the best offer I've heard all day, CB."

"CB?"

"Commander Beetlejuice."

GRAYSON PICKED CONSUELO'S from among the half-dozen greasy-looking mom-n-pop cooking trailers we passed along a three-mile stretch of US 92.

"Who knew Plant City was a taco-lover's paradise?" Grayson said after we placed our order through the screened window of the rusty white food truck. He waved away a fly. "No wonder people retire to Florida."

We'd barely placed our bottoms on the bench of a picnic table when a woman stuck her sweaty face out the window of the traveling taco stand.

"Beezelshoes!" she hollered.

I smirked. "Looks like you're up, boss."

Grayson shot me a look, then got up to retrieve our food. He returned with two greasy cardboard plates heaped with tacos, beans, and yellow rice.

My mouth watered despite the images still buzzing around in my head. "Those pictures of Jenkins were really gross," I said, then picked up a fish taco and crammed half of it into my mouth. "Poor guy."

"Should've kept up his gym membership," Grayson said, eyeing me for my reaction. "The slob really let himself get soft."

I nearly choked on a mixture of disgust and chopped cabbage. I rolled my eyes, but I had to admit, Grayson's gallows humor was growing on me. So were his looks.

Except for the cheesy moustache.

Given his lean build, his intense, indecipherable eyes, and his rakishly angled fedora, half a century ago, Grayson would've been typecast as the bad guy in any black-and-white movie. Lucky for him, the line between the good guys and the bad guys had long since blurred into a million shades of gray.

I chewed my mouthful of taco. "So, what's your goal?"

Grayson focused his green eyes on mine. "Goal?"

"Yeah. What do you want to try and accomplish here?"

Grayson's brow furrowed. "Collect hard evidence on whatever alien or cryptid is involved in this. I thought you knew that when you climbed aboard the good ship lollipop. Or, in your case, Tootsie Pop."

Grayson stared at me and rubbed the small, blue bruise just below his right eye. I'd given him the mark a few days back when I'd beaned him in the face with a slightly used sucker. In my defense, at the time I'd thought he was a psycho killer. In hindsight, I knew he was no killer. The psycho part, however, was still up for debate.

I shook my head. "*You're* the one collecting evidence of aliens or whatever. I'm just here for the P.I. training."

His eyes narrowed. "No, Drex. As my new partner, you signed up for both."

"Geez." I chewed my lip. "Seriously, Grayson. Do you think chasing monsters is a job for sensible adults?"

Grayson's back stiffened. "We don't chase monsters. We chase the *truth*. And in case you haven't noticed, Drex, being a so-called sensible adult isn't all it's cracked up to be. In fact, it's nothing but a trap."

I stopped sucking down my soda. "What are you talking about?"

Grayson studied me for a moment. "Unless you absolutely love it, a job is a gilded cage designed to keep you *just comfortable enough* so it can suck the life out of you, like you're doing to that bottle of pop."

I grimaced. "Geez. That's pretty dark."

Grayson's left eyebrow arched. "Is it? I think it's pretty enlightened. Think about it. Whether you're counting gold bricks or pushing a broom, no amount of cash can buy back the time you waste doing something you hate."

I crinkled my nose. "It's not *that* bad out there."

Grayson's green eyes locked on mine. "Don't tell me you're having second thoughts, Drex. Do you really want to go back to ordering mufflers for busted Buicks and wiping strangers' dipsticks? If so, I'll take you back to Point Paradise right now."

He stood.

I grabbed his arm. "No! That's not what I meant!"

I bit my lip. "I guess ... I'm just wondering ...." I stared at the table.

"What?" Grayson said. "Just say it, already."

I cautiously looked up into Grayson's eyes. "Why *me?*"

He stared at me for a moment. "What do you mean?"

"You *know* what I mean. Why did you pick *me* to be your partner? Be honest. If I didn't have this thing going on with my brain—the twin—would you have even considered me for the job?"

Grayson sat back down and sighed. "You're broken, Drex."

I winced. "What?"

"I chose you because you're *broken.*"

My eyes narrowed. "What are you saying? That you felt *sorry* for me?"

Grayson laughed. "No. That's not what I meant at all. Just the opposite, in fact."

Grayson leaned across the table toward me. "You've been broken by the world, Drex. You played their game and lost. And now, if I'm right about you, you're ready to tell them all to go shove it where granny hides her gin-spiked Geritol."

I leaned back and chewed my lip. Grayson's analogy was dead-on. But I didn't want him to know it. I wasn't sure *I* wanted to know it.

Grayson tilted his head and looked me in the eyes. "Am I right?"

I shrugged. "How does chasing monsters tell the world to shove it?"

Grayson's face lit up with an almost sinister delight. "Don't you see? It's the ultimate color-outside-the-lines kiss-off. No one can discredit you from an already unaccredited career. Am I right?"

My lips curled into a tentative smile. "Yeah, I suppose. But Grayson, even *you've* got to admit that's a pretty low bar."

"Bar, shmar. This whole idea of goal setting is nothing more than a no-win scenario designed by society to prove we'll never live up to its expectations. Let it all go, Drex. Sit back, let go, and breathe in the freedom."

I sat back and sniffed the air. "Right now, freedom smells like sweat and burnt tortillas."

Grayson laughed. "And here's the best part. If we …. No. *When* we come up with hard, irrefutable evidence that one of these cryptid creatures exists, there's no banana cream pie big enough to cover the egg that'll be all over their faces."

I grinned. Grayson messed up his metaphors, just like my Grandma Selma used to when she was alive. It was the one thing about him I was totally onboard with.

Something deep inside me relaxed. I sighed and reached for a taco. "So what do you think really happened to Jenkins, anyway?"

"Too soon to tell. We'll need to examine the body first."

"Wha—?" A piece of taco tumbled from my gaping mouth.

Grayson eyed the mangled glob on the table. "Or at least get our hands on the autopsy report."

I wiped my mouth with a paper napkin. "Ugh. I was afraid you'd say that."

Grayson locked eyes with me again. "By the way, how are you feeling? You know, with the whole vestigial-twin gonad thing going on in your skull. Had any more weird hallucinations?"

"None that spring to mind."

Grayson's face grew serious. "We're partners, now, Drex. If you want me to help you master your gift, you're going to have to let me know whenever you see something weird."

"*Gift?*" I scowled at Grayson. "If this was really a *gift*, I could return it."

Grayson shook his head. "Women. Even *God* doesn't know what to get them."

I sneered and took a savage bite of taco. As I chewed, I glanced over at the slob seated across from us. I nearly choked.

The man appeared to have just survived an attack by giant moths. His T-shirt was peppered with gaping holes which offered innocent bystanders glimpses of his doughy side-rolls and curly armpit hair. A long, gray beard hung down from his face and spilled onto his impressive beer gut. His neck and arms bore enough tattoos to qualify him as a human sandwich board.

If God really knew what women wanted, that guy wouldn't exist.

I nodded my head in the man's direction. "We're in Florida, Grayson. When you ask whether I've seen something weird, you're gonna have to be a lot more specific.'"

Grayson's eyes shifted to the tattooed man, then back to me. "I see your point. How about this: Have you seen anything that *shouldn't* be there?"

I nodded toward the tattooed man. "Yes."

Grayson snorted. "Okay. Anything you *wish* wasn't there?"

I nodded toward the man again. "Too many to count."

Grayson grinned. "All right, Drex. Have you seen anything that makes you question your traditional concepts of reality?"

I sighed. "No. But that picture of Jenkins reduced to flesh pudding comes close."

Grayson nodded and glanced back at the food truck. "That reminds me. I want to see a dessert menu. Flan, perhaps?"

"Ugh! You're incorrigible!"

Grayson laughed and ogled a laminated menu.

"You said our next step is to talk to that vet guy. Rexel, right?" I asked.

"Yes. I gave him a call while you were in the ladies' room. He said he could meet us at two o'clock."

I glanced at my cellphone. "That's in like, twenty minutes."

"No problem. It's just around the corner."

"Around these parts, Grayson, nothing is just around the corner."

His eyebrow shot up. "No? In that case, I suggest we get going, cadet."

Our eyes simultaneously shifted down to the last remaining taco on the table, then back up.

We both grabbed for it.

Grayson was quicker.

He shot me a victory grin, took a huge bite from the taco, and handed me the rest.

I smiled and took it.

I guess partnering with Grayson has its privileges, after all.

Chapter Six

The derelict RV shimmied southbound along the Redman Parkway that divided Plant City—the strawberry capital of the world—in half. As we crossed over SR 60, the parkway turned into SR 39. Not that the change in numbers made any difference. Everything along that strip of highway was the same, ubiquitous shade of forgettable.

As we passed through the tiny town of Hopewell, I began to wonder just exactly what the hell the people around here were hoping for.

I looked down and squinted at the tiny map on Grayson's smartphone. "Swiney ... or is it Swilley Road? Anyway, it's supposed to be around here somewhere. On the right. Before you get to Keysville Road ... or is it Keystone?"

Grayson shook his head. "Grab a pair of glasses out of the glove compartment, would you? You look like a politically incorrect emoji. All you're missing are chopsticks and a pointy hat."

I scowled. "Do it yourself, then."

I shoved his phone back at him. Grayson refused it.

"Nothing doing. Driving while operating a cellphone is worse than playing Russian roulette. Over a quarter of all accidents are caused by cellphone usage."

I rolled my eyes. "You and your so-called facts. Why don't you just let me drive, then?"

"Uh ... *because you can't see?*"

I scowled again. "I can see well enough to shoot."

"You've got presbyopia, Drex. Your near vision is deteriorating. Welcome to the short-arm club."

I frowned. "But I'm not even forty."

Grayson smirked. "You're an overachiever. Congratulations. Now grab a pair of specs so you can read the display, already!"

"Ugh!" I jabbed the button on the glovebox. It dropped open. I picked out a pair of cheap, plastic eyeglasses and settled them on my nose. When I glanced back down at the phone, I nearly gasped at the amount of detail it displayed.

"There it is," Grayson said. "Swilley Road, right?"

I looked up. The blur from the lenses made me instantly nauseated. "Ugh. Yeah. Right."

I looked down at the phone again. Grayson hooked a sharp right, sending me lurching sideways.

"Geez, Grayson!"

He snorted. "Come on, grumpy. Where's your sense of adventure?"

"Where granny hides her Geritol, apparently."

I took off the glasses. "That Garth guy said Rexel is a stickler for protocol. I don't want to look like a dimwit again. What was that thing you two were talking about? An M and M?"

"EME. It's ham radio jargon for a moon bounce. That's when you use the moon as a passive reflector to establish a signal path. Earth-Moon-Earth equals EME."

"Right." I still didn't understand what the hell he was talking about. But did it really matter? When would that subject ever come up again in my lifetime? *Never*. "Hey, after Rexel, then what?"

Grayson came to a stop sign and looked both ways. "We'll check out Operative Garth's brother on the force. Jimmy Wells."

"I thought we didn't use real names. And how'd you find out *his*, anyway?"

"It was on the mailbox. They live together."

"Oh." *Two guys, no gal. Well, that explains the filth.*

"So much for anonymity," I quipped.

Grayson's eyebrow ticked up. "And so much for your observational skills."

I frowned. Grayson noticed.

"Listen," he said. "You're new at this. Everybody's got to start somewhere. So be a good intern, would you? Keep an eye out for a small tower. That'll be Rexel's repeater. He said we can't miss it."

I licked my wounds as we drove through a half-finished subdivision. The place appeared to have been abandoned by its developer decades ago. Like some wannabee Chernobyl, a smattering of houses dotted the crumbling asphalt lanes and empty cul-de-sacs. The rest of the lots lay vacant and weedy.

We turned a corner. Amongst a stand of pines, I spotted a crude metal structure that resembled the Eiffel Tower—if it had been built by a scrap metal salesman after downing a bottle of mescal.

I jabbed a finger at the windshield. "Is that it?"

"Yes. Good eye, cadet."

I perked up and I allowed myself the edges of a smile. "Turn there," I said.

Grayson made the turn and rumbled down the road to the end. He pulled the RV onto a tidy, crushed-shell driveway leading to a modest, well-kept block house covered in brick a shade too red to be real. The lawn, trees, and bushes bore the precision trim jobs of a seriously hard-core anal-retentive.

Grayson shifted into park. Before we could even open the doors, a short, wiry old man emerged from the house, checking his watch. His bald, liver-spotted head glistened in the sun. When he looked up, his face appeared frozen in a state of permanent condescension. He probably could've played General McArthur if he wasn't the height of George Castanza.

"You take the lead on this," Grayson said, smirking as he threw me under the bus. "Get one under your belt."

"Wha—?"

"Like I said, just follow my lead."

"You're a minute and thirty-eight seconds late," Rexel barked as we climbed out of the RV.

"I ... we're ..." I fumbled.

"Excuse our delay, Mr. Rexel," Grayson said. "My partner, Pandora here, was overcome with admiration for your magnificent repeater."

Rexel peered over his bifocals at me. His skeptical frown softened into a smile that seemed so foreign to his face I was afraid it might crack. "Why thank you, young lady."

"That's some repeater," I winged.

Rexel beamed. "Built it myself."

"You don't say!" I cooed. "Truly impressive. You ever do EMEs with it?"

Rexel's face went disconcertingly dreamy. "Been known to do an EME a time or two, young lady."

I looked over at Grayson just in time to see his eyes finish rolling. I turned back to Rexel. "Mr. Rexel, we're here investigating the sad demise of Mr. Lester Jenkins."

Rexel sneered. "Not *that* sad, if you ask me."

I blanched. "Why?"

The skinny little man's face twisted as if he'd sucked a lemon wedge. "Damned amateur. Jenkins barely knew what he was doing. Always skimming the guidebooks and skimping on the rules." Rexel shook his angry, turtle-like head and spat. "That lazy scumbag was always ker-chunking on my repeater."

I shot Grayson a quick, wide-eyed glance.

He grinned, but offered me no lifeline.

I nodded at Rexel sympathetically. "I hate when that happens."

Rexel gave me a sharp nod, then continued his tirade.

"No matter how many times I told him, Jenkins never gave out his call sign when he keyed up his radio. Pinged off my repeater without even so much as a 'How do you do.' It was annoying as all get out, I tell you."

What the hell?

I shot Grayson a *Mayday* look. He finally took the lead.

"So, Mr. Rexel, how did you know it was Jenkins if he didn't give his call sign?"

Rexel turned to Grayson and doubled up on his sour expression. "He was at that disgrace of a shack he called a cabin near 'bout every Friday. He'd always ping my repeater around the same time. Quarter to six. Right before happy hour at Blarney's Bar. It was the only thing that sorry S-O-B ever did on a reliable basis."

"I see." Grayson rubbed his chin. "And what about his last transmission? You heard it, correct?"

"Yeah. The idiot was yelling, 'They're here. They're here.' Sounded like he'd already had a few. I asked for his call sign ... you know, to keep a decent level of protocol. The man didn't bother to reply. I'm telling you, Jenkins had no manners whatsoever."

I sighed. *He was probably too busy dying.*

Rexel snorted derisively. "Jerk never even bothered to get more than a Technician Class license. Me myself? I went all the way to Amateur Extra Class."

Wow. Where's that extra class now?

Grayson acknowledged Rexel with a nod. "Did Jenkins say anything after that?"

"Nope. Let me tell you, I gave him a piece of my mind over not using his call sign. But the jerk didn't give me so much as the courtesy of a reply to that, either. Typical Jenkins."

Grayson's brow furrowed. "How far away is Jenkins' cabin from here?"

"Half a mile, maybe. It's down there, at the end. Where the road cuts off." Rexel pointed down a paved road that appeared to lead to nowhere. "Jenkins would park his truck down there and follow the trail in the woods."

"What happened here?" I asked, glancing around at the vacant lots and weedy sidewalks. "Why didn't they finish the subdivision?"

Rexel's expression told me I'd hit a nerve. "They were supposed to build more houses, but then the EPA said the land's too swampy. Damned EPA cares more about the life of some stupid toad-frog than it does its own war veterans."

Grayson gave the old man a sympathetic look. "Mr. Rexel, who do you think Jenkins was referring to when he said, 'They're here.'?"

Rexel shrugged. "Those damned toads for all I know. Like I said, he was a real booze hound."

Grayson nodded. "Well, thank you for your time, sir."

"Sure. Always happy to help out a fellow ham radio operator."

I nearly snorted. *Right. Unless he's Lester Jenkins.*

I plastered on a smile and climbed into the RV. Rexel came up to my window and looked at me as if he expected something.

"Uh ... that really is a really nice tower you've built there, Mr. Rexel," I offered.

Rexel shot me a lascivious grin. "You really like my little elephant, don't you?"

Yuck. "Uh...sure." I rolled up the window and locked the door before Rexel climbed in and gave me a hug or something.

Grayson turned the ignition, and as he slowly backed down the drive, Rexel winked at me and waved.

I groaned. "I feel like I've been slimed."

"What?" Grayson asked. "You mean like Jenkins?"

"No. Worse."

Grayson's right eyebrow flat-lined. "What's going on?"

"What did Rexel mean with that crack about me liking his little elephant?"

Grayson opened his mouth to answer.

"Wait!" I blurted. "If it's gross, I don't want to know."

Grayson laughed. "He was referring to his tower, Drex. A repeater that can receive further than it can transmit. You know, big ears, small mouth. Like an elephant."

"I'd say Mr. Rexel has big ears *and* a big mouth."

Grayson shrugged. "He seems harmless enough. A man needs his hobbies, after all."

"I guess."

Grayson reached below the dash and fiddled with the knobs on his ham radio. It crackled to life.

As static filled the cab of the RV, I frowned. All that stupid radio jargon the men had used with each other. Who in their right minds would care about any of that crap?

"I don't get it," I said finally. "What's so great about this amateur radio stuff?"

"What?" Grayson nearly veered into the gutter. "It's only like the *original internet*, Drex. With a ham radio you can talk to folks all over the world. Even in outer space."

"Outer space? Gimme a break. Don't tell me you believe all that stuff Garth said about talking to aliens?"

"Well, I believe it's *possible*, sure," Grayson said defensively. "Ever since Russia launched Sputnik, amateur radio buffs have been monitoring the skies for space transmissions."

Grayson smiled wistfully at the windshield. "The Apollo missions were a dream come true. As a kid, I remember tuning in to the astronauts' live broadcasts from space. Good times." He turned to me. "*That* was possible. So, why shouldn't we be able to tune in to space alien's transmissions?"

I shook my head. "I guess. But what are the odds of that happening?"

"I'd say pretty good. You may not realize it Drex, but there are over three million amateur radio operators around the world. Tuning in to an alien life form on a subspace channel is bound to happen. It's just a matter of time."

I snorted. "Meanwhile, you know, while you guys are waiting for ET to phone home and all, what else do you do for fun? Swap Tang recipes with each other?"

"No. We ...." Grayson coughed. "We exchange weather updates and whatnot."

I smirked.

"Don't knock it until you've tried it." Grayson turned a knob on the ham radio. "You can also monitor police transmissions with this baby. And airline pilot chatter. There's even some spooky 'black channels' out there broadcasting encrypted messages twenty-four seven. I think you'd be surprised what ham radio operators can pick up."

"No offense, Grayson, but if they're all like Garth and gramps back there, I'd be surprised if they could *pick up* anything."

Chapter Seven

A finger of dread ran a cold, sharp nail down my spine as I inched behind Grayson, mimicking his movements along each zig and zag in the narrow trail that meandered through the boggy Florida scrubland.

The terrain was flat and sandy, covered in a thick carpet of waist-high palmetto bushes. Amid the sea of jagged, silver-green palmettos, patchwork islands of dwarf, moss-covered scrub oaks and towering, red-barked pines jutted out.

The only sounds were our footsteps and my own groaning complaints. In the distance, the shrill, laugh-like call of a pileated woodpecker rang out. I wondered whether he'd just told a joke at our expense.

"Two buffoons walk into a forest …."

Not only wasn't I in the mood for tromping through the woods—I wasn't dressed for it, either. The thorny palmettos clawed snags in my sweater, and the boggy mud collected on the bottoms of my new, white tennis shoes, weighing them down like Frankenstein clodhoppers.

When Rexel pointed out we could access Lester Jenkins' cabin at the end of the lane, Grayson had put our plans to interview Officer Jimmy Wells on the backburner. We'd left Rexel's house and driven directly to the stub-end of the unfinished road where the trailhead started.

As we tromped down the switchback path leading to Jenkins' cabin, the postmortem pictures of Jenkins flashed in my mind anew.

I shuddered.

This trail is a maze designed by a madman. A dead *madman! I hope there's not any more out here ….*

35

My cellphone chirped, startling the crap out of me. I made a mental note to change my ringtone from the theme of *Psycho* and pulled my phone from my pocket.

It was a text from Beth-Ann. *You OK?*

I smiled. She was on speaking terms with me again. I texted back. *Yes. With Grayson. Can't talk now.*

She texted, *Hope UR not alone in woods w/him. Ha Ha.*

I swallowed a knot that cropped up in my throat. *Don't be silly. Call U later.*

I shoved the phone back in my pocket. Beth-Ann had ripped me a new one for taking off with a man I barely knew and whom she'd never met. Her concern had been well meaning, but I couldn't take on her fears, too. I already had enough of my own. I crossed my fingers and hoped her dire prediction that I'd be found murdered by Monday didn't pan out. I'd just begun to feel I could trust the man in the black fedora. Maybe I shouldn't ....

"Grayson." I tugged on the backpack strapped to his back. "I don't get it. Why all these random switchbacks in the trail? Wouldn't it have been easier to make a straight path between the pines?"

Grayson turned to face me. "Either Jenkins was trying to disguise the trail, or he had the worst sense of direction of all time."

"Or he was crazy."

Grayson nodded. "A third, viable option."

I chewed my lip. "I think Jenkins *was* trying to hide the trail. But why? And Garth with his prison compound guarded by a hound from hell. Who exactly are these guys worried is going to get them?"

Grayson's eyebrows lifted. "Who, or *what?* That's the sixty-four thousand dollar question, isn't it?"

My nose crinkled. "For that kind of money, I'd like to take a stab at an answer."

Grayson's shoulders broadened. "Fine. But first, you have to name the game."

"Game? What are you talking about?" *Murder me by Monday?*

"You know. The *game*. The universal mind is playing with us again. I can feel it. Didn't you hear it laughing at us?"

"That was a woodpecker."

"And who put it there?"

I scowled. Grayson had an infuriating way of being right and wrong at the same time.

He smiled deviously. "We're following the clues for the next game."

Right. And the challenge for this round is, which one of us is the bigger lunatic?

I shot him a hard stare. "You really think so?"

Grayson nodded. "Absolutely. Now that the game is afoot, what's your next move, cadet?"

Flop-sweat broke out on my forehead. I'd never been any good at being put on the spot. "I ... I have no idea, Grayson. I wouldn't know where to begin."

Grayson's face grew somber. "Sure you do. You already figured out the biggest clue."

"What?"

"I see it on your face. *Fear*." He locked eyes with me. "Never forget that. The game is *always* about fear. Identify your fears, and you have a chance of conquering them."

"Thanks, Yoda." My confidence might've fled like a bad blind date, but I couldn't shake my sarcastic wit to save my soul.

The woodpecker's shrill laugh sounded again.

"That must be Obi-Wan," I quipped. "I've been told he's our only hope."

Grayson squelched a grin, then turned and continued down the narrow trail. I sighed and followed suit.

A few switchbacks later, his backpack caught on a palmetto frond. As it came free, the frond flew back like a slingshot, jettisoning a passenger—a cockroach the size of a mouse.

It spread its wings and flew right at my face.

"Aaargh!" I screamed.

Grayson whirled around, eyes wide. He saw me swatting wildly at my insectoid nemesis and laughed.

"Scared of a little bug, are we? Yet another irrational fear you need to tackle, Drex."

"What do you mean, *another?*" I stopped waving my arms. "For your information, palmetto bugs aren't *little*, Grayson. They're *disgusting*. And they carry diseases! So it's not irrational to be afraid of them."

Grayson's lips twitched with amusement. "Right. And here I thought you were a true-blue country gal. So tell me, what's a roach ever done to you?"

"I grew up in the *South*, Grayson. Not in a *dump*. Roaches are filthy!"

Grayson's right eyebrow shot up. "Really? Then why do roaches clean themselves after coming in contact with humans?"

I scowled. "You just made that up."

Grayson smirked. "Did I?"

A lizard scurried across the trail. It took a flying leap onto a twig and grabbed the roach in its mouth. I grimaced.

Grayson snorted. "Come on, Princess Leia. Let's go before Jabba the Lizard gets you."

Chapter Eight

After another ten minutes or so of dodging insects and insults, Grayson and I came upon a clearing at the end of the zig-zagging trail through the pines and palmettos.

We came face-to-face with the dark, ominous husk of a falling-down log cabin. The shattered front window had been crudely sealed with cardboard and duct tape. A tattered, camouflage-patterned tarp sagged over its broken roof.

"Oh, look. The honeymoon suite," Grayson said.

"Yeah. In *Apocalypse Now.*"

A torn strip of yellow crime-scene tape waved lazily at us from a post on the front porch. Grayson rubbed his chin. "I guess we're not the first to arrive."

My upper lip hooked skyward. "You're not thinking of actually *going in*, are you?"

Grayson shrugged. "The scene's already been compromised, so we can't do too much more damage." He swung the backpack from his back and unzipped a pocket. "Here. Put these on."

I stared at the surgical booties in his hand. "Are you serious?"

"Yes. Over your shoes. We don't need to add our biology to whatever's already in evidence."

I slipped the booties over my muddy tennis shoes. Grayson donned gloves and picked the lock on the dilapidated cabin door. It took him mere seconds. The man had skills, I'd give him that. Where he'd gotten them, I wasn't sure I wanted to know.

Grayson slipped his lock-picking tool back into his pocket and turned to me. "Here we go, cadet. Our first official crime scene investigation together." He held up his cellphone. "Want a picture for your scrapbook?"

"I'll pass."

"Your loss." He slipped the phone back into his pocket and motioned for me to step inside. "Come on, then. Ladies first."

I grimaced. "I think this is a case of ladies *not* going first."

"Have it your way. But keep close."

"The place is the size of an outhouse. Do I have any choice?"

Grayson disappeared into the cabin. I made a few reluctant steps, then gave up and followed him inside.

The stale air in the log cabin smelled vaguely of fish.

And turpentine.

And putrefying flesh.

Yuck.

"What's that?" I pointed toward a corner heaped with electronics.

"Jenkins' ham radio equipment."

"No. Above it."

I raised my finger up, toward a clothesline strung high along the back wall. Draped over the line hung ragged, reddish-brown slabs of what appeared to be drying flesh.

My heart began to thump so loudly I was sure Grayson could hear it echoing off the log walls. But I was wrong. He hadn't noticed.

"Huh," he said, and walked over to the hunks of flesh hanging from the clothesline like Dahmer's dirty laundry. "Not your typical cafeteria mystery meat," he said as he took a piece of flesh from the cord.

He sniffed it. Then—against every normal, human instinct I knew—he opened his mouth to take a nibble.

"Stop!" I screeched.

He looked up, giving me time to run over and slap the meat out of his hand.

"What?" Grayson said. "It's not *human*."

"Ugh!" I hissed. "It's *deer* meat, Grayson. Venison."

"Huh," he said, studying the meat in his hand. "How do you know that?"

"My cousin Earl hunts deer, remember? And if it were human flesh, I doubt the cops would've left it hanging here."

Grayson nodded, apparently approving of my reasoning. "So, you think Jenkins was making deer jerky in here?"

"Yeah." I nodded toward the crude kitchen in the corner. "And from the looks of that meat grinder clamped to the table over there, deer hamburgers and meatballs as well."

Grayson looked impressed. "So *that's* what that thing is. I thought it was a giant pencil sharpener."

"Kind of looks like one. But it's a vintage LF&C hand-crank meat grinder. The pioneering homemaker's friend. My Grandma Selma had one. They're made out of galvanized steel. Practically indestructible."

Grayson's lip twisted to the left. "I don't get it. Why would anyone want to grind their own meat? I'm pretty sure we passed at least one Wendy's and two McDonald's on our way to Rexel's."

I snorted. "You really *are* a city boy, aren't you? Well, Mr. Fancy Pants, outlasting the apocalypse with store-bought goods doesn't come cheap."

Grayson shot me a wide-eyed stare. "Who said anything about the apocalypse?"

I picked up a wrapper from the floor. "I think this guy Jenkins was a prepper."

"A prepper?"

"Yeah. A survivalist. He was 'prepping' for the imminent breakdown of society as we know it."

Grayson scratched his chin. "I thought that already happened. You know, when they made Sharknado II."

I smirked and walked over to a plastic container the size of a breadbox. It was lying on its side near a corner of the cabin. The lid was off, and the container was covered in small, dirty handprints.

"See these wrappers strewn all over the floor? This container had a good month's worth of food in it ... before the raccoons got to it."

Grayson's eyebrow ticked up. "A month's worth of food in that small cooler?"

"It's not a cooler. It's what preppers call a portable food storage kit. This thing was packed with freeze-dried meals."

I handed Grayson a shredded foil pouch.

His nose crinkled. "Freeze-dried tuna fish. Yum." He let the wrapper fall back to the ground and picked up a small, gray tin marked ThermaFuel. "Well, look at that. Who knew doomsday survival included fondue?"

I snorted. "That's diethylene glycol. Kind of like Sterno on steroids. But it's for *heating*, not cooking. A small can like that could warm up this place for the better part of a day."

"What about this?" Grayson held up a lumpy object roughly the size and shape of a small loaf of bread. It was ashy white. "Let me guess. Fire log? Wait. Petrified fruitcake?"

I shook my head. "I dunno. I've never seen one of those. But if it's fruitcake, that would explain why the raccoons haven't touch it."

Grayson grinned. "Only a true sadist would include fruitcake in somebody's survival gear. Could you imagine if this thing was your last meal on Earth?"

Grayson dropped the misshapen brick onto the floor. It landed with a thud that rattled loose a few shards from the broken window.

I smirked. "Thick as a brick. Just like the ones my Aunt Lucy used to make. We used 'em for doorstops. They're not pretty. But you've got to admit, that thing would certainly last you a while."

Grayson stared at the ashy clump on the floor. "True. I think our family re-gifted the same fruitcake for over twenty years. But ours never turned white."

I shrugged. "Maybe it's mold. Or some kind of protective coating. Anyway, it's gotta be survival rations."

Grayson crinkled his nose. "If that's surviving, count me out."

I laughed. "Coming from the man who got hungry staring at Jenkins' man-pudding photos, that's rich." I looked over at a stack of empty Dr Pepper cans. "Meat and sodas. How long can someone survive on that?"

Grayson held up a magazine. "As they say, man cannot live by bread alone. I suppose that's why Jenkins also hoarded these lovely issues of *Paranormal Underground*."

I lifted Lucky Red and scratched my scalp. "So he *was* a UFO freak after all."

Grayson set the magazine down and turned back toward the radio equipment. "Hey. At least he was aiming for the stars."

I was about to groan at Grayson's lousy joke when something erased the notion from my mind.

It was the unmistakable sound of a gun's trigger-hammer locking into place behind me.

I started to turn around, but something poked me hard in the spine.

A strange voice spat out words usually reserved for old Clint Eastwood movies.

"You two. Put your hands where I can see 'em. *Now!*"

Chapter Nine

"What are you doing in here?" the man behind me demanded. He poked the hard, pointy thing against my spine again. I had a feeling it wasn't a churro. I stared ahead at Grayson, afraid to look back for fear it might compel the man to blast a bullet through my guts.

"We're private investigators," Grayson said. He shot me a quick glance he must've meant to be reassuring.

It wasn't.

Not even close.

Grayson reached slowly for his jacket pocket. "Here. Let me show you my credentials."

"Don't even think about it," the man barked. "P.I. or not, you're disturbing a crime scene."

Grayson displayed his open palms. "True. But the crime scene tape was already broken when we got here. And, technically, you're disturbing it, too."

"I'm a police officer."

Grayson eyed him skeptically, making me think the man holding the gun didn't fit the part.

"Where's your uniform?" Grayson asked.

"I'm on plain-clothes patrol."

"Oh." Grayson's face relaxed a notch. "Well, in that case, nice to meet you, Officer." Grayson extended his hand.

The man behind didn't reach for it. Instead, he jabbed his gun in my back again and said, "Show me some I.D."

As Grayson reached inside his jacket, I slowly turned my head and caught my first sideways glimpse of the man holding us at gunpoint.

He was white. Short haircut. Surprisingly young—maybe mid-twenties—and dressed in camouflage hunting fatigues. He could've been a military hero or the Unabomber.

I shot the man a weak smile. "We're working for Chief Warren Engles."

The young man eyed me sourly. "Yeah, well ain't that special. Shut it, ma'am. And assume the position."

The position? What am I supposed to do? Bend over and squeal like a pig?

"What do you mean?" I squeaked.

"Put your hands behind your back." He glanced at Grayson's I.D. "You, too, mister. I'm cuffing you both. Put your tin badge away. You can explain what you're doing here to my captain back at the station."

The man's gun stopped poking my back. A trickle of relief washed over the dread standing on my throat, making it hard to breathe. As ice-cold cuffs slid around my wrists, my old sidekick, cynicism, wasn't about to miss this golden opportunity.

Well, I guess I can mark "get arrested" off my bucket list.

A touch of hysteria made me giggle at the utter absurdity of the situation—a bad habit I just couldn't' seem to break.

"You think this is funny?" the man with the cuffs spat at me. "We'll see who gets the last laugh here." He slapped a second pair of cuffs on Grayson and shoved him toward the cabin door. "All right. Let's go. And no funny business."

Grayson shot the man an incredulous look. "Funny business? Officer, I wouldn't dream of it."

GRAYSON AND I STAGGERED, single file, ahead of the man claiming to be an out-of-uniform cop. He'd refused to show us any identification, and we weren't in a position to argue. Cuffed like fugitives, we formed a strange, stumbling, six-legged centipede as we zigged and zagged through the narrow, maze-like trail carved in the palmettoes.

About midway along the path, Grayson called out from in front of me. "Officer, couldn't we solve this whole situation with the help of my old friend, Ben Franklin?"

"Ben Franklin?" I asked. "What about Warren Engles?"

"Wait a minute," the man said. "You trying to bribe me, mister?"

Grayson coughed. "Uh. Not as far as you know."

"That's it!" the young man yelled angrily. "Hold it right there!"

Grayson and I froze in our tracks.

"Turn around," he demanded. "*Slowly*."

I shot Grayson a dirty look. Had his big mouth just cost us our lives? What if this guy was no cop? What if he was the one who'd killed Jenkins in the first place? I had to get us out of this mess!

I winced and turned my pleading eyes to the young man with the gun. "Sir, we're sorry." I studied his face for signs of mercy, then a niggling thought wormed its way into my brain.

I've seen this guy before.

"Let's see that P.I. badge of yours again," the man demanded of Grayson.

Grayson shrugged. "I'd love to oblige. But I can't. It's in my jacket pocket."

The hard-faced young man brushed past me and snatched Grayson's wallet from the breast pocket of his jacket. While the man examined Grayson's badge, I studied his face and racked my brain over his features. That square jaw. That dimpled chin. Those pale-blue eyes ....

Where have I seen him before? On TV? At Walmart? A wanted poster at the post office? Match.com? Come on, think!

The man looked up at Grayson and sneered. "Well, Mr. Nicholas Grayson, looks like you won't be needing this anymore." He waved the tin badge in the air. "Bribing a cop is pretty good grounds for suspension of your license. And I think my father, the Chief of Police, can make it stick. I'll be sure and let him know all about your friend Ben Franklin, though."

Grayson winced as if he'd been punched in the gut. "I didn't mean any harm."

"Save it. Let's get going."

As the young man sidled by me again, the angle of his face and curve of his lips set the final pieces of the puzzle into place.

"Wait a minute," I said. "You're Jimmy Wells, aren't you?"

He eyed me suspiciously, but said nothing.

"It's you, all right," I said. "I recognize you from a picture at your brother's place. You two looked mighty cute cozied up together with that giant bong."

The man's smug smile flew away from his face. "Crap."

I shot a glance at Grayson. He was grinning at me like a proud professor.

"Don't worry, Officer," he said. "I'm sure we can work something out."

Chapter Ten

"So you met my brother, Gary," Officer Wells said after releasing Grayson and me from the handcuffs he'd kept us in until we'd cleared the path in the woods.

"Yes. Grayson and I met him this morning." I rubbed my wrists and attempted an ingratiating smile. "And his little lapdog, Tooth."

Wells' eyes widened. "Wait a minute. You two. You're not ...?" He closed his eyes and blew out a breath. "Tell me you're not Mr. Gray and Pandora."

"The very same," Grayson said.

Wells shook his head. "I thought Gary was just making that whole thing up. It's hard to tell with him sometimes. Crap! What other family secrets did my brother spill?"

"Besides the bong?" I asked. "Well, he said you were the first to discover Jenkins' body. He showed us the pictures."

A vein began to throb in Wells' neck. "That little twit! I'm going to kill him!"

Grayson took off his backpack and tossed it onto the seat of the RV. "Where'd you find Jenkins, anyway? Inside the cabin?"

"No." Wells glanced around to see if anyone else was within earshot. "Look. I shouldn't be speaking with you about this."

"We're professionals," Grayson said. "We keep our sources confidential."

Wells' eyebrow shot up. "Like you did with my brother, Gary?"

Grayson grimaced. "Oops. Well, we'll keep the bong confidential. Scout's honor."

Wells looked as if he might throw up. He swallowed hard and said, "I found Jenkins in a clearing by the side of the cabin."

"Was he still alive when you found him?" I asked.

"I thought so, at first. He was lying there, eyes open, like he was gazing up at the stars. I thought he might be alive, but when I grabbed his arm, it felt soft ... kind of like mashed potatoes."

My nose scrunched involuntarily. "What do you think happened to him?"

"I dunno. I've never seen anything like it."

Grayson cleared his throat. "Garth ... uh ... *Gary* told us that Jenkins' head was covered in slime."

"Yes. Some kind of lubricant or something."

Grayson nodded. "Anything else unusual?"

Wells chewed his lip. "Well, this is kind of weird, but I found Jenkins' ammo belt and boots first. They were on the ground in front of the cabin steps. The boots were standing up in the middle of the ammo belt, still laced up—like Jenkins had been jerked from his gear by some enormous power."

Grayson's eyebrow rose a notch. "Power?"

Wells studied his shoes. "I didn't put this in my report, but I saw a strange ray of light in the sky. White, like a search beam, sort of. It was off in the distance, but it still gave me this creepy feeling."

"What do you mean?" I asked.

"It's just ... argh." Wells shook his head. "Nah. You'll think I'm crazy."

He looked up. Grayson locked eyes with the young man. "Believe me, Officer Wells, we're the last people who'd do that."

Wells pursed his lips and blew out a breath as if he'd given up on something. "It's just that ... this idea came over me that Jenkins had simply *vanished* from that exact spot. You know ... that the boots and ammo belt were left behind when he got ... uh ... beamed up in that ray of light."

Wells studied our faces. I wasn't sure what he was looking for, but he must have found it, because he continued talking.

"Like I said, I just got this major case of the creeps, you know? Like that feeling you get when you think something's watching you. Anyway, I freaked a little and started running back toward the trail. I wanted to get the hell out of there before I got zapped myself. But then I spotted Jenkins lying in the pine straw and realized he hadn't been beamed up after all."

"Why would Jenkins have been wearing an ammo belt?" I asked.

Wells shook his head. "I don't know. Maybe he'd seen a panther or something. They're pretty sneaky predators. Maybe that was what was watching me." He glanced back toward the woods. "I honestly couldn't tell you. But what I don't get is why he left his AK-47 behind. I found it on the floor inside the cabin."

"Interesting," Grayson said. "Did Jenkins have any other weapons on him?"

"Not that the crime-scene techs found in their search yesterday. He didn't need anything else. An AK-47 usually does an adequate job in most scenarios."

Grayson nodded. "In combat situations, sure. But why would Jenkins feel the need to have an automatic weapon and all that ammo out here in these woods? It seems to me like he was preparing for some kind of showdown."

Wells shrugged. "You'd be surprised how many wild animals are out here. Lots of things with fangs and claws. Alligators. Wildcats. Rattlesnakes. Brown bears."

"Is that how you got those scars on your neck?" I asked.

Wells reached up and absently touched the fine, white lines on his neck. "These? No. Tooth gave me these—when he was still a puppy. He's not too keen on strangers, in case you didn't notice."

I grimaced. "I noticed. So they're treating this as a crime scene?"

"Well, it sure wasn't suicide," Wells said sourly.

"Any suspects?" I asked.

"None at present."

"What about aliens?" Grayson asked.

The young cop blew out a breath. "You talkin' Mexicans or Martians?"

Grayson shrugged. "Either one. I'm flexible."

Wells shook his head. "I knew I shouldn't have mentioned the light beam. Don't tell anyone, okay?"

"Absolutely," Grayson said. "It's just that I noticed Jenkins had a stockpile of UFO magazines along with his ammo. And your brother Gary said he intercepted a ham radio signal where Jenkins was yelling 'They're here!' over and over again. Could he have meant space aliens? Like you said earlier, could Jenkins have been 'beamed up' and then spit back out?"

Wells kicked the jagged line of asphalt where the paved road disappeared into greyish-white sand. "Look. Lots of folks around here think they see UFOs. My brother Gary's the worst. He's always going on about it. It was probably all his jabber that put that crazy thought in my head in the first place. UFOs aren't real. Like all the other times, this'll turn out to be something stupid."

"All the other times?" Grayson and I asked in unison.

"Sure. People call into the station all the time about lights in the sky. They turn out to be emergency flares. Beacons on cellphone towers. Even lightning bugs. One time, I actually had a woman run up to me all freaked out about 'flying monsters.' Turned out to be dragonflies. *Dragonflies!* People can be downright nuts."

"How about Jenkins?" Grayson asked. "Was he what you'd call a nut?"

Wells shrugged. "No more than any of the other old drunks who come down here to spend their golden years turning us locals' lives to crap. Jenkins had a fondness for getting blasted at Blarney's Bar. From what Gary tells me, Jenkins would drink his fill of Jack Daniels and blabber on about the end of the world to anybody who'd listen."

"The end of the world?" I asked.

"You know. Alien invasions. A woman president. Eight-dollar gasoline. That sort of crap."

Grayson smirked. "Was Jenkins prone to hallucinations?"

"Not that I know of. But once at Blarney's, he did mistake some other gal for his wife, Arlene." Wells snickered. "I remember Gary coming home one night and telling me Jenkins thought Arlene had shown up at the bar ready to clobber him with a frying pan. Gary said Jenkins ducked under the counter and hightailed it out the back door. That old bastard might've talked a tough game, but I think his wife was one showdown he wasn't prepared to deal with."

Grayson shot Wells a man's-man smile. "Thank you, Officer Wells. You've been a great help."

The two men shook hands, but when it was time to release the grip, Grayson didn't let go.

"Just one more thing," Grayson said, holding firmly to the young cop's hand. "I'd like to have access to Jenkins' body, or at minimum the coroner's autopsy report."

Wells' eyes widened, then narrowed. "No way!" He jerked his hand free. "Our deal was *your* freedom for *my* bong. That's it. We're done here."

"Right. But what about these pictures?" Grayson took out his cellphone and flashed a picture of Jenkins doing his human Jell-O impersonation. "Who should I say is the source?"

Wells crumpled. "Look. I'll see what I can do. Okay?"

Grayson nodded. "I appreciate that. Is Jenkins going to be cremated?"

Wells shrugged. "I don't know. His wife Arlene hasn't claimed the body yet."

"Why not?"

The young cop pursed his lips and shrugged. "Probably because no-body's seen her since the night Jenkins died."

Chapter Eleven

"What's your take so far?" I asked Grayson as he hooked a left out of the desolate subdivision Rexel and a few other residents had been swindled into calling home.

He stomped on the accelerator. "Don't buy swampland in Florida."

"Har har. I mean, what do you think is going on with Jenkins?"

Grayson shrugged. "Hard to say. Like I said before, we need to get a look at his body, or the autopsy report."

"What about his wife, Arlene? She might be missing. You think she could've met the same fate as her husband?"

"Beamed up by aliens?"

I blew out a breath. "No. I meant do you think she's dead somewhere in those woods back there?"

"I don't know. Wells mentioned panthers and bears as potential killers. But the terrain around here is also the perfect habitat for Sasquatch—or as you Floridians like to call him, the skunk ape." Grayson's lip twisted to one side. "Now that I think about it, the Boggy Creek monster would find this area to his liking, too."

"What?" I smirked. "No giant spider or scaly iguanodon?"

Grayson grinned and showed me the palmetto scratches on his knuckles. "Nah. Too many sharp objects."

"So, I take it then that you think it was an animal that turned Jenkins into baby food?"

Grayson smirked. "There you go again, making me hungry."

He turned the RV onto SR 39. "Let's pick out a restaurant for dinner. I'm suddenly in the mood for venison and mashed potatoes."

I crinkled my nose. "You're sick, Grayson."

"I prefer the term 'desensitized.'"

I snorted. "Yeah. You keep living *that* dream."

Grayson laughed. "You're in a good mood. How about an evening on the town? I hear you can't beat Blarney's Bar for cheap beer and disgruntled wives."

I smirked. "To be honest, I could use a drink. But first, I'm gonna need a wig. I'm not going into a bar wearing a Redman chewing tobacco cap. In a redneck town like this, I might be accused of crossdressing. How far is it to Walmart from here?"

"Look it up on your phone."

I scowled. "Why? You know the way."

"Come on. You look so cute when you do your Mrs. Magoo impersonation."

"Very funny."

I got out my cellphone and tried not to squint as I punched the Google mic on the display. "Address of nearest Walmart."

The voice spilled out the answer.

I turned to Grayson. "Got that?"

"Affirmative."

I sat back and watched the shabby little town of Hopewell fade in, then out of view.

"I'm curious, Grayson. Why didn't Wells care when I mentioned that we were working for Chief Warren Engles?"

Grayson's eyes met mine. "That only works for the FBI. And even then, only under certain circumstances."

"Why's that?"

Grayson turned his gaze back to the road. "Right now, cadet, you don't need to know."

AN OLD MAN STOPPED in his tracks and looked me up and down as I climbed out of the RV in front of Walmart. Apparently, my ball cap and buzz cut didn't jive with my boobs. The judgmental sneer on his face could've made Jesus weep.

"Promise me you're coming back," I said to Grayson through the RV window. "I'm not dressed for long-term survival here."

"Don't be silly. I'll be back in twenty minutes, tops. I'm just going to find a UPS store and mail something off for analysis."

"The Mothman scat from the last job?"

"Bingo. As with any treasure, the value lies in its authentication."

"I thought it was the lies about authentication that added value to the treasure."

Grayson shook his head. "Drex, Drex. Always the skeptic. Hey! Pick me up a bag of Cheetos while you're in there, would you?"

"Sure. See you in a bit."

As Grayson drove away, a sudden wave of insecurity caused my gut to flinch.

Am I crazy? What am I doing in this strange town with this strange man?

What did I really know about Nick Grayson?

Not even enough to be sure he was coming back.

I checked my purse for my lifeline. A ping of relief flooded through me as my fingers found my cellphone in the bottom of my bag. I tucked it back in my purse and headed into Walmart.

Like a confused nomad wandering into a strange oasis, I was no longer certain what part of my life was real, and what was a mirage.

But at least I had four bars.

And a full battery.

Chapter Twelve

For a guy who was completely OCD about keeping his RV spic-and-span, making a living selling cryptid crap seemed totally out of character for Grayson. But then again, the need to make a living could trump anything.

I knew that all too well.

After my father died, I'd wasted the better part of a year trying to prove to his ghost that I could run the family auto repair business. I'd failed him on all levels—even at being his biological daughter. As it turned out, my cousin Earl had been both the real mechanic *and* the real relation.

I'd spent twenty-five years blaming Earl for stealing my job and my father's affections, only to find out it wasn't his fault at all. I'd been a real jerk to my cousin. And good-old Southern guilt was telling me I needed to make it up to him.

As I wheeled my cranky Walmart shopping cart past a display of ball caps, I took it as a sign to give Earl a call. But as I dialed his number, I realized sarcasm makes a better master than a servant. Dropping my caustic, barb-slinging routine with him was going to take some serious effort.

"Hey, Earl," I said sweet enough to make me nearly gag.

"Hey, there, Bobbie. Still alive, I see."

The snide tone of Earl's voice sounded like ... *home.*

I smiled. "You run the family business into the ground yet?"

He laughed. "Gimme another day or two. You know I can't work that fast. Thanks for turning out the light, by the way."

I cringed. As I'd driven away from Point Paradise last night, I'd shot out the lousy hole-in-the-wall's only claim to fame—the flashing yellow light hanging over the intersection of nowhere and oblivion.

"You all right, Cuz?" Earl asked.

"Sure. Sorry about the light. It was kind of ... symbolic for me."

"I get it. I'd a done a lot worse if I'd just found out my pappy wasn't my pappy. How's it going with Grayson?"

"I survived the night. And we're on a new case in Plant City. Some prepper guy got killed at his cabin. Someone—or some*thing*—mooshed him into a human Slurpee."

"That don't sound too good Bobbie. Be careful. You still got Lucky Red to protect you?"

"Yes." I touched the cap atop my head. "Don't worry. Your precious cap is safe with me. I'm at Walmart now looking for another one. I need a wig, too. Thanks to Mothman and your duct tape, my last one was shot to hell. I'll grab a new cap here and mail Lucky Red back to you."

"No. You keep ol' Red for as long as you need him. You deserve some better luck, Bobbie." Earl laughed. "Hey, maybe you'll get lucky with Grayson."

I rolled my eyes. "Is that all you think about, Earl?"

"That and pistons. What's so bad about that?"

"Nothing, I guess. Be good. I've got to go."

"I'm always good," Earl quipped. "At least, that's what all the gals say."

I clicked off the phone and smiled. So much had been upended in my life over the past few days, it was nice to know one thing had remained the same. My cousin Earl would always be a wisecracking pain in my ass.

And for some reason, I loved him all the more for it.

Chapter Thirteen

I was standing amid the towering eyeglass racks in Walmart trying on "cheater" specs. Amidst the jumble, I found a pair of 2.5 magnification lenses in pink frames. I tried them on, but when I looked through them, all I could see was colorful donuts dancing in the air.

Weird.

I looked down. Slices of pepperoni pizza wiggled in a bright yellow background above a pair of red, leopard-spotted tennis shoes.

This can't be right. Am I having another hallucination?

I took off the glasses and rubbed my eyes.

"You gonna keep those?" a man asked.

My eyes blinked open.

I blinked again.

It hadn't been a hallucination after all. Suddenly, I realized that having 20-20 vision wasn't always an asset.

A short, pudgy, sweaty man in his late thirties was eyeing the glasses in my hands, licking his lips. The fabric of his shirt was imprinted with life-sized donuts—his pants likewise with pizza slices.

I couldn't decide whether I felt hungry or nauseated.

"Well?" the man asked.

"Uh ... no." I held out the glasses. "You can have them. They're a bit too strong for me."

He grabbed them from my hand. "Thanks. You're lucky. My eyesight is terrible."

Well, that'd be one *explanation for that outfit.*

"It sucks getting older," I said, and reached for a pink pair with 1.5 magnification.

"I know that's right." The man looked in my cart. "I see you picked a wig from the new Lucy Goosy line. Good choice."

I suddenly lost confidence in my prospective coiffure selection. I eyed the wig dubiously as the man plucked a dozen pairs of glasses from the racks.

"Why all the eyeglasses?" I asked.

He shrugged, causing the donuts on his shirt to undulate. "Buy one, get one sale. If all hell breaks loose, there won't be any glasses anymore."

There won't be any donut shirts, either. At least, I hope not.

"Wait a minute," I said. "Are you a prepper?"

The man glanced around, then whispered, "Yes. You?"

"Yes."

He gave me the once-over. "I haven't seen you at any of the meetings."

"I'm new in town."

"Oh. Well, listen. A couple of us are meeting at Blarney's tonight. You know the place?"

"Sure do."

"Stop by. Introduce yourself. We'll be there around seven."

"Thanks. I appreciate that."

He smiled. "The guys will like you. They're always on the lookout for breeding stock."

My back stiffened. What was *that* supposed to mean?

I was about to give donut dude a piece of my breeding stock mind when Grayson walked up. He eyed my cart full of cheap clothes, toiletries, Tootsie Pops and Cheetos.

He grinned. "All that scat cash burning a hole in your pocket?"

I glared at donut man and pasted on a fake smile. "Awe, you know me, honey." I gave Grayson a peck on the cheek. Pizza man's hopeful face collapsed like punched dough.

"Well, I better get going," he said. "Nice chatting with you."

"Yes," I said, too enthusiastically. "See you tonight!"

As the guy wheeled his cart away, Grayson turned to me. "I had no idea you're such a tease, *honey*."

I dropped the girlfriend charade. "Tactical diversion. Pizza Pants invited us to a prepper meeting tonight."

Grayson snorted. "*He's* a prepper? What kind of camouflage is that? In case he's attacked by a horde of health-food zombies?"

I shook my head. "I just pray the fabric's not scratch-n-sniff."

Grayson guffawed. "Well, honey, looks like we've got ourselves a hot date tonight."

"Hot date?"

"A ménage á trois—with chocolate sprinkles."

"You have one sick sense of humor, Grayson."

He grinned. "You love it. Admit it, B.H."

"B.H.?"

"Breeding hips."

Crap. He'd heard our conversation after all.

Chapter Fourteen

One step inside the hotel room and my nostrils shriveled. I turned to Grayson. "Ugh! This place reeks! I thought I told you to ask for a *non-smoking* room."

Grayson plopped a small duffle bag onto one of the saggy twin beds. "I *did*."

I followed the worn trail in the nicotine-colored carpeting to the bathroom. The cheap laminate countertop and bathtub rim were pockmarked with amber cigarette burns. I stomped back into the main room. "Then who's the chain-smoker? The maid?"

"Actually, I think she died of emphysema a while back." Grayson pulled back the comforter on one of the beds. The threadbare sheets were rumpled and dirty. "Nobody's changed these since the Nixon administration."

My mouth puckered. "Gross. And I thought Jenkins' cabin was bad. Listen. I'm gonna get a shower, but I'm not touching either of those beds."

"Suit yourself."

I thought about the small lizard Grayson kept in a terrarium on the windowsill above the RV's banquette table. "Don't even think about bringing poor Gizzard in here."

Grayson's nose wrinkled. "I wouldn't. I have too much respect for the reptilia phylum."

I cocked my head and shot him a side-eyed sneer. "But not too much respect for *me*, apparently."

"Your habitat isn't under threat by Cuban invaders."

"It is if you count Miami." I glanced back into the ratty room and got the willies.

No self-respecting cockroach would stay in this place.

I couldn't bring myself to shower in the RV. It just seemed too—*up close and personal.* After that romp in the woods, my *Secret* was out.

I clamped my molars, grabbed my duffle, and marched into the bathroom. Both the countertop and floor were too disgusting to set the bag down on, so I hung it on the doorknob.

After locking the door, I pulled back the shower curtain, revealing what could only be described as a laboratory experiment gone horribly awry. I blew out a sigh and unbuttoned my jeans. A thought made me quickly refastened them.

I jerked open the bathroom door and yelled at Grayson.

"Is this a setup to make me want to stay in the RV? There's not even any toilet paper in here, for crying out loud!"

Grayson grinned. He was lying atop a bath towel he'd laid over the dirty bedspread. "Hey. You want toilet paper, lady, you've got to pay more than sixty-eight bucks a night."

I chewed my lip. "What am I supposed to ... you know, take care of my business with? A pillowcase?"

Grayson nodded toward the other bed. "I think someone already beat you to that idea."

I tried not to look. Failing at that, I closed my disgusted eyes and sucked in a deep breath. On the exhale, something hit me square in the gut.

I gasped and opened my eyes just as Grayson's football-sized travel bag tumbled to the floor in front of me.

"My emergency kit," he said. "Never leave home without it."

With the weight of my biological emergency pressing down on my bladder, I didn't bother to complain about being used for target practice. "What's in there?"

"Spray bleach. Disinfectant wipes. Toilet tissue. Rubber booties."

"Booties? *Again?* What is it with you and booties?"

"Hey. You get off on toenail fungus, be my guest."

"Gawd, Grayson! What are we doing in this dump?"

"Trying to stay on budget. Now you know why I camp in RV parks and Walmart lots. The bathroom facilities are much nicer. And cleaner."

I did the math. Staying in decent hotels would cost over four grand a month.

"Fine." I skulked back into the bathroom with Grayson's emergency kit.

As I showered in booties amongst a live studio audience of assorted flora and fauna, my lousy couch-bed in the RV slowly transformed into the penthouse suite at the Ritz-Carlton.

Grayson was a diabolical genius.

Either that, or he was pathologically cheap.

"NICE JOB ON THE BATHROOM," Grayson said as he emerged showered and dressed in black jeans and booties.

I finished putting on lipstick in the vanity mirror while he pulled a black T-shirt over his muscular chest.

"Yeah. You owe me dinner for that one."

Grayson smiled and nodded. "Fair enough. Nice wig, by the way."

"Thanks." I adjusted the shoulder-length, bob-cut I'd bought at Walmart. I wasn't sure if the auburn color clashed with my new pink blouse or not, and I didn't care. It was better than looking like a redneck cross-dresser.

I turned to face Grayson. "You ready to meet the preppers?"

Grayson glanced up from his phone. "It's just six. We've got time."

"Not if I'm going to get a drink in me first. And something to eat. I don't want to take the chance those prepper guys'll make me lose my appetite."

"Okay, Miss Early Bird Special. Just let me put on a belt and shoes."

I shot a glance at his feet. "You're not keeping the booties on?"

"No. They clash with my outfit."

I laughed. "Why do you wear black all the time, anyway?"

"I thought I just covered that. So I never have to worry about clashing."

"Right. You wouldn't want to mix your donut shirt with your pizza pants."

Grayson grinned. "Exactly."

Chapter Fifteen

Grayson shifted the RV into park in front of a wooden structure that appeared to have been constructed entirely from the remains of old moonshine still explosions.

He let out a low whistle. "So this is the infamous Blarney's Bar."

My nose crinkled. "I think I'm gonna need a bigger glass of vodka."

A car door closed nearby. I glanced over and spotted the eyeglasses hoarder from Walmart. He ambled toward the bar's entrance, still sporting his fast-food couture.

"Damn," I said. "There goes my head start—and my hankering for pepperoni pizza."

Grayson smirked. "Come on, Drex. A man has a right to make his own unique fashion statement."

"Yeah. His is, 'Kill me before I accessorize.'"

Grayson laughed and nodded toward Blarney's. "Hey, you think they serve tacos in there?"

I shrugged. "Why not? They obviously serve troglodytes. But earlier, didn't you tell me you wanted venison and mashed potatoes?"

"Can't a guy change his mind?"

"Sure. So long as a girl can, too."

Grayson studied me with his green eyes. "Fair enough. Let's go check out the locals, shall we?"

"I can't wait."

We climbed out of the RV and walked across the dirt lot to the falling-down front porch that served as the entrance to Blarney's. Once inside, I made a beeline for the bar. But even though I gave it my best shot, I wasn't fast enough.

"It's you!" the guy in the pizza pants called out. "You came! Come join us!"

As the pudgy pizza man approached, I gave him a weak smile. "That's okay. We were gonna get a bite to eat first."

He squinted through pink glasses and shook his head. "Nonsense! We already ordered enough chicken wings for everybody in the place."

"Does that include me?" Grayson asked.

"Uh ... sure."

Grayson eyed me playfully. "Then count us in."

I scrunched my nose. "You've never seen Grayson eat," I warned.

"You've never seen *me* eat, either," Pizza Pants rebutted.

I sighed. "No, I haven't. Lucky me. Looks like it's going to be a banner night."

The man grinned. "Follow me."

The colorful donuts on his shirt wobbled up, down, and sideways like a Fruit Loops acid flashback, rendering me slightly seasick by the time he led us to a dark corner booth in the rear of the bar. I was surprised to see the back of a blonde head poking up from the booth.

What do you know? Pizza Pants brought a date.

Then the head turned around.

"Pandora! Mr. Gray!"

Operative Garth stood up and pushed his black glasses higher on his nose. "Welcome!"

Pizza Pants' eyes were almost the size of the donuts on his shirt. "*The* Pandora and Mr. Gray?"

"One and the same," Garth said. "I see you've met my colleague, Dr. Freddy Crum."

"Doctor? As in Ph.D.?" I stuttered.

"General physician," Garth said.

My jaw went slack. "You're kidding."

Grayson elbowed me. I blushed and fumbled out an apology. "Sorry, Dr. Crum. You just ... it's just that ...."

"It's okay," Crum said. "I like to keep a low profile. These crazy scrubs are intentional."

"*Intentional?* What do you mean?"

Crum slid into the booth across from Garth. "They make me invisible."

My left eye ticked involuntarily—my built-in woo-woo alarm. "Uh ... pardon the pun," I said to Crum, but I just don't see it."

Crum laughed. "As a physician, I mean. People don't see me as a doctor when I dress like a clown."

I cocked my head. "I still don't get it."

Crum shrugged. "Ever had an old woman lift her shirt and show you her boob?"

"I have," Grayson said, raising his index finger.

I shot him a dirty look and turned back to Crum.

"You see, in this getup, people don't constantly pester me for medical advice while I'm out buying groceries, walking the dog, and generally trying to have a normal life."

"Oh." I smiled at the doctor. "That's actually kind of brilliant. But you have to admit, that's some really 'out there' camouflage."

"The fast-food combo is one of my personal favs," Garth said, and high-fived Crum across the table. "In that getup, nobody even asks us what *time* it is."

Crum grinned up at us, then he suddenly appeared startled. "Oh, my! Where are my manners? Please! Have a seat, you two."

Garth patted the open stretch of brown vinyl beside him. As I slid into the booth next to him, Garth said, "Mr. Gray, you can sit by Dr. Prepper."

"Dr. Prepper?" Grayson asked and stared at Crum. "So, you really *are* a prepper?"

Crum glanced around the room, then gave a quick nod. "That's me. Dr. Prepper."

Suddenly, Garth belted out an old advertising jingle, giving us an exhibition of his buck teeth as he sang, "He's a prepper, I'm a prepper, Rex's a prepper, they're a prepper. Wouldn't you like to be a prepper too?"

Crum groaned. "I told you never to do that again."

Garth's laugh sounded like a donkey's bray. "Come on. Nobody can resist Dr. Prepper!"

Crum groaned again and glanced at the end of the booth. "Speaking of Rexel, looks like we'll need to pull up a chair for him. He won't be too happy about that."

"It's *his* rule," Garth said. "Last one here has to sit on the end."

Crum looked concerned. "Strange. Rexel's almost always the first one here."

Garth sneered. "'Bout time he got a taste of his own protocol. He's the original Debbie Downer."

Crum sighed and nodded. Then his eyes lit up. He rubbed his pudgy fingers together and said, "Quick! Tell us about your adventures before Rexel gets here."

I shrugged. "Well, there's not much to tell—"

"We just captured Mothman," Grayson said.

Garth's eyes nearly popped out of his skull. "The creature from Point Pleasant?"

Grayson grinned proudly. "The very same. Well, either him or a near cousin."

Crum's eyes widened. "No way! That must've been super exciting!"

"Exciting?" Garth aimed the word at Crum, his chin nearly touching his neck. "More like *freaking amazing!* Didn't I tell you their lives rocked?"

"Sheesh," Crum said. "The most exciting thing I've done lately is lance a boil on a kid's buttocks. Are you two working on a case here in Plant City?"

Garth answered for us. "They're investigating Lester Jenkins' death. They think Grays did it."

"Grays?" Crum whispered. "As in *Gray aliens?*"

Grayson cleared his throat. "Well, yes. That's one possibility. However, we haven't come to any conclusions yet. Pandora told me this was a prepper meeting. Do you two know much about prepping?"

"Enough," Garth said, and nodded at Crum. "Freddy and I are on the same survivalist team. I'm security and communications."

Crum raised an index finger. "I'm in charge of medical and safety."

Grayson nodded. "Makes sense. And Rexel?"

Garth scowled. "He takes care of inventory and supplies."

"Was Lester Jenkins part of your team?" I asked.

The two men looked at each other and burst out laughing.

"Lester? No way," Garth said. "He was too much of a hot head."

"And unpredictable," Crum said. "And, I might add, a slob."

I smirked. *That's rich coming from a guy wearing his own grocery list.*

"I agree with you about his lack of fastidiousness," Grayson said. "His cabin was a wreck. You'd think Jenkins would've kept it in better repair, considering the whole upcoming apocalypse and all. There's a hole in the roof the size of a basketball."

"Maybe that's why he went there," I said. "To repair his cabin."

"More like to get away from his old lady," Garth said. "He was always pissing and moaning about her. Couldn't keep his mouth shut."

Crum nodded. "Shoot first and ask questions later. That applied to Jenkins' *gun* as well as his mouth."

The waitress arrived with enough chicken wings to permanently ground an entire migrating flock. My stomach gurgled in anticipation, but I didn't want to be the first to reach for one.

"Help yourself," Crum said, heaping his plate with the barbequed wings.

"Thanks." My fork at the ready, I stabbed at the wings while I aimed my conversation at Garth. "We uh ... ran into your brother, Jimmy, today. He told us he found Jenkins' ammo belt and boots outside by the front steps, about fifty feet from his body. Why would a prepper like Jenkins take his boots off? According to my weather app, it was nearly freezing that night."

Garth shrugged. "Maybe they got wet and he was drying them."

I mulled over the idea. "Why do you think he had so much ammo with him?"

Garth licked sauce from his lips. "Because Jenkins was a total doomsday prepper."

"Isn't *every* prepper?" Grayson asked.

"No," Crum said. "Some of us are simply hoping to outlast the food and power shortages inevitable with an economic collapse."

"What do you mean?" I asked.

"The reign of Retail Man is coming to an end," Crum explained. "We can't continue to spend our way out of dips and recessions. The national debt is like an iceberg getting ready to sink our economic boat."

"That'll never happen," Grayson said.

Crum snorted. "That's exactly what they said about the Titanic."

"If the economy doesn't get us, global warming will," Garth said.

My nose crinkled. "Can't we just outrun the tide?"

Garth shook his head. "Rising sea levels are just a minor symptom. Pandora. Global warming's gonna change the entire weather pattern. Probably even the flow of the Gulf Stream itself. When it does, we're talking killer tornados. Droughts. Ice storms all the way to Havana. Not to mention the ten or twenty million folks along the shorelines with nowhere to live except in a tent in our backyards."

"Don't forget earthquakes," Crum said.

"Like the San Andreas?" Grayson asked. "But they've been saying that thing's going to blow for the last two hundred years."

Crum set down the bony remains of a chicken wing. "No. I'm talking about the New Madrid fault line along the Mississippi River. Lots of folks think when it blows, it'll leave a two-hundred-mile-wide gap running north to south right down the middle of the US."

"So much for the *United* States," Garth quipped.

Grayson shook his head. "Hold on a moment. I'm trying to wrap my head around this. How was Jenkins—or any prepper for that matter—going to solve any of those issues with a bucket of freeze-dried deer meat and a loaded AK-47?"

"They're not," Garth said. "That's short-term thinking. But you gotta make it through the short term to get to the long term."

Grayson nodded, his eyes thoughtful. "Your brother Jimmy told us Jenkins shot out the window in his cabin. Then he left his gun behind and went outside carrying a fully loaded ammo belt. Have any idea why would he do that?"

Garth licked barbeque sauce from his buck teeth. "Maybe his gun jammed when he fired it. It would've been useless."

"So, *then* what?" Grayson asked. "He was going to beat his assailant to death with his ammo belt?"

Crum laughed derisively. "Don't discount that idea. Jenkins has had more than a few screws loose lately."

I looked Crum in the eye. "What do you mean by *lately?*"

"Sorry," Crum said. "Client-patient confidentiality. But I'll say this. Over the past few months, he's been acting more paranoid than usual."

"Any idea why?" Grayson asked.

"Yeah." Crum's lips twisted into a wry smile. "A little condition called 'life.'"

Grayson drummed his fingers on the table. "Could carbon monoxide make someone paranoid? We found some spent fuel canisters in the cabin."

"What kind?" Garth asked.

Grayson deferred to me.

"ThermaFuel," I answered.

Crum shook his head. "No. That wouldn't do it. That stuff's made of diethylene glycol. It's non-toxic. Doesn't even smoke. You can use it indoors or out without worrying about carbon monoxide poisoning."

Grayson's brow furrowed. "What else could've pushed Jenkins over the edge?"

"Besides his wife Arlene, you mean?" Garth quipped.

Grayson's eyes narrowed, as if he'd noted Garth's comment on some list inside his head. "The scene at Jenkins' cabin indicated he must've felt an imminent threat. That whatever he was afraid of was right outside the cabin door. What would—"

"Hey guys," a familiar voice sounded.

Engrossed in conversation, none of us had noticed Officer Jimmy Wells approach. The young cop stood beside the empty chair at the end of the booth. His expression made me think he was trying to piece together how Grayson and I'd managed to crash his private prepper party.

"Sit down," Garth said to his brother. "Looks like Rexel is a no show. Somebody should search Google to see if Hell's frozen over."

Garth and Crum laughed, but Wells' face remained stoic.

"I was afraid of that," Wells said. "I just heard over the police radio that his truck was found abandoned by the side of SR39 this afternoon. I thought maybe one of you had heard from him."

We all shook our heads.

Wells eyed Grayson and me suspiciously. "Weren't you two out there earlier today?"

"Yes," Grayson said. "But just to check out his repeater." He locked eyes with me. "My partner has a thing for little elephants."

Wells' jaw tightened. "Was he acting strangely?"

Grayson shrugged. "Impatient. Paranoid. Angry at the world."

"That's Rexel's normal," Garth said.

Wells blew out a sigh. "I know."

Chapter Sixteen

As Grayson pulled the RV out of Blarney's parking lot, he gave his pathetic Southern accent another try. It was almost as painful as my heartburn from the chicken wings.

"Cryin' shame 'bout Rexel," he said. "But it sure was mighty neighborly of Garth and Dr. Prepper to invite us to join their friendly little, Sunday-go-to-meetin' survivalist clan."

I shot him some side-eye. "Where'd you pick up that shtick? *Hee Haw?* And don't flatter yourself, Grayson. They're just looking for someone to take over Rexel's job of handling their inventory."

Grayson smirked. "Given those breeding hips of yours, darlin', I suspected as much. So, just how good are you with 'handling inventory' anyway?"

"Ugh!" I squelched a grin. "Shut up!"

I whacked him one on the bicep. "And can the corn-pone accent. I've already warned you about it once."

"You breeders are all the same," Grayson muttered, shaking his head. "Well, I guess it's your choice, ma'am. Do we turn right and head to the Walmart parking lot? Or left and go back to our lovely hotel suite?"

I sneered. "Anything but that ashtray of a motel."

"Walmart, it is," he said, and hung a right.

I breathed a sigh of relief, then punctuated the end of it with a rather impressive burp.

"Nice one," Grayson said. "Practicing for the Guinness Book?"

My ears grew warm. "Excuse me. It's just that I haven't had that many chicken wings—or leers from creepy guys—since ... uh, let's see ... *ever.*"

Grayson grinned, then his expression went introspective. We traveled along in silence for a few minutes, watching the lights from one unmemorable business after another flash by like uninspired background filler.

As he made the turn onto the Redman Parkway toward our supercenter stop for the night, Grayson finally broke the silence.

"Relationships are hard."

Crap.

The mention of the word 'relationship' always made me squirrely. I glanced over at Grayson, unsure where he was going with his statement. Random thoughts began ping-ponging around inside my skull like a nuclear reactor gone haywire.

Was Grayson interested in me as more than a business partner? Were my breeding hips really that alluring? Geez. Why hadn't anyone told me earlier? Why did I waste all that money on a ThighMaster? Wait! Maybe he decided our partnership isn't working out.

I'm too flippant.

Too naïve.

Too ... *gassy!*

I cringed. *Is he going to* fire *me?*

Grayson turned his head to face me. "Let me ask you something."

I closed my eyes and braced for the worst. "Okay."

"Jenkins and his wife obviously didn't get along that great. What made them think they could survive the end of the world together in that rattrap of a cabin?"

Relief washed over me like a tsunami. It was quickly followed by a small wave of disappointment. Then, to my surprise, a trickle of anger.

"I don't know," I said, opening my eyes. "But I'll tell you *this*. If I was Jenkins' wife and he tried to drag me to that crappy cabin to ride out the apocalypse, he'd be the first casualty on my list."

"That's what I figured," Grayson said, and turned his eyes back to the road. "Rather than go willingly, she'd put up a fight, right?"

"In my book, yeah."

"But how much of a fight? Do you think Arlene would kill him?"

I shrugged. "Push comes to shove? Why not? If Jenkins was half the jerk those guys said he was, living with him would've already primed Arlene for the job."

Grayson whistled. "Granted, the guy was no husband of the year. But *murder?*"

"You forget, Grayson. From what we've been told, she's a survivalist, too."

Grayson blew out a breath. "Right. I guess you can't be squeamish about the whole kill-or-be-killed thing when the end of the world is breathing down your neck."

"Yeah." I smiled to myself, enjoying his botched metaphor.

Grayson pursed his lips. "You know, until tonight, I never really thought about how many ways it could happen."

"Murder?"

"No. The end of the world. Nuclear power-plant meltdowns. Polar icecap meltdowns. Economic meltdowns. Societal meltdowns. I gotta say, the sheer weight of worrying about all of that doomsday stuff is *insane*. I wouldn't be surprised if the stress caused Jenkins to have his own *personal* meltdown."

I shrugged. "Maybe. But honestly, obsessing about the end of the world isn't much different than watching the network news."

Grayson eyed me, then chewed his lip. "I guess you're right about that. The news is loaded with doom and gloom stories you can't do anything about."

"Exactly." I stifled another burp. It felt like it could've been a record-breaker. "What else can a person do in this crazy, cruel world but stockpile a few creature comforts and hope for the best?"

Grayson smirked. "Thanks. I think I finally understand the whole twenty-four-seven Walmart thing."

I laughed.

Grayson pulled up to a stoplight and studied me. "So let me get this straight, Drex. Am I right in believing you think these prepper folks are just sensible people preparing for a future that, at the moment, isn't looking so bright?"

I shrugged. "I wouldn't go *that* Pollyanna. But look. All I'm saying is that maybe they're not *all* completely bonkers. Some of their fears are justifiable."

"Maybe you're right." Grayson pulled through the intersection. "But whatever happened to enjoying the moment? Maybe I'm wrong, but it seems like these prepper folks are so busy worrying about some post-apocalyptic *tomorrow* that they've forgotten to have a good time *today*."

"I dunno about that. Tonight, Garth and Dr. Prepper seemed pretty happy to me."

Grayson smirked. "True. Beer has that kind of magical power over men."

I laughed. "Chicken wings, too. Who could possibly be sad with a nice, big gutful of chicken wings?"

"Uh ... *the chickens?*"

I laughed again. "Okay. The chickens."

Grayson pulled into the Walmart parking lot. It was surprisingly empty. As he parked the RV at the back-end of the lot, I stared at the yellow, flower-shaped icon on the store's blue sign. Was it my new emblem for "home sweet home?"

"Home sweet home," Grayson said, as if on cue.

I didn't know whether to laugh or cry.

"You can have the bathroom first if you want," he said.

I shook my head. "Thanks, but I already brushed my teeth in the restaurant washroom. I'm good to go."

Grayson smiled. "Low maintenance. I like that."

While I pondered what to make of *that* remark, Grayson cut the ignition. I undid my seatbelt and started to stand, but Grayson gently put his hand over mine.

The feel of his fingers on mine was electric.

"You know, all this prepping stuff?" he said. "Say it actually worked. Say you survived whatever horrific meltdown scenario played out. *Then* what?"

"I dunno."

"Me either."

He pulled his hand away, sending my emotions colliding against each other all over again. Relief. Disappointment. Anger. I really did need to get a grip. I concentrated on his words, and let logic iron over my rumpled feelings.

"To be honest, I just don't get prepping," Grayson said. "Struggling every day simply to keep your belly fed and your heart beating. It just doesn't seem like much of a life to me."

"You forget, Grayson. For most of human history, that's the way it's been."

His lips curled into a slow, thoughtful smile. "Life before Netflix. I almost forgot."

I matched his smile. Grayson's face grew serious again. "Call me crazy, but I think I'd rather go on to my reward—whatever *that* may be—than to survive and be forced to scrounge like a rat for whatever scraps remained in our decimated world. Wouldn't you?"

I nodded. "Probably, yes. But honestly, until the crap actually hits the fan, I don't think anyone knows whether they'd chose to live or die. I guess preppers are simply trying to keep their options open."

"Like Garth said, short term for the long term."

"Yeah."

From the dim light of the streetlamp shining through the windshield, I could almost see the gears turning in Grayson's mind. Finally, he said, "Fair enough," and got up from the driver's seat.

I followed him into the main cabin of the RV. He continued on to his bedroom. I stayed in the living quarters and took the cushions off the couch to access the storage bin underneath.

As I pulled a set of sheets from the bin to make up the couch, Grayson came back into the room.

"You need any help?" he asked.

The tenuous look on his face made me wonder if he was debating whether or not to kiss me.

I nearly dropped the sheets.

"Uh ... no. I'm good."

He turned to go, then stopped and turned around again, causing my heart to beat like a jackhammer. He smiled at me wistfully.

"You know, I can't stop thinking about Jenkins holed up in that disgusting cabin, surrounded by rotting deer meat and ammo. What kind of life is that?"

Definitely not thinking about kissing me.

"I dunno," I said.

"And that AK-47 bugs me," he said. "Why did he leave it in the cabin? Why would he have it in the first place? I'm thinking something in those woods must've been spooking him for a while. Not just this past week. Whatever it was, it had to be something he saw as a major threat to himself, and possibly even to his wife, Arlene."

I fluffed a pillow absently, my thoughts and heartbeat slowly returning to their usual paces. "Grayson, do you think Dr. Prep—I mean Freddy Crum, or Garth ... or even *Rexel* for that matter .... Do you think any of those guys might've killed Lester and abducted Arlene?"

"Why?"

"You know. For ... breeding stock. None of them seemed to like him. And with her husband conveniently out of the picture ... well, it's possible, isn't it?"

Grayson grimaced as he thought about it. "Yes. I suppose. But I doubt it. Those guys didn't seem like they had enough wits about them to be able to keep a woman against her will."

A sudden chill made me shudder. *What kind of wits did it take?* "Maybe you're right."

Grayson studied me. "What about you, Drex? Are you ready for the end of the world?"

"You mean like *prepper* ready?"

"Like *any* kind of ready."

Grayson peeled off his black T-shirt as he waited for my answer. I couldn't help but notice his six pack, and the yellowish, almost healed bruise between his neck and shoulder. Whether he'd gotten the wound from his RV accident or a bite from the Mothman he'd been chasing would be, it seemed, forever up for debate.

"Yeah," I said. "I guess you could say I've got a plan for the end of the world in the back of my mind."

Grayson's green eyes lit up. "Really? What is it?"

"I'm going to head straight for ground zero. My plan is to run head-long into the abyss."

Grayson cocked his head. "Why?"

"Like you said. What's the point of scrounging like rats in a destroyed world? When the time comes, I think I want to be the first to go."

Grayson winked. "Right after Jenkins, you mean."

I smirked. "Hopefully not *that* soon."

Grayson laughed. He reached into a drawer and pulled out a foil pouch. He opened it and tossed Gizzard a couple of freeze-dried crickets. "Listen. I'm gonna hit the hay. Sleep well. I'll see you in the morning—that is, provided we survive any random, overnight apocalypse."

Grayson grinned, held up crossed fingers, then disappeared down the hall.

I slipped into a T-shirt and sweatpants and lay down on the couch. In the dim light, I could just make out my new shoulder-length auburn wig hanging sideways off the side of ET's ugly, square-shaped head.

I smiled to myself. I'd survived the first day of my new life—my first day as a P.I. intern, and my first day as Grayson's partner.

I sighed, settled my five-foot-four frame into the lumpy couch cushions, and listened to the blood coursing through my veins. For the first time since I could remember, I felt ... what was the word for it?

Alive.

I whispered into the darkness.

"Goodnight, Grayson."

A tingle ran down my spine when, to my surprise, he whispered back.

"Goodnight, Drex."

Chapter Seventeen

I was lying on my back. I couldn't see my hands in front of my face—not even the emerald ring I always wore—the one Grandma Selma had left me when she passed away.

My fingers searched the inky darkness to my left. Then to my right. Above. Below. No matter which direction I tried, my fingertips collided with a rough, flat surface mere inches from my body.

OMG! I was trapped inside a box. No ... a coffin!

Somewhere close by, a dog howled mournfully. The coffin was too short. My head was jammed in sideways. I tried to move, but I was wedged in tight.

Either that, or I was paralyzed. Or was I already dead?

The howling grew louder. Closer.

Heavy, slobbering intakes of breath sounded in the darkness, drawing nearer ... nearer.

Suddenly, something began scratching at the coffin.

Someone was digging me out! Or—oh crap!—trying to get in!

My mind froze with terror as the coffin lid first cracked, then flew away as it were caught in a tornado. Above me, the fangs of a hellish hound flashed white against the pitch black night.

It was Garth's dog, Tooth!

The beast's yellow eyes locked on mine. He let out a low, sadistic snarl, and lunged for my throat. I grabbed for my neck.

Suddenly, Tooth farted. He covered his muzzle with his paw and laughed like Scooby Doo ....

I woke up drenched in sweat, my head crammed sideways against the armrest of the couch.

Ugh. Damned chicken wings.

Forced into an odd angle, my neck ached like a stab wound. Stars danced in my eyes as I sat up and rubbed my shoulder blades.

Suddenly, an unearthly yowling sounded close by.

Instantly, I was wide awake. My spine jerked ramrod straight. My eyes darted wildly as I tried to decipher from which direction the horrible sound was coming. A vertebrae in my neck popped as I honed in on the culprit.

Then a grin crept across my face.

It was Grayson. In the bathroom.

The guy was either dying, or he was in dire need of singing lessons.

I laughed. *Huh. Maybe Mr. Perfect isn't so perfect after all.*

I hauled myself up off the couch, grabbed my wig off ET's sickly gray head, tugged it on, and fumbled my way around the tiny kitchen, trying to get a pot of coffee on the make.

The lifespan of an entire generation of fruit flies ticked by as I waited for the coffee to finish brewing. With mug in hand, I was about to do the old carafe-cup switcheroo when Grayson's voice sounded behind me, startling me so badly I nearly dropped my cup.

"Morning, cadet. Coffee smells gold star."

I turned around to find him wearing nothing but a pair of black jeans. No booties this time.

"Thanks," I said. "It's almost ready."

"Good. I thought this morning we would—"

I mashed an index finger over Grayson's lips. "No coffee, no talkie."

Grayson grinned. "My mistake. I'll go finish dressing."

I nodded, and watched Grayson shuffled off to his bedroom. Mercifully, the coffee machine beeped, signaling it was done. I poured myself a mugful. After downing a life-resurrecting slurp, I placed the warm mug against the aching crick in my neck.

"How's it working out with the couch?" Grayson asked from behind me.

Unable to turn my neck, I crab-stepped my body around to face him. Grayson's head, shaved bald a little over a week ago, was now covered in dark stubble like a 1970s-era G.I. Joe.

"I'll get used to it," I said. "But the singing in the shower? That's another story. I gotta say, *Bad to the Bone* is your song, Grayson. And I mean that in more ways than one."

Grayson started to smirk, then stopped. "You could hear that? My apologies. Not used to having an audience."

"No prob." I poured him a cup of coffee and added a pinch of salt. "At least you didn't quit your day job."

"Well, in case you haven't noticed, I kind of *did*." Grayson took a sip of coffee. "Mmm. Good stuff."

It *was* good coffee. Less than one cup in and I already felt nearly completely coherent. "Why did you quit?"

Grayson cocked his head. "What do you mean?"

"You know. How'd you go from being some noted MIT physicist to rambling around in an old RV chasing monsters?"

Grayson's face fell an inch. "I'm gonna need a bigger cup of coffee if I have to spill *that* story."

He flopped into the booth of the small banquette. I put a couple of Pop-Tarts in the toaster, reinforced my coffee mug, and slid into the bench opposite him.

"So?" I asked.

"Well, it all started when—"

A knock on the RV door turned both our heads, but I was the only one who winced from the effort.

"You expecting anybody?" I asked, rubbing my neck.

Grayson shrugged. "No. You?"

I started to shake my head, but thought better of it. Instead, I got up and opened the door.

Officer Wells was standing at the bottom of the steps, holding a kite. I knew the kid was young, but *really?*

"Did someone tell you to go fly that?" I asked, unable to stop myself.

Wells' brow furrowed, then he smirked. "No, ma'am. It was tangled up on your antenna, flapping against your roof. Couldn't you hear it?"

Now that you mention it, yeah. But I thought it was Tooth scratching at my coffin.

"Want some coffee?" I asked.

"Maybe a quick cup. Is Mr. Grayson decent?"

"Sure. Why do you ask?"

His eyes darted up and down, then away. I suddenly realized I was still in my T-shirt and sweatpants, minus any lift and support. I cringed and folded my arms over my boobs. "Come on in."

"Morning, Officer Wells," Grayson said cheerily. "What's up?"

I poured the cop a cup of joe and scooted to the bedroom where my new Walmart clothes awaited. The pink jeans, pink long-sleeved button-down, and white, fringe-covered fake-leather jacket were stuffed into the closet next to Grayson's all-noir collection. There was plenty of room. The man's entire wardrobe consisted of two pairs of black jeans, three black T-shirts, a black suit, and two black dress shirts. He was prepared for any occasion—as long as it was a nighttime stakeout or a funeral.

Comparing the clothes side-by-side made me realize maybe I'd gone a touch overboard in the girly department. But after being mistaken for a boy most of my life, and posing as a garage grease monkey for the past six months, I guess the pendulum was bound to swing a tad too wide on the rebound.

As I donned my town-tramp couture, I kept the bedroom door open a crack and listened in on the guys' conversation.

"I can't stay," I heard Wells say. "I snuck Jenkins' autopsy report out of the file on my boss's desk. I've gotta get it back before he misses it."

"What does it say?" Grayson asked.

"Read it yourself. With the exception of his skull, nearly every major bone in Jenkins' body had been fractured."

"What could do that?"

"Hell if I know."

I hurriedly buttoned my blouse as I scurried out of the bedroom and down the hall. Forgetting that it only took a few steps, I nearly tripped on Wells' long leg extending out from the banquette like a grasshopper's.

He pulled it in and apologized. "Whoa. Sorry about that, ma'am."

"My bad," I said, and glanced at the photo of Jenkins doing his roadkill impression. "Have you ever seen a man crushed like that before?"

"No, ma'am. Only in cartoons—usually with a steamroller."

Grayson pursed his lips. "I'd say we can rule out Wile E. Coyote. I mean, how would he get a steamroller into the middle of a swamp?"

My eyebrows ticked up a notch. "*That's* your problem with that theory?"

Grayson scanned the report, ignoring me. He locked eyes with Wells. "What else could explain it?"

Wells cleared his throat. "Being dropped from a high altitude would do it."

"Like from an alien craft?" Grayson asked.

Wells sighed. "I was thinking more like from a skydiving plane. It happens every once in a while out near Zephyrhills. A skydiver's chute fails and they hit the ground like a sack of wet cement."

Grayson's eyebrow ticked up. He turned a photo toward Wells. "Did any of them look like this?"

Wells grimaced. "Not exactly. Plenty of broken bones, sure. And pretty much smashed to a pulp, too. But when you're dropped from that kind of height, your body usually busts open like a watermelon."

I crinkled my nose. "What's the minimum height you'd have to fall from to get Jenkins' kind of injuries?"

Wells shrugged. "Offhand, I couldn't say."

Grayson rubbed his chin. "He's right. It's impossible to accurately calculate falling injuries."

"Why's that?" I asked.

"Every case is different." Grayson took another sip of coffee. "People have fallen off horses and died. Then others fall thousands of feet and end up with just a few scratches and bruises."

"Well, Jenkins' body wasn't 'busted open like a watermelon,'" I said. "The only cuts were around his head and neck. What could cause that?"

Grayson bit his lip and looked up at Wells. "You've heard about cattle mutilations, right?"

Wells sat up a little straighter. "Uh ... sure."

"They say some of them have broken bones, like they've been dropped from an aerial vehicle."

Wells shook his head. "I'd say that's a stretch."

Grayson eyed the autopsy report and grunted. "Well, whatever did it, one thing's for sure."

"What's that?" I asked.

Grayson shot me a look. "It's still out there."

A cold streak ran down my back. I wanted to change the subject. "Officer Wells, has there been any news on Jenkins' wife?"

"No, ma'am. She's still missing. We checked the house with a fine-tooth comb. She's not there." Wells stood. "Thanks for the coffee. But I've got to get this report back before anyone notices it missing."

Grayson stood and held out the report. "Thank you for letting me take a look at it."

"Keep it. That's yours. I made a copy at Walmart, in case you weren't up yet." He looked Grayson hard in the eyes. "We're even now, right?"

"Absolutely."

Wells' face relaxed a notch. "Good. Now do me a favor. Stay away from Jenkins' cabin. I don't need to be cleaning up any more piles of potted meat."

Grayson nodded and dropped the report onto the banquette table. He got up and opened the RV door for Wells. "Thanks again, Officer."

"We're even," Wells repeated as he stepped out the door.

Grayson nodded. "As far as you know." He shut the door, leaving Wells staring up at him like a deer in the headlights.

I shook my head. "So, what now?"

"Eat your Pop-Tart and put on your pink boots, Dolly. We're going to Jenkins' place."

Chapter Eighteen

Slack-jawed, I stared at Grayson as he took a casual sip of coffee. "You really think it's a good idea to go back to Jenkins' cabin after you just told Wells you wouldn't?"

"Tsk. Tsk." Grayson shook his head. "You should listen more carefully. I said no such thing."

"You're impossible, Grayson! And in case you're not keeping tabs on these things, a guy just got himself murdered out there!"

"Who says he was murdered? And besides, when I said Jenkins' place, I meant his *other* place. You know, where he used to play house with his wifey."

"Oh." I studied my Pop-Tart. "Why didn't you say so in the first place?"

"Do I have to spell out every little detail for you?"

Grayson blew out a breath, and I suddenly worried he was thinking I was more trouble than I was worth. I swallowed hard and tried to come up with the kind of intelligent questions a proper intern might ask. I couldn't think of squat.

Maybe he should *fire me.*

"So, what's the plan?" I asked sheepishly.

Grayson set down his coffee mug and pointed an index finger to the sky. "Find the motivation, find the killer. At least, that's what most investigators focus on. But the game we're playing isn't quite the same."

"What do you mean?"

"Everybody we've talked to says Jenkins was a jerk, right?"

I raised an eyebrow. "That's putting it kindly."

"Right. So there was ample reason to, shall we say, help speed the man along to his own personal doomsday."

"So you *do* think he was murdered. By an actual human, I mean."

Grayson shrugged. "Jenkins' death could be a simple case of ticking off the wrong person. He could've gone to Blarney's, inadvertently pissed off some clodhopper, and became the hottest new dance floor for a hillbilly stomp fest."

My eyes narrowed. "Or his wife did him in and ran off with said clodhopper hillbilly."

Grayson nodded thoughtfully. "Another fine possibility. But then again, what if our killer *wasn't* human? What would be the motivation then?"

I held up my half-eaten Pop-Tart. "Uh ... breakfast?"

Grayson smirked. "*Typically*, yes. But Jenkins' body wasn't eaten."

"Hmm." I pursed my lips. "What if he taunted the animal until it finally fought back and killed him just for sport?"

Grayson took a slug of coffee. "A reasonable theory. But what if the killer wasn't an animal at all, but something more otherworldly than that?"

I groaned. "Everything leads back to aliens with you. Don't tell me these 'superior beings' you're so fond of were able to navigate billions of miles to get here but couldn't find a better test subject to probe than Lester Jenkins' sorry old ass."

Grayson laughed, then his eyes flashed with seriousness. "That's a pretty good point, cadet." He sighed, got up, and rinsed his cup in the sink. "I hate to admit it, but I think you're right. I just don't see anything *that* out of the ordinary going on here."

I frowned. "What are you saying?"

"Simple. No monster, no paycheck."

"We're giving up?"

"Cutting our losses."

I frowned. "What about that whole radio transmission thing? Jenkins yelling 'They're here,' and all?"

Grayson shrugged. "Like Rexel said. He was probably drunk." He dried his mug with a dishtowel and hung it on a hook. "I say we hit the road."

My back stiffened. "Come on, Grayson. We're here. We might as well check out Jenkins' house like you planned. If we don't find anything there to support this alien invasion theory, *then* we can go."

Grayson's mouth curled into half a smile. "Now *there's* that scrappy intern I hired."

I gave him some side-eye, then laughed. "Okay. Suppose Jenkins *was* abducted by aliens. And these other-planetary beings dropped him back to Earth without the courtesy of a parachute. What could possibly be their motivation?"

"Easy," Grayson replied. "Entertainment."

Chapter Nineteen

G rayson turned off the ignition. The old RV shuddered wildly, giving my sore neck a pleasant little mini-massage. It was midmorning, and we were parked on the street in front of a remarkably uninspired single-story house.

To call it a crackerbox would've been an insult to Saltines.

Not much more than a concrete-block rectangle with a door and a couple of windows punched out of it, the house was one of a street-full of nearly identical homes, each somehow more unremarkable than the last.

I tipped my head and glanced over my sunglasses. My upper lip hooked skyward. "Geez. How would you ever find your house in the dark around here?"

Grayson snorted. "I doubt anyone around here stays up past sundown. Come on. Follow me."

I climbed out of the RV and tried my hand at the kind of P.I. stealth mode I'd seen in the movies—head down, eyes darting around for danger. I glanced over at Grayson to see if I was doing it right.

I nearly choked. He was high-stepping it straight up the driveway like the leader of a marching band.

I scrambled up the drive and caught up to him just as he rang the bell. "What the—?" I asked, staring at him as if he'd lost his mind.

"What?" He mashed the doorbell again. "Just making sure no black sheep relatives are here pilfering through the family jewels."

Grayson's screwed-up metaphor made my eyes itch to orbit around their sockets. He mashed the bell a third time. No one came to the door. I figured his next move would be to pick the lock. But he surprised me again. He merely shrugged and walked around to the side yard.

I shook my head as I trailed after him.

Either he's the worst P.I. in the world, or I am.

"What are you doing?" I hissed at his back as we edged our way across a lawn that hadn't seen a mower in at least a month.

He turned around. "*Think*, Drex. The cops already checked the house and known relatives. So what's left? Where could Arlene Jenkins be?"

"Uh ... the garden shed?" I nodded toward a rusty metal structure in the corner of the lot.

Grayson shrugged. "Worth a shot."

He turned, took a step, and fell face-first onto the ground, letting out a loud grunt. He was up and back on his feet before I could even bite my lip to keep from laughing.

"You okay, there?" I asked, trying to appear concerned instead of amused.

"Yes." Grayson shook himself out and picked up his fedora. "Sizeable hole in the ground there. Watch your step."

He placed his hat back on his head, dusted himself off, and switched his gait from a cavalier jaunt to cautious, creeping steps as he approached the metal shed.

I stood back as he yanked on the handle.

The rusty door squealed open. Something fluttered inside. Then, like something from a bad horror movie, a dozen or so bats came darting out of the shed right at us.

Grayson covered his face with his arms and screamed like a little girl. "Aaaahhhh!"

I nearly bit through my lip, but it didn't help. I burst out laughing anyway. "Don't tell me the great monster chaser is afraid of bats!"

Grayson's eyes scanned the sky with disgust. "Rats with wings. That's all they are."

I pouted. "Even poor Batman?"

Grayson shot me one of his unreadable expressions. But if I had to guess, I'd say I'd just stepped in bat crap. I squelched the giggles banging against my tonsils. It wouldn't do to get fired on my second day at work. I was still in awe that I'd survived day one.

"What now?" I asked.

Grayson took a deep breath and picked up as if nothing had happened. "Arlene's definitely not holed up in there. It's worse than their cabin."

I shook my head. "Gross. Don't remind me. No woman in her right mind would stay in that filthy, falling-down hole in the woods."

Grayson gave a quick nod. "So either Arlene's run off, or there's another place she and Lester were supposed to meet when the end of the world hit the fan."

I smirked. Grayson's messed-up metaphors were becoming part of his charm. Like the cute guy in high school I let get away with saying "supposably."

"But where else could she be?" I asked, glancing around the backyard. I waved my hand, and the thorn from a straggly rosebush pricked my skin. For some reason—maybe the pain—I thought of my mother.

The day after my father's funeral, she'd run off with a guy named David Applewhite, who, I found out a couple of days ago, was my biological father. Maybe she hadn't wanted to waste another second of her life with the wrong man.

Maybe the same thing held true for Arlene Jenkins.

"Maybe she really *did* run away," I said to Grayson. "You heard those guys at the bar last night. None of them wanted Lester Jenkins on their prepper team. Maybe his wife didn't, either."

Grayson mulled over the idea as he inspected a rusty bicycle half buried in weeds. "Why would she have stayed with him this long, then?"

"Two reasons," I said. "One, he was alive. Two, he owned an AK-47."

Grayson smirked. "Fair enough." He dusted his hands off. "I guess that marks the end of the line for this case."

I sighed. "I guess you're right," I said as I stepped up onto a raised, wooden deck. It was the only thing in the backyard that seemed in halfway decent repair.

The heels of my new boots made hollow tapping sounds as I crossed the boards. I thought I heard the sounds echo back.

Strange.

"Did you hear that?" I asked.

Grayson looked up from the garden gnome he was examining. "What?"

"I thought I heard tapping. Or something. I'm not sure."

Grayson's eyes locked on mine. He put an index finger to his lips to shush me, and scanned the yard. I walked across the deck toward him. The echoing taps sounded again.

"Listen!" I said. "Did you hear that? Like muffled banging. Maybe from behind the neighbor's fence?"

Grayson grabbed my arm. "I think it's coming from under your feet."

I shot him a look. "Well, duh, but I'm talking about—"

"No. I mean from under the deck."

My eyes widened. "What?"

Grayson tugged me off the deck and scanned its perimeter with the intensity of a cougar on the hunt. He grabbed a plank and pushed.

A sinister glee swept across his face. "Aha!"

Chapter Twenty

Grayson yanked upward, and half the deck behind Arlene Jenkins' house rose up like a cellar door. Underneath it was a concrete floor. In the center of the concrete was an oval, metal door I figured must've been salvaged from a submarine.

"What the hell is that?" I asked.

Grayson gave me a sideways glance. "Don't tell me you've never seen a bomb shelter before."

"Bomb shelter? In Florida? Dig too deep here and you hit water."

Grayson stared at the gunmetal gray door. "It's a fallout shelter, all right."

Grayson picked up an abandoned rake and banged it against the metal door. From inside, the same number of beats repeated.

My mouth went dry. "You think Lester locked his wife down there?"

Grayson shrugged. "Who else could it be?"

"Cripes, Grayson! The guy's an animal! Help me get this open!"

I knelt down and yanked on the industrial-sized combination padlock bolting the door closed. Whoever was inside banged out a few more beats. I looked up at Grayson. "We need a welding torch to cut through this thing."

"Hold up a second."

Grayson ran off down the side yard toward the front of the house. The faint banging resumed again.

"It's okay," I yelled at the bunker door. "We're here to help."

The banging stopped. Either whoever was down there had heard me, or they'd given up. I wrung my hands until Grayson finally reemerged from around the side of the house.

My jaw dropped open. Grayson had a stethoscope around his neck. In his hand he toted a grapefruit-sized, white crystal.

What the hell?

Caught between a weirdo above ground and one below, I wasn't sure what to do next. I eyed the crystal, then the stethoscope. "You gonna perform a séance or an EKG?"

Grayson shot me some side-eye. "I left my shrunken heads in my other RV. Now shut it and watch the master at work."

Grayson cracked his knuckles, knelt down, and laid the crystal on the ground beside him. He put on the stethoscope, then placed the end on the padlock. He twirled the dial on the combination lock to the right. His eyebrow ticked up. He turned the dial to the left. One more turn to the right and he looked up at me triumphantly.

"Voilà."

He yanked on the lock.

It didn't open.

I smirked as his victory face collapsed.

"Crap. Hold on a second."

Grayson tried the same routine again. Right, left, right. This time, the padlock released. He picked up the crystal and glanced my way. "Brace yourself. Here we go."

"What's the crystal for?" I asked.

"To cold-cock the sucker."

I swallowed hard, then held my breath.

With the crystal in his right hand, Grayson's left hand slid the lock's thick, metal pin from the latch. He glanced up at me, licked his lips, and curled his fist around the handle to yank open the door.

He never got the chance.

The portal door flew open as if kicked by a mule. It struck Grayson squarely under his chin. He sailed backward and landed flat on his back on the deck, knocked out cold.

"Grayson!" I screamed. But then a shadow caught my eye. I turned back toward the bunker. To my horror, something pale and hairy peered out from the opening like a giant, grotesque pupa hatching from an underground cocoon.

Reeking of death and smeared with blood, the creature flashed its savage eyes at me.

I froze in place.

Paralyzed, I was helpless as it lunged at me—bloody teeth snapping—red claws flailing.

I heard a gunshot.

Something struck my head.

My knees hit the deck.

The rest of me quickly followed.

Chapter Twenty-One

Someone slapped my face.

Not woman-gently. Man-gently.

In other words, not gently enough.

"Ow!" I yelped and opened an eye. A black silhouette stood over me, the midmorning sun burning a corona around its edges.

"Thank goodness," a man's voice said. "I thought I was going to have to take you to the hospital."

I squinted up at Officer Wells. The glare off his belt buckle burned holes into my eye sockets.

"No hospitals," I muttered.

He offered me a hand. I took it. As he pulled me to my feet, I couldn't help but notice blood smears all over his nice, crisp uniform.

"What happened to you?" I asked. Then it all came flooding back to me.

The bunker. The submarine door. The monster!

I grabbed Wells by the shoulders and nearly jumped into his arms. "Where is it?" I screeched. "What the hell *is* that thing?"

"Calm down," he said, patting me on the back. "You're okay. You found our missing person, Arlene Jenkins."

I felt woozy and sick to my stomach. "That ... *thing* ... in the bunker? That was *Arlene Jenkins?* But ... she looked like ... she ... she came at me like an *animal!*"

Wells took me by the arm, steadying me. "She was a bit on the wild side, I'll give you that. Tried to put out my lights with a socket wrench. I had to wrestle her all the way to the front yard." Wells shook his head.

"Pinning her down wasn't easy. If you ask me, that woman could turn pro."

I rubbed the knot on my head. "She attacked you?"

"I wouldn't go so far as to call it an attack. The poor woman wasn't in her right mind. Freddy says she's hysterical. Who wouldn't be? She's been locked down in that bunker for God knows how long."

I shuddered at the thought. "Where is she now?"

"Inside. Freddy—I mean, *Dr. Crum*—is examining her right now."

"Here?"

Wells nodded and tipped his hat. "Yes ma'am. That's one of the perks of living in a small town. Doctors still make house calls."

"Where's Grayson?"

"*Now* you think of me," he called out. "I'm okay, by the way."

I turned to see him sprawled out in a deck chair. He waved at me weakly with the hand that wasn't busy holding a baggie of ice to his chin.

"Can you stand?" Office Wells asked him.

"Yeah."

"Come with us, then."

Wells held me up by my elbow and led me into the house. Grayson followed behind us, grousing the entire way to the kitchen.

I rubbed the knot on the side of my head, then examined my fingertips. No blood. I looked up at Wells. "I thought I heard a gunshot."

"You did. It was me." Wells patted his holstered gun. "I was responding to a call a couple doors down. Shot a four-foot rattlesnake curled up on Mrs. Dolan's welcome mat."

I grimaced. "Oh."

"Saw your RV and figured I'd stop and see what you two were up to." Wells shot us both sour looks. "You guys seem to have a penchant for trespassing on the Jenkins' private property."

I bit my lip and looked down.

"But seeing as how you found Arlene, I'll let this one go."

A flashback of the bloody monster coming at me made me flinch. "How'd you figure out that thing was Arlene?"

Wells shrugged. "Process of elimination. Not too many platinum blondes around here. Especially ones with inch-long red nails and gold front teeth."

Geez. I would certainly hope not.

Wells picked up a framed photo from the countertop. "See?"

I crinkled my nose at the photo of the bleach-bottle blonde smiling next to a dour-faced Lester Jenkins. She was flashing a set of grillz that would've given Urkel street cred. "What's with the gold teeth, anyway?"

Wells opened the refrigerator and pulled out two bottles of water. He handed me one. "Portable wealth."

I twisted open the cap. "Huh?"

"You know," Grayson said, then winced. "Like during World War I and II. Whenever the economy tanks, gold remains a valuable form of legal tender." Grayson wiggled his jaw from side to side like a snake, then pressed the baggie of ice back up against it.

"For real?" I asked Wells.

He nodded. "Pretty standard prepper protocol."

I grimaced and tried, unsuccessfully, not to think about how one actually conducted a transaction involving one's own teeth. An incisor for a sack of groceries? A molar for a tank of gas? Would Arlene have to knock out her teeth herself, or would her creditor do the deed? As a post-apocalyptic form of currency, it seemed to me that no one had actually thoroughly thought that plan through.

"Seems like a painful way to do business," I said. "Yanking out your own teeth."

"Grillz slip on over your teeth," Grayson said.

Huh. Maybe they did *think it through.*

Wells handed Grayson a bottle of water. "Y'all drink up. You need to stay hydrated. *And* stay put. I'm going to check on Dr. Crum and Mrs. Jenkins."

Wells disappeared down the hall. Grayson tapped me on the shoulder, making me jump. "Jittery, are we?"

I scowled. "Bats. Monsters. Rattlesnakes. What next? And don't say aliens!"

Grayson grinned, then winced. He pressed his baggie of ice into my hand. "Hold this. I wanna get a peek inside that bomb shelter."

"Grayson! Stop!"

But he was already at the sliding glass door. I held my breath as he opened it, scrambled across the deck, and disappeared into the underground bunker.

Great. How am I supposed to stall Officer Wells? Ask for more ice?

I slunk down the hallway and peeked inside the room I'd seen Wells go into. He was talking to Dr. Crum, who had somehow managed to find an outfit even more absurd than the donut shirt and pizza pants.

The doctor was wearing Birkenstocks and a burlap sack-dress tied at the waist with twine.

What the?

A moan drew my attention to Arlene Jenkins. She was lying in bed, her hands tied to the bedframe with what appeared to be strips of torn sheet. Her fingers were raw.

Double what the?

I stepped inside the room. "What's going on in here?"

Arlene's wild eyes locked on me. "Witch!" she hissed.

Both men's heads jerked in my direction.

Wells rushed over, grabbed my forearms, and pulled me out of the room while Arlene screamed her head off.

"Why is she tied down?" I asked angrily. "Her hands ... the blood. Is she injured?"

"Calm down," Wells said. "Nothing serious. She broke a few finger-nails digging at the door trying to get out. We've got her restrained, but just until she calms down and comes to her senses."

Crum joined us in the hallway. "Keep it down. I just gave her a sedative."

I stared at the doctor. "She thought I was a witch."

Crum shrugged. "Don't take it personally. She thought I was a space alien trying to conduct experiments on her."

"Really?" I studied Crum's burlap ensemble. "From where? Planet Bedrock? What's with the potato sack?"

Crum sighed. "It's part of—"

Arlene screamed again.

Crum glanced at the door. "Listen, I'll explain later."

I frowned. "What's going to happen to her?"

Crum slapped on his soothing doctor face. "She'll calm down. She's just a bit panicked. Trauma from being trapped in that bunker. I'll stay here with her until she comes out of it."

I frowned. "Doesn't she have any relatives nearby? A sister, maybe?"

"No," Wells said. "But Lester has a half-brother. Hank Chambers. I've already called him. He's on his way."

Grayson came hobbling down the hallway toward us. He eyed Crum's sack-dress. "What's up, doc? Laundry day?"

Crum blew out a breath. "I was on my way to Dreadmore when Wells called me."

"Dreadmore?" I asked.

"It's a kind of Medieval-themed survivalist camp," Wells explained. "Preppers go out there to practice living off the land."

Grayson nodded at Crum. "I can definitely see the appeal. I mean, why wait around for some lousy apocalypse when you can live today like it already happened?"

Chapter Twenty-Two

"You sure you're okay to drive?" I asked Grayson as we walked down the Jenkins' driveway. "You might have a slight concussion. And it looks like you've got an alien creature trying to hatch out of your chin."

Grayson shrugged. "I've lived through worse. How's your bean counter?"

I felt the lump on the side of my head. "Lived through worse."

We climbed into the RV. Grayson turned the ignition, hit the gas, and the Jenkins' rundown, cookie-cutter neighborhood slowly disappeared in the rearview mirror. I turned to Grayson. He appeared deep in thought.

"Let me guess. Dreaming of joining the Dreadmore clan?"

Grayson snorted. "Hardly. Just trying to wrap my head around this whole thing. Jenkins locking his wife in that bunker. What if we'd never found her? Makes me wonder how many preppers might've already met a similar fate."

I shuddered. "I don't want to think about it. Where are we headed now?"

"I say let's grab some lunch and get out of here. Lester Jenkins got his butt kicked by some disgruntled country boy. Arlene got locked in a fallout shelter by her husband. Preppers have a penchant for burlap and AK-47s. Case closed." He turned to me. "I've seen enough. Agreed?"

"No."

Grayson shot me a surprised glance. "Really?"

I shrugged. "Arlene thought Dr. Crum was an alien. That he wanted to do experiments on her. Doesn't that seem strange to you?"

"Meh. Not that strange."

"You're kidding, right?"

Grayson laughed. "Listen, Drex. Nobody's willing to admit it, but deep down inside, everybody fantasizes about being anally probed."

Total sicko.

"Grayson, the poor woman was trapped underground for days! She was traumatized! Hysterical!"

"Exactly my point. It was psychosis. Aliens had nothing to do with it. I'd be off my rocker, too, if I'd been buried in a tin can with nothing but deer jerky and a stack of old Chuck Norris DVDs."

My nose crinkled. "That's all that was down there?"

"That and a few freeze-dried pot pies."

"Gross." I reached into my purse and pulled out two Tootsie Pops. "You want one?"

"Sure."

I handed him a disgusting green one.

He smiled. "My favorite."

That totally figures.

Grayson stuck the sucker in his mouth. The bulge it made in his right cheek balanced out his swollen chin. Topped off with the fedora, he looked like the Monopoly banker on the get-out-of-jail-free card—*if* he'd just gotten out of jail, but not scot-free.

I smirked at him.

"What?" Grayson said.

I turned my gaze to the road. "Nothing."

"Right. Keep your eye out for a taco stand, cadet. Let's get some gas and blow this town."

I wasn't sure if that counted as another messed up metaphor or not. I was cooking up a snarky comeback when Grayson's cellphone chirped.

His green eyes glanced my way. "Get it, would you?"

"Sure." I grabbed the phone from his jacket pocket and hit speaker. Wells' voice came on the line.

"Grayson?"

"Speaking."

"Wells here. Can you meet me at McGreggor Funeral Parlor?"

Grayson shot me a curious glance. "What's up?"

"It's about Lester Jenkins."

"Oh," Grayson said, and smiled. "Don't worry. I'll destroy the autopsy report. I promise."

"No. That's not it."

"What then?"

"It's ... about ...." Wells let out a shaky-sounding exhale. "Jenkins' body is missing."

Grayson let his foot off the gas. "Missing? How?"

"That's what I'm hoping you can tell me. Because from where I'm standing right now, it looks like he just got up off the slab and climbed out the funeral home window."

Chapter Twenty-Three

When we reached McGreggor Funeral Parlor, Officer Wells was leaning against his patrol car, his head hanging down as if he'd just lost his best hunting dog.

I rolled down the window. "You okay?"

The young cop looked up, his eyes bright and angry. "I'm a laughingstock at the station now. If my father wasn't chief of police, I'd probably already be fired."

I blanched. "Why? It's not your fault Jenkins' body disappeared."

"That's not it. It's *why* ...." Wells slammed his palm on the hood of the patrol car. "My brother Gary told his friends I was working with you guys—'Mr. Gray and Pandora, the alien hunters.' Word got back to the station ...." He closed his eyes, grimaced, and blew out a breath. "I am *so* screwed."

I winced in empathy. I knew exactly what Wells was going through. I'd felt the same way not much more than a week ago, when I'd first met Grayson. Joining him in his lunatic pursuits had been a leap of faith.

Off a cliff.

Without a parachute.

In other words, the choice hadn't been an easy one to make. To most people, the gap between normal and abnormal was galactic. But like most things, the more familiar you got with something, the less gonzo it seemed. As it currently stood, I wasn't totally convinced whether I was a legitimate P.I intern helping establish new scientific frontiers—or I was a fool helping out on an even bigger fool's errand.

Like Officer Wells, slowly but surely, what constituted "normal" was becoming increasingly unclear in my mind. Was that enough to make someone bitch-slap a patrol car?

Absolutely.

"What can we do to help?" I asked Wells softly.

He studied the pavement for a moment, then struggled to explain. "It's hard to .... Ugh! I dunno. Maybe .... Aww, crap." He looked up at both of us. "Could you just follow me inside? I need to show you something."

I glanced over at Grayson. "Sure," he said.

Wells stared blankly at the ground while Grayson and I got out of the RV.

"Ready?" Wells asked.

"Absolutely," Grayson said. "Lead the way, officer."

Wells turned and slowly dragged his feet toward the entrance, as if he were about to attend his own funeral. Grayson and I exchanged glances, then followed him like a pair of indentured pallbearers.

As we entered McGreggor Funeral Parlor, an older gentleman in a charcoal suit spotted us. He ducked into an office and discretely closed the door. A placard on the wall read, Jeremiah Simpson, Funeral Director.

"This way," Wells said, his face red and sheepish. He led us past the director's office and down a long, narrow hallway filled with photographs of funerals. Happy customers, I supposed. But not too many repeaters, I'd bet.

At the end of the hallway, Wells opened a door. We followed him into a room that smelled worse than the time Grandma Selma tried to make dill pickles in an old laundry tub. My face puckered.

"Jenkins was being prepped for embalming in here," Wells said.

Grayson's nose crinkled. He waved his hand in front of his face. "Looks like Glade beat me to my idea for a fresh new scent."

Wells nodded toward a long metal table with a sink on one end. "Mr. Simpson told me that he and his assistant put Jenkins' corpse on that table by the window. According to him, they went out to lunch. When they returned, his body was gone."

"Did they leave the window open like it is now?" Grayson asked.

"Yes. Mr. Simpson told me that in cooler weather, it helps with the uh ... smell." He pointed out two slashes in the window screen. "He said those weren't there when they left for lunch."

Grayson sniffed the screen, making me wince. "Is he sure?" he asked.

"Uh ... yeah," Wells said. "I asked him the same question. Mr. Simpson's pretty particular about his screens. You know, for keeping out ... you know ... the ... uh ... *flies*."

"Hmm."

While Grayson rubbed his chin and pondered, Wells appeared to edge closer and closer to the verge of panic. After chewing off another fingernail, he blurted, "What do you think happened, Mr. Grayson? Have you ever seen anything like this before?"

Grayson frowned. "Not exactly."

Wells' brow furrowed with hope. "But something similar, right?"

Grayson nodded and exhaled. "Yes."

Wide-eyed, Wells asked, "What was it?"

"I'd say this is the work of your basic, run-of-the-mill body snatcher."

Wells' mouth fell agape. "Body snatcher?"

Grayson shrugged. "Either that or Jenkins got up and climbed out the window himself. Your pick."

"That's it?" The young cop's face twisted in anguish. "So you really don't think aliens had anything to do with this?"

Grayson shook his head. "Absolutely not. Aliens don't cut window screens. They just go right through them."

I stared at Grayson. Now *my* mouth was agape.

Really? Your answer to this whole crazy mess is that aliens don't carry pocketknives?

I shot Wells a sympathetic expression. Poor kid had dared to go out on a ledge and believe, just to be shot down by a stupid hole in a window screen.

"How can you be so certain," I asked Grayson. "What about the way Jenkins was crushed? What would a body snatcher want with a body pulverized like that?"

Grayson shrugged. "Meat popsicles?" He turned to Wells. "Sorry, Wells, but I think we're going to wrap this up and go—"

"Wait! You can't do that!" Wells grabbed Grayson by the shoulders. "Please! At least, not yet."

Grayson studied the cop's earnest, boyish face. "You got another reason for us to stick around, son?"

Wells let go of Grayson and took a step back. "I ... I just think you shouldn't be so quick to rule out the possibility Jenkins' death was due to some kind of ... you know ... *extraterrestrial* involvement."

Grayson sighed. "Sorry, Wells, but you're going to have to do better than that to pique my interest. That story of seeing lights in the sky and getting a creepy feeling won't cut it. If you're going to convince me, I need solid evidence. You got any of *that* handy?"

Wells slumped, bit his lip, and studied the floor.

"Thought so. Sorry, kid." Grayson patted Wells' shoulder and headed toward the embalming room door.

I grimaced with empathy. "Sorry." I turned to follow Grayson out the door, but a firm hand gripped my shoulder, stopping me.

"Hold on a second," Wells said.

I turned to find the young cop no longer slumping or wheedling. Wells' jaw was set. His eyes flashed with determination. "Miss Drex, tell me the truth. Do you believe in all this alien stuff?"

I winced. "I *want* to believe. Does that count?"

"It's going to have to. Help me. *Please.*"

"How? What can *I* do?"

"Convince your partner to hear me out."

I shook my head. "Sorry. I want to help. I really do. But you've got to have something better than anecdotes and hearsay to make Grayson change his mind. We've already got that out the yin-yang."

Wells nodded. "I understand. And I think I do."

I trailed the young cop down the hallway and out into the parking lot. Grayson revved the RV engine and waved for me to get inside. As I walked up to the driver's side window, Grayson rolled it down.

"What's the holdup?"

"Just give the poor kid a second, would you?"

Grayson took off his fedora and let out a sigh that could've filled a hot air balloon. "Okay."

"Thanks."

We watched as Wells pulled a plastic bag out from under the front seat of his patrol car. He walked up to us.

"I found this in Jenkins' cabin." He held up a cheap spiral notebook. "I submitted it as evidence, but it was dismissed—along with the pile of UFO magazines it was in amongst. To be honest, I dismissed it, too, at first. I mean, who'd take something like this seriously?"

Wells thumbed through the notebook until he found what he was looking for. He flipped it around and showed us a centerfold spread. The pages were covered in grade-school doodles of aliens, most of them in compromising sexual positions.

Grayson shook his head. "Thanks for the intergalactic anatomy lesson, kid. But unless there's more in there than some lecher's sick Martian fantasies, you don't have a case."

Wells closed the notebook. "There's more. Trust me." He pulled a small cassette recorder from his jacket pocket. "If what's on here doesn't convince you, nothing will."

Grayson eyed the recorder and licked his lips.

"Okay, Wells. You've got yourself one hour. Let's go get some tacos and talk."

Chapter Twenty-Four

We were sitting in a booth at a tiny, strip-mall restaurant called Tacos Locos. Officer Wells was making his last-chance pitch to Grayson. The young cop had to convince him that something *way* past normal was going on around Plant City, or we were hitting the road, pronto.

"Lester Jenkins could be a jerk, for sure," Wells said as he eyed Grayson's frosty mug of beer with envy. "But he just didn't seem like the kind of guy who would lock his wife up to die alone in that bunker."

"You sure about that?" Grayson said. "From what I hear, the guy was no Gandhi."

"Believe me," Wells said. "I've been called out to the Jenkins' to settle more than a few domestic disputes. But their fights were always about Lester drinking too much or Arlene spending too much. Never anything that would drive him crazy enough to bury her alive."

Grayson leaned back in the booth and eyed Wells. "But he *did* bury her alive. Didn't even leave her a cellphone. He wanted her dead."

Wells drummed a finger on the table absently. "No. I just don't believe that. I think he was trying to punish her somehow. I'm sure he planned on letting her out. He just never got the chance."

Grayson's lips twisted to one side. "Okay. Let's say you're right. That still doesn't answer the question of why he locked her up in the first place. There are easier ways to stop a shopaholic. Just take away her credit cards."

Wells acquiesced with a nod. "I know. That's what has me stuck. Jenkins must've had a really good reason."

"Maybe it was *Arlene* who wanted *Lester* dead," I offered. "So, he stuck her in there to protect himself."

Wells pursed his lips. "If she was trying to murder him, Jenkins didn't mention anything about it in his notebook."

"What *did* you find in that thing?" Grayson asked.

"Mostly ramblings about the end of the world. This may sound weird, but I think in his own way, Jenkins may have been trying to *protect* Arlene."

"From what?" I asked.

"Listen and decide for yourself." Wells set a small tape recorder on the table, then pulled a tiny cassette from his shirt pocket. "I only caught the beginning of this before I got the call about Jenkins' body disappearing."

"Then you don't know what's on the tape?" Grayson asked.

Wells hesitated. "Well, not exactly. No."

Grayson's eyes narrowed. "So you were bluffing."

Wells cringed. "Sort of. But I figured if it was anything like the notebook—"

Grayson grinned and nodded his head. "Well played, kid. You got me. Now don't waste any more of my time. Let's hear it."

"Yes, sir."

Wells mashed a button on the recorder. As it began to play, a waitress delivered a pile of tacos to the table. I started to reach for one, but the words on the cassette made me lose my train of thought.

"*static* ... don't know what to think. The metal casing is definitely extraterrestrial ... *static* ... the earth's atmosphere usually tears holes in a meteorite. This thing is smooth ... *static* ... cylindrical shape."

I locked eyes with Grayson. "Is this for real?"

Grayson's green eyes flashed. "Shhh!"

The recording played on. "Something's happening ... *static* ... end of the thing is beginning to ... *static*."

Grayson barked at Wells. "Turn it up a notch."

Another voice came over the recording. "She's moving ... *static* ... keep back, there! Keep back, I tell ... *static* ... it's red hot, they'll burn to a cinder! Keep back there. Keep those idiots back!"

A gong-like sound reverberated, as if a huge chunk of metal had collided with the ground. Grayson and I exchanged glances as the voice on the tape resumed.

"Someone's crawling out of the hollow top. Someone or . . . *something*."

Screams in the background overwhelmed the man's voice, making the next words barely audible. "Something's wriggling out of the shadow like a gray ... *static*."

The tape went silent. I stared at Grayson. "Was that last word 'gray'?"

"I think so."

I nearly choked. "Gray, as in *aliens?* Is it possible that Jenkins really could've been ... *you* know?" I looked up at the ceiling.

"Possibly," Grayson said. "It would fit the autopsy findings. Aliens beamed Jenkins up, then did experiments on him that left those weird cuts on his face."

My brow furrowed. "What about the fact that most of his bones were broken?"

Grayson sat back in the booth and sucked his teeth. "Let's think about this. According to most reports, Grays are small creatures. If they used a transport tube designed for *their* anatomy, Jenkins would be too big for it. He would've been crushed when they tried to suck him up."

Grayson stopped for a moment. His eyes flashed, then he resumed his analysis. "Or, if the Grays used a transport beam, maybe it malfunctioned and Jenkins' DNA got scrambled into goo. In either scenario, Jenkins would be in no condition for anal probing, so they must've decided to jettison his carcass. It fell back to Earth and splat—Jenkins-flavored man-pudding."

I shot a glance across the table at Wells. The poor guy was slumped in his seat, his mouth hanging open wide enough to shove a doorknob into.

"You okay?" I asked.

My question broke Wells' stupor. His eyes flickered wildly, then he bolted out of his seat and yelled, "Are you *kidding* me? *Hell, no,* I'm not okay! Didn't you hear that tape? Earth is under attack by aliens!"

"But—"

Wells pulled his gun out of its holster and scrambled out of the restaurant like a madman on fire.

I stared at Grayson. "Is he right? Are we under attack?"

Grayson stopped chewing the side of his mouth. "It's a distinct possibility."

My gut flopped. "What are we going to do?"

"What we always do. *Investigate.*"

A shiver of dread ran down my spine. Grayson, on the other hand, seemed alarmingly unfazed. He sighed, grabbed a taco, and scooted out of the booth. I started to get up and follow him, but he stopped me.

"Sit tight, cadet. I've got this. But do me one favor."

"What?"

"Don't let the Grays eat all the tacos before I get back."

He shot me a wink, and a sudden wave of peace came over me. My body relaxed as if I'd been hit with a tranquilizing dart. As I watched Grayson sprint out the door, I realized that if Earth really *was* under attack by creatures from outer space, he was exactly the kind of calm-under-pressure leader I wanted by my side.

I only hoped for humanity's sake that the aliens didn't turn out to look like bats.

Chapter Twenty-Five

While I waited in the restaurant booth for Grayson to talk Wells down off his alien-invasion ledge, I flipped through Lester Jenkins' bizarre notebook entries and wondered why any form of intelligent life would bother with our crazy asses in the first place.

On page 43, Sasquatch was doing it doggie style with a Gray. On the opposite page, a reptilian was putting his forked tongue to lascivious use on an insectoid's spread antennae .... *Ugh.* From every angle, humans—especially guys—were disgusting creatures, indeed.

I chewed my lip and wondered if perhaps Grayson was right. Maybe the only reason humans existed was to entertain the gods.

Maybe we're all merely fleas in the great cosmic flea circus of life ....

I glanced through a few more pages of Jenkins' sick drawings and lunatic ramblings, and found myself empathizing with the aliens.

I don't blame them. If I had a spaceship, I'd be soooo *outta here.*

"Stop ogling those poor, exploited aliens," Grayson's voice sounded above me.

Startled, my gaze shot upward. Grayson was standing at the end of the booth, his arm around poor Officer Wells' shell-shocked young shoulders. My ears burned.

I closed Jenkins' notebook full of home-drawn galactic porn and cleared my throat. "I was only reading it for the articles."

Grayson snorted.

Wells jerked away from his embrace. "How can you two laugh at a time like this?"

Because it's either that or start sucking my thumb, I thought.

"Look around, kid," Grayson said. "We're not under attack at the moment. And even if we were, this isn't a problem you can solve with a six-shooter. Jenkins had an AK-47, and look what it got *him*."

Wells' lip quivered. Grayson put a hand on his shoulder.

"Sit down, Wells. Have a taco. Drink a beer. I think if an alien invasion were imminent, we'd have heard something about it on the news by now."

"Network news never tells the whole truth," Wells muttered.

Grayson nodded. "That's why I never watch it. Now sit down and eat. You're going to need your strength to kick all that alien butt later."

Wells gave in and plopped into the booth. I reached across the table to hand him back Jenkins' notebook. "Did you show this to your brother, Garth?"

Wells glanced at me with eyes more confused than ever. "You mean *Gary?*"

I cringed. "Yes. Sorry. We know him as Operative Garth. Has he seen the notebook or heard the tape?"

"No!" Wells shook his head. "That's all I need. Gary'd get on that stupid radio of his and the whole town would know in five minutes. I'd lose my job for sure!"

Wells slumped back in the booth and muttered to himself like a mental patient. "Not that it would matter, once the aliens take over."

Grayson munched on a taco. "Before we jump to any conclusions, I think we should go talk to your brother."

Wells glared at him, his eyes narrow slits. "Why?"

Grayson cocked his head. "You're a cop. You know why. Like you just said yourself, Garth's connected to the local underground communication channels. Don't you think we should gather some corroborating evidence before we call CNN and tell them the aliens are out to get us?"

Wells sighed. "I guess," he said sullenly. "But we can't right now. He's at work."

I tried to picture Garth at a place of employment. I liked to think I had a good imagination, but my brain couldn't stretch that far. Who on earth would hire him? Walmart? Taco Bell? An orthodontist?

"Where's he work?" I asked.

Wells' eyes shifted to the floor. "Dreadmore Village."

My eyebrows ticked up a notch. "That prepper place Dr. Crum was talking about?"

"Yes."

Grayson's lips took on a sadistic curl. "Well then, what are we waiting for?"

Chapter Twenty-Six

Officer Wells' battered old pickup bounced and swerved along the muddy, rut-scarred backroad like a sadistic carnival ride. I was on the bench seat, sandwiched between the young cop and Grayson. I hung onto the ashtray for dear life, wishing I had a mouth-guard to keep my teeth from chipping.

"This isn't a road," I said between bumps. "It's a collection of pot-holes."

As if on cue, the truck's right front tire sunk into a hole so deep it sent me lurching toward Grayson. He grabbed me to keep me from flying out the window. I ended up in his arms, both of us pinned against the side of the cab.

I'd have thought up another complaint if I hadn't been distracted by the feel of Grayson's skin against mine.

It was electric.

Heat shot through every part of me that made contact with his taut, muscular body. If Grayson felt the same buzz from my somewhat less slim and less muscular body, he didn't let on. Instead, he pushed me back upright and asked, "How much farther?"

"Another quarter mile or so," Wells said.

"Great," I groaned.

Wells shot me a sideways glance. "Dreadmore's a prepper colony, not the Holiday Inn."

"Cheery name," Grayson quipped. "How'd they come by it?"

"It's an intentional community with an intentional name," Wells said defensively. "It's designed to discourage unwanted visitors."

"Oh. Kind of like Cockroach Bay," I said. "Not high on the tourist list, but one of the prettiest places in Florida."

"Exactly," Wells said. "Keeps the gawkers away."

"So, are you a member of Dreadmore?" Grayson asked.

Wells blew out a breath. "I asked not to be listed on the official books. But yeah, I do my share of helping out. Security mostly. They're not a bad bunch of folks. Just looking to survive when the storm hits."

"So, Wells," Grayson asked. "Just exactly what kind of storm are you all planning for?"

Wells shrugged and shifted into low gear. The pickup bucked forward like a branded bronco.

"Varies," he said. "Some prep for a mega hurricane. Others a massive EMP. But most are worried about economic collapse. If China sells off its US currency, a wheelbarrow full of dollars won't buy a lima bean."

"What's an EMP?" I asked.

"Electro-magnetic pulse," Grayson said. "A solar flare."

"A big enough one could fry every electronic circuit on the continent," Wells said.

Grayson waved his hand across the windshield. "Picture it, Drex. No TV. No cellphones. No computers. We'd be back to the stone age before sundown."

"Exactly," Wells said. "That's what Dreadmore's about. Figuring out how to survive without electricity or commercial food supplies."

"Sounds like a hardscrabble existence," I said.

Wells shrugged. "Electricity and indoor plumbing are luxuries, Miss Drex. They've only been around for a few generations. Most of our grandparents grew up using outhouses and wood-burning stoves."

I chewed my lip. "Still, I mean, what's the likelihood of one of these EMP's hitting, anyway? A trillion to one?"

"More like a twelve percent chance in the next ten years," Wells said. "Or whenever the military decides to drop another one."

I nearly choked on my tonsils. "*Another* one?"

"In '62, they caused an EMP over the Pacific," Wells said. "It fried electrical circuits all the way to Hawaii—over nine hundred miles away."

The old truck lurched forward, sending me careening into its dented metal dashboard. "Geez! That wasn't a pothole. It was a meteor crater!"

"Good call on vehicles," Grayson said. "My RV would've never made it."

Another pothole sent my knee banging into the dashboard. I shot Wells a sour look. "It would've been nice if you'd sprung for some shock absorbers. What year is this truck, anyway? Or would you have to check the fossil record? I guess being a cop doesn't pay well enough for you to have a decent vehicle."

Wells shot me some side-eye. "You done?"

I pouted. "Yes."

"I can afford a new truck, ma'am. But I prefer this one. No electronics."

"So it's EMP proof," Grayson said.

"Right. No circuits to fry, no engine will die." Wells hit the brakes. "We're here."

I glanced up at the dusty windshield. Through a stand of pines, I made out a collection of thatch-roofed huts and rough-hewn, wood-framed buildings, none bigger than a two-car garage. The sharp, acrid smell of a campfire hinted at my nostrils.

"Stay in the truck," Wells said. "I need to get clearance before you can enter. People around here don't take kindly to snoopers. Like I said earlier, our goal is to keep this place off the radar."

Wells climbed out of the truck and headed toward the shantytown. I turned to Grayson.

"What are you *really* hoping to get out of talking to Garth?"

Grayson tipped his fedora up a notch. "A second opinion on that radio transmission, for one. You heard it. It's hard to deny it sounds pretty authentic—as far as alien invasions go."

My eyebrows shot up in shock and surprise. "You weren't joking? This may actually be *real?*"

Grayson shrugged. "We'll see."

I reached in my purse and pulled out a Tootsie Pop to calm my nerves. I stuck it in my mouth, then turned to Grayson. "Want one?"

"Sure. Green if you've got it."

"No problem. I save those just for you."

Chapter Twenty-Seven

"**I**s it the Tootsie Pop?" I asked.

All the burly men dressed in burlap sacks appeared to be staring at me.

"Probably the pink jeans," Grayson said.

Officer Wells shook his head. "More likely the fact that you're a girl. And your hips are wide. Good breeding stock."

Geez! Not this breeding stock crap again! I never thought I'd miss those damned work coveralls I left behind in Point Paradise.

I gritted my teeth, stuck my head down, and, ironically, wished I looked more like a guy. But there was nothing I could do to make my hips less "shapely." If there had been, I'd have figured it out years ago and sold my idea for a gazillion dollars.

A leer from a tattooed dude sent a creepy feeling wrapping around the back of my neck. I switched places with Grayson, putting myself in the middle between him and Wells. I thought about holding Grayson's hand, but I didn't want to give *yet another* guy the wrong idea.

As the three of us walked along the dirt path cutting through Dreadmore Village, we passed sights I never thought possible outside a low-budget caveman movie.

To our right was a makeshift clothesline—a length of rope strung between two hand-hewn posts. On it hung half a dozen stiff, raw deer hides. Next to that, a sweaty guy wearing one of the hides for a shirt pounded on a red-hot metal rod, then stuck it back into a pile of molten coals.

A grubby, nearly toothless man riding bareback on a donkey leered at me. As his burro trotted by, I saw it was pulling a small wooden cart stacked with rolls of barbed wire.

This is like a medieval fair—without the fun.

A few yards down to our left, we passed an open shack, its ceiling strung with upside-down bouquets of drying herbs. Next to the shack, a man was pumping water from a hand well into an animal-skin bag.

Just past the pump, Officer Wells stopped in front of a faded wooden shed. Its old tin roof was covered with more patches than one of Grandma Selma's quilts.

"Gary should be in there," Wells said. "I've got a couple of things I've gotta do. Go on in. I'll be back soon."

Wells opened the shed door and motioned for us to enter. I followed Grayson inside, glad to leave the set of *Grogg vs the Deerosaur.*

After everything I'd just seen, I didn't know what I'd expected to find inside the shack. I only knew that what I saw was definitely *not* one of the possibilities.

The room was glowing neon green.

I took a quick glance around. A hodge-podge of metal shelving units lined the wooden walls of the shed. Stacked on the shelves were thirty or so brightly lit aquariums. I didn't see any fish. Instead, each tank seemed to glow emerald-green from the filmy water contained within it.

My lip snarled in disgust. I pulled the red Tootsie Pop from my mouth and waved it at Grayson. "I'm not a hundred percent sure about this, but I think this may be where green flavoring comes from."

"Actually, spirulina is virtually flavorless," a voice sounded behind us.

I whirled around to see Operative Garth emerging from between the dirty, opaque-plastic flaps hanging over the back entryway.

"Spiro Agnew?" I asked.

"Spirulina," Garth said. "Edible algae."

I grimaced. "Uh ... I'm no scientist, Garth, but I don't think *any* algae is edible."

Grayson laughed. "People pay good money for it in health food stores, *Pandora*."

Garth gave a quick nod. "That's right, Mr. Gray. But we don't plan on selling it. Spirulina's part of our alternative renewable foods program. ARF, for short."

I glanced around at the slimy aquariums. The thought of that gunk in my mouth made me want to ARF, all right.

"Interesting idea," Grayson said. "But why bother?"

"Excellent question," Garth said in a tone reminiscent of an evil genius. "Did you know that Florida's got the fourth biggest population of all the states? If the food supply chain collapsed today, grocery store shelves would be empty within days. Hours, maybe. That's why we're working on growing our own renewable supply."

I sneered. "And you have the added bonus of never having to worry about thieves."

Grayson shot me a look, then turned to Garth. "I thought you were in charge of *communications*."

"I am. But since Rexel went missing, I got stuck taking over his projects."

Grayson glanced around. He looked impressed. "So, Rexel set all this up?"

Garth nodded. "Yeah. I help him out sometimes. Keeping the tanks in balance is a lot of work. I didn't want to see his latest batch go bad."

If it did, how could you tell?

I slapped on a smile and tried to look less disgusted than I felt. "So, why algae, Garth?"

Garth beamed. "Another excellent question, Pandora. Compared to growing crops, spirulina is a lot less labor intensive. And you don't have to worry about GMO cross-pollination. Or the toxins and radioactive fallout that can happen with field crops."

I took a close look at one of the tanks and swallowed hard. "But ... I mean, how much of this stuff would you have to eat to survive?"

Garth grinned proudly. "That's the beauty of it. One and a half tablespoons of spirulina delivers all your daily vitamin needs."

Grayson nodded. "Impressive. But what about protein?"

"Got that covered, too, Mr. Gray." Garth grinned, then gestured like a snooty butler. "This way, if you please."

I followed the two men through the nasty plastic flaps of the back entryway. We emerged into an outdoor area sheltered from the sun by a loose, flappy roof made of white plastic draped over tall, wooden posts.

A breeze caused the sheets of plastic to flap like dingy ghosts above a jumbled row of narrow, wooden boxes. The boxes themselves were all up on raised platforms constructed of chain-link fencing that had been laid out horizontally and nailed to meter-high sections of tree trunks.

What the hell is in those boxes?

As if reading my mind, Grayson eyed the makeshift operation and plucked the Tootsie Pop from his mouth.

He turned to Garth. "So. What's for dinner?"

Garth licked his lips. "Let me show you."

He opened the wooden lid on one of the boxes and stuck a hand inside. When he pulled it out, his fist was covered in dirt as black and fine as coffee grounds. Between his fingers, a mass of reddish-pink creatures wriggled like spaghetti on LSD.

"Earthworms," Garth said with more enthusiasm than the word deserved. His blond eyebrows waggled above the dark frames of his glasses. "Six of these babies a day is all the protein you need."

My gut dropped four inches. "You're kidding."

Garth grinned. "Nope. Algae and earthworms. Rexel says after the apocalypse, they'll be the new pesto and pasta."

Forget Calgon. Chef Boyardee, take me away.

I sucked hard on my Tootsie Pop, hoping to abate the heaving feeling rising up from my gut. I didn't *want* to know, but couldn't stop myself. I *had* to know.

"How do they taste?" I asked. "I mean, *really?*"

Garth shrugged. "Not that bad with a little A-1 Sauce. Here. Try one." He plucked a squirming worm from his fist and held it toward me.

"Uh ... no thanks."

I'd rather eat the soles of my shoes—after walking through a dog park.

My stomach turned as Grayson plucked the worm from Garth's hand and popped it into his mouth. He chewed it enthusiastically for a second, then his face puckered into a wince.

"I hope you stockpiled a ton of A-1," he coughed.

I'd have laughed if I hadn't been overcome by disgust. I turned to Garth. "*That's* what you're going to live on? Worms and algae?"

Garth shook his head. "Of course not. You also need a bit of roughage. You know, to keep the system moving. Leaves, roots, bark. Anything non-poisonous will do the trick."

The look on my face snuffed out Garth's glow of confidence. He toed the ground with his army boot. "If you don't like that, there's plenty of other choices."

I eyed him suspiciously. "Like what?"

"Well, I don't know all the specifics. Rexel was our entomophagy expert."

"Ento *what?*"

Grayson elbowed me. "Expert on edible insects."

My skin squirmed with imaginary—and hopefully inedible—creepy crawlies. I whispered to Grayson out of the side of my mouth. "Do me a favor. If you ever hear of an impending apocalypse, just shoot me."

Grayson smirked. "Gladly."

I shot him some side-eye. Grayson cocked his head playfully. "What's wrong with bugs, Drex? Insects are a nutritious, highly replenishable food source. Am I right, Garth?"

"Absolutely, Mr. Gray. Algae, insects, and worms. They're all part of a healthy, balanced diet."

I nearly retched. "Yeah. If you're a gecko. Thanks anyway, Garth. But I think I'll go eat double-bacon cheeseburgers until I keel over."

Grayson laughed out loud, catching the attention of a man walking by Dreadmore's Earthworm Emporium. Garth saw him and ducked behind Grayson.

"Who you talking to, Gary?" the man in burlap asked.

Gary, aka Garth, sighed and said snippily, "They've already been approved by security, Jake. Don't bother—"

"Who approved them?" Jake demanded, barging into our circle. "Wait. Don't tell me," he scoffed. "Your brother Jimmy, right? And why aren't you in uniform?"

Garth looked down at his jeans. "Burlap makes me itch."

Jake studied Grayson and me as if he were sizing us up for his freezer. He was thin, wiry, and had the hard, sinewy face of a man who ate only for survival. From the sound of his tone, he took no pleasure in people, either.

"This is Jake," Garth said, then blew out a breath. "He's Rexel's ARF partner. He specializes in wild renewables like—"

"Lots of folks foolishly think they can rely on wild game," Jake said, talking over Garth. "But animals like deer and hogs'll be decimated within a year of the big one. Smart folks'll be eatin' rapid-producing animals. They're the only truly sustainable meat."

"Rapid producing?" Grayson asked. "You mean *re*producing? Like rabbits?"

"Rabbits," Jake hissed. "What a newb." He scoffed again and shook his leathery head. "I'm talking *field mice,* man."

I nearly choked on my Tootsie Pop. "You've got to be joking."

"Don't knock it until you've tried it," Jake said. "That sucker in your mouth? It has nearly the same calories as a field mouse. But candy's all carbs. With field mice you get fats, proteins, and essential minerals."

Garth sneered. "Along with tapeworms, parasites, and salmonella."

Jake glared at Garth as if he were a Cossack. "That's why you *cook* 'em, genius. Mice taste a hell of a lot better than them worms you're growin'."

"Says who?" Garth argued. "You'd have to eat like what—a couple dozen mice to get enough calories to last a single day?"

"*Seventeen*," Jake growled.

Garth shook his head. "That's a lot of rodent roulette with your gut, man. No thanks. I'll take my chances with earthworms."

I swallowed hard. "If those are the only two options, I think I'll take my chances with Tootsie Pops."

Jake stared at me in a way that made me wish my hips were smaller. "Gimme that," he snorted, and grabbed the sucker from my mouth.

"Hey! Watch it! You could've chipped my tooth!"

"Who needs teeth when you're dead?" Jake sneered. "You know this thing is lethal, right?"

I pouted defensively. "The FDA hasn't definitively linked red dye number—"

"That ain't what I mean."

Jake slapped the sticky head of the Tootsie Pop into his palm and closed his fist around it. The stick-end protruded between his knuckles. He shook his fist at me like an angry, homeless caveman. "See this here? Makes a pretty decent puncture weapon. Just aim for the soft tissue areas."

Grayson glanced at an imaginary watch on his wrist, then over at Garth. "Well, look at the time. Speaking of *areas*, could we find a private one to continue our conversation?"

Garth's face melted with relief. "Absolutely, Mr. Gray. You and Pandora follow me."

We left Jake and his deadly sucker-fist standing by the worm boxes and went back into the wooden shack full of aquariums. Officer Wells was inside, listening to the tape again. He hit a button on the recorder. The garbled buzz of the tape rewinding echoed like ghostly babble off the glass tanks lining the shed's walls.

"So what's going on?" Garth asked.

"We've got a tape we want you to hear," Wells said. "I want you to listen carefully, little brother. This could be the end of the world as we know it."

Garth's eyebrows met his mullet. "Good thing the spirulina's almost ready. Let's hear it, bro."

Chapter Twenty-Eight

Officer Wells pursed his lips and hit the play button on the tiny recorder. The eerie green glow of the aquariums provided the perfect backdrop to the otherworldly words emanating from the small device.

"*static* ... don't know what to think. The metal casing is definitely extraterrestrial ... *static* ... the earth's atmosphere usually tears holes in a meteorite. This thing is smooth ... *static* ... cylindrical shape."

I glanced over at Garth. To my surprise, he didn't seem very impressed.

"Something's happening ... *static* ... end of the thing is beginning to ... *static*. She's moving ... *static* ... keep back, there! Keep back, I tell ... *static* ... it's red hot, they'll burn to a cinder! Keep back there. Keep those idiots back!"

Garth started laughing. "Is this some kind of joke?"

Wells jabbed a finger at the recorder, silencing it. "No! Why the hell would you say that?"

Garth shrugged. "That's *War of Worlds*, man. Orson Welles."

I shot a glance at Grayson. His index finger was pressed against his lips, and he was nodding as if he expected just such a logical explanation—or maybe even confirmation of something he'd suspected all along.

As for Officer Wells, he seemed as stunned as I was.

Wells stared at his brother. "Who?"

Garth snorted. "Orson Welles, bro. That famous broadcaster dude? Did that big radio prank back in the '30s?"

Wells' face exploded into an undecipherable jumble of emotions. "But ... but ... *that doesn't make any sense!* Jenkins recorded this over his ham radio. You can hear him breathing in the background. I thought ... I mean *Jenkins* thought ...."

"That it was real?" Garth asked. He snickered. "You and Jenkins and a ton of other boobs." Garth shot a look at my chest, then his eyes moved to my face. "No offence."

Wells' brow furrowed. "But how is that possible? And *why?*" He shook his head. "Rexel ... could he have pranked Jenkins to get back at him for being rude on the radio?"

"Perhaps," Grayson said. He chewed his lip, then shifted his gaze to Garth. "But I'm thinking the culprit is more likely a Cassini bounce."

Garth's eyes lit up. "Yeah. Of course, Mr. Gray!"

As usual, I was at a loss. "What are you guys talking about now?"

"I got this one," Garth said, and turned to face me. "Long story short, in 2004, the Cassini spacecraft buzzed around Saturn. When it did, it recorded a human radio signal bouncing around the planet's rings."

Grayson nodded. "Thus, the Cassini bounce."

"I still don't get it," Officer Wells said, saving me the trouble.

"Don't you see?" Garth said. "Radio signals never die. They just bounce around the solar system like pinballs. They're called skywave transmissions."

I finally got it—sort of. "Okay, let me get this straight. You think Jenkins just happened to randomly pick up the original broadcast of *War of the Worlds* on his radio?" I shook my head. "That just seems so ... *improbable.*"

Grayson nodded. "Yeah. You'd think so. But it happens."

Garth bobbed his mullet. "Mr. Gray's right. In 2014, some guy named Palboya was testing his radio equipment and picked up the skywave transmission of the Hindenburg disaster. It was broadcast back in the 1930s, too."

Wells' face was an unsolved puzzle. "The Hindenburg disaster?"

Garth crinkled his nose. "Come on, bro. From history class? That Zeppelin that caught fire? You know. That reporter guy yelling, 'Oh, the humanity!'"

Oh, the humanity, indeed.

"Ahem." Grayson cleared his throat. "Well, I guess that solves our little alien invasion problem, men. Looks like our work here in Plant City is officially completed."

"Wait!" Garth said. He turned to his brother. "What about Rexel? Is he still missing?"

"Yes," Wells said.

"So, don't you see?" Garth said. "You can't leave yet, Mr. Gray."

Grayson shook his head. "People go missing all the—"

"Yeah, I get that," Garth interrupted. "But what about Jenkins' body *disappearing?* I mean, how'd a dead guy get out a window? There's *gotta* be something funky about *that.*"

Jimmy Wells joined his brother's campaign. "Gary's right. This morning, I noticed something weird on one of Jenkins' autopsy photos." He took a picture from his front pocket and handed it to Grayson. "See those marks on Jenkins' neck?"

Grayson peered at the photo. "Where?"

Wells pointed a finger at the picture. "The two triangular marks. Here."

Grayson squinted at the photo.

"Here. Use these," I said, and pulled my pink cheater glasses from my purse. I handed them to Grayson. He didn't appear particularly grateful, but he put them on anyway.

"Do they look like alien implants to you?" Wells asked.

Grayson studied the photo. "More like something stomped on Jenkins with its cloven hoof."

Garth took a step back, his eyes as big as saucers. "You talking *Satan,* Mr. Gray?"

Grayson glanced at me. His eyes danced with amusement. "Uh ... I'm afraid that would be a *no.*"

I stifled a grin.

"What then?" Wells asked. "You think Jenkins might've been attacked by a wild boar?"

Grayson shrugged and bit his lip. "Maybe. Or a deer." He turned to Wells. "Do deer attack people?"

"Not usually," Wells said. "Unless Jenkins covered himself in pheromones and a randy buck took a shine to him. But it's not even rutting season."

"So, what could it be?" I asked.

"Something outside the normal range of possibilities?" Garth asked hopefully. "Something paranormal?"

"There is this one other possibility," Grayson said, and rubbed his chin. "A half-goat, half-man with a mean urge to stomp."

"A chupacabra!" Garth blurted. "Oh! That would be so cool, man!"

Grayson shook his head. "No. As fun as that would be, I don't think so. No sucking injuries."

Garth's face collapsed.

"So, what made those weird marks then?" I asked.

"I was just speculating," Grayson said. "But now I'm thinking maybe it *could* be him."

"Who?" Wells asked.

Grayson chewed his lip as we all waited anxiously for him to speak. Finally, he said one word.

"Pan."

"Pan?" Garth, Wells, and I said in unison.

"Yes. Pan."

"Who the hell is Pan?" Wells asked.

"Oh. Sorry," Grayson said. "Pan's a mythical creature. A Greek legend. He has the legs and horns of a goat, but walks upright like a man. The horns would explain the marks on Jenkins' face. And, well, because

Pan is bipedal, that could explain how he was able to stomp Jenkins flat with his cloven-hooved feet."

Wells' face sagged. "Now I've heard everything."

Garth nodded as he mulled over Grayson's theory. "Interesting concept, Mr. Gray. But what would a Greek goat-man be doing down here in Florida?"

Grayson shrugged. "The same as everyone else, I suppose. Just looking for a place to ride out his golden years."

Chapter Twenty-Nine

"Sorry Grayson, but I don't buy your Pan theory."

Grayson poured maple syrup over a steaming pile of blueberry flapjacks. "What? You don't like panpipes?"

"I *love* pancakes."

He shook his head. "For a P.I. trainee, you don't listen worth a crap, Drex. I said pan*pipes*. It's a musical instrument. Pan invented it. Thus, panpipes."

"Okay, I *get* it," I said sourly. "Pan*pipes*. So what else did this Pan creature do?"

"Well, legend has it he was the original Fred Astaire."

"Dancing? Let me guess. His favorite move was the stomp. And he liked to get his groove on with old white guys."

Grayson's upper lip hooked into a snarl. "Please! I'm *eating* here."

"I meant that he liked to stomp on—. Wait. *That* bothers you? Aren't you the guy who just ate a freaking *earthworm*, for crying out loud?"

Grayson shrugged. "And your point is?"

My eyes made a trip around the top of their sockets. "Okay, let's put a pin in Pan for the moment."

Grayson winced. His forkful of pancakes paused midway to his mouth. He started to say something, but didn't. Instead, he stuffed the pancakes into his mouth and mumbled, "Proceed."

"Jenkins didn't mention anything about a goat man in his notebook," I said. "But he did blather on and on about strange lights in the sky. And, of course, there's always the possibility he got more than one of those Luke Skywalker things you were talking about."

Grayson's head cocked to one side. He took a sip of coffee to wash down his pancakes. "*Star Wars?*"

"Those bouncing radio signals—you know, off Saturn's rings and all."

"Oh. Skywave transmissions."

"Yeah. Those thingamajigs. Well, what if that happened, but kind of in reverse?"

"What do you mean?"

"What if aliens picked up one of our old transmissions, and thought *they* were under attack?"

Grayson's left eyebrow flew up. He chewed on the idea along with a bite of bacon. "Huh. We've been broadcasting radio signals into space for over a hundred years. I guess one of them is bound to be intercepted and misunderstood at some point."

I tapped a finger on the rim of my coffee cup. "But what I don't get is, if that's what happened, why would aliens hone in on Jenkins as their first point of contact? I mean, what could be so compelling about the ramblings of some drunk old coot in a falling-down shack?"

Grayson's eyebrows met above his furrowed brow. "Lots of people who've changed the world came from humble beginnings, Drex. In fact, I'm of the opinion that the creator of the universe actually *prefers* an underdog."

I shook my head. "Then why crush him like a cracker?"

Grayson sighed and set down his coffee cup. "Good point. But wait a minute. As I recall, didn't God like to smite folks now and again?"

"Smite?"

"Yeah. That's what they called it when ...." Grayson's face shifted. His green eyes twinkled. "Hey. Maybe that's it."

"*What's* it?"

"What happened to Jenkins. Maybe that's what *smiting* is. You know, getting pulverized into pudding. Huh. No wonder you don't hear the term used much nowadays."

I fought a sneer and lost. "Yeah. I heard smiting went the way of verily and thee." I shook my head. "Earth to Grayson. In case you haven't noticed, God doesn't make house calls anymore. Or should I say, *cabin* calls."

Grayson smirked. "Right. Not since he farmed all his smiting out to the Grays."

I laughed despite myself. "Come on, Grayson. If little green men are running all over the cosmos, why haven't they tried to contact us? I mean, besides the smiting, of course."

Grayson locked eyes with me. "Who says they haven't?"

"Well ... duh! Only *everybody*. Except UFO nuts. Like you're always saying, where's the proof?"

"Oh ye of little faith. The proof is everywhere, if your eyes and mind are open enough to see."

"You're right, Jehoshaphat. My bad. I should've never let my subscription to the *National Enquirer* lapse."

Grayson snorted. "Okay, you want proof? How about this? When Nicola Tesla sent out his *very first* radio communication, he reported making contact with beings from outside our planet. Do you consider *him* a crackpot?"

"No. But you have to admit, he was a tad eccentric."

Grayson nodded. "Fair enough. Here's one. In 1977, a news broadcast in the UK was taken over by a being claiming to be Vrillon of the Ashtar Galactic Command."

"You're making that up."

"Nope. All across the UK, TV sets went blank, and this weird, inhuman voice droned on for something like twenty minutes. Vrillon said he was part of an alien race making first contact with us, and that they came in peace."

"That's ridiculous."

Grayson shrugged. "You can listen to it yourself on the internet. So far, no one's been able to satisfactorily debunk it."

"I can. It was *the Brits*, for crying out loud."

Grayson eyed me. "Tough crowd today. Okay. How about this? In 1974, the Voyager—a good-old *American* space probe—was launched into the cosmos. Onboard, it carried a pictographic image of the human body and our DNA helix. Flash forward twenty-seven years to 2001. A crop circle in England bore the *identical* basic format as the Voyager pictograph, only the body shape and DNA helix had been altered to reflect alien anatomy and genetics."

I picked up my coffee mug. "This crop circle. Was it in wheat or barley? I've heard you should never trust barley."

Grayson sat back in his seat and sighed. "See? That's the basic problem with humanity. Nobody wants to stick their neck out to believe. Everything's a hoax, no matter how good the evidence."

He threw up his hands in mock despair. "I mean, gimme a break. Take that Patterson film of Bigfoot. What more do you want? Nobody's willing to believe anything's real until we kill it and parade its head around town on a stick. We're still just dumb animals, Drex. Animals with cellphones and nothing worth saying."

An idea sparked in my brain. "Maybe that's *it*, Grayson."

"What do you mean?"

"Why alien life doesn't bother trying to contact us anymore. Maybe we're just too primitive. We're simply not worth talking to. Either that, or our technology is too inferior. Think about it. To an advanced civilization, even our cellphones might seem like two tin cans and a string."

"Maybe," Grayson conceded. "Or it could be that we've been forever shunned by the IWW for our bad manners."

My eyebrows inched closer together. "The IWW?"

"Intergalactic Welcome Wagon."

"What are you talking about?"

Grayson leaned toward me. "Remember the 'WOW signal'? You know, that radio signal Ohio State University got back in '77? It was the first and only signal their radio array ever detected that had all the hallmarks of extraterrestrial communication."

"Yeah. I've heard of it. But it was just a blip. The signal never repeated."

"Correct. And you know why?"

"No."

"Because we were rude."

My eyebrows shot up. "What?"

Grayson shook his head. "We didn't answer back right away. In fact, *nobody even noticed the signal for two solid days*." He sat back and sighed. "By the time they tried to respond, it was too late. We failed a basic manners test, Drex. And quite possibly blew our chance at ever meeting that alien race or being invited to their next cosmic cocktail party."

I bit my lip. "Geez. Maybe you're right. I know I've dropped guys I was dating for less."

We both sat in silence for a moment, watching my over-easy eggs congeal on my plate.

"Grayson, if there *is* a cosmic consciousness out there trying to communicate with us, how can we tune in to it? Like your ham radio gizmo—do you think there might be a 'God frequency' out there somewhere? Could it be that we have built-in receivers in our brains, but forgot how to use them?"

Grayson studied me. "Big questions, Drex. And to be honest, I don't have all the answers. It's a massive universe out there. And it's full of unlimited possibilities. What's a mere mortal to do? Hell, I can't even decide what to watch on Hulu."

I smiled, but I wasn't ready to drop the topic. "I'm serious, Grayson. How do you think this so-called creator of the universe communicates with us?"

Grayson shrugged. "Lots of ways. Dreams. Thoughts. Visions. Feelings. Experiences. Insights."

"Keep going with that list and there won't be anything that's *not* a communication from God."

Grayson grinned. "Bingo, cadet."

I frowned. "You're nuts, Grayson. But at least we have one thing in common."

"What?"

"We like breakfast for dinner."

Grayson smiled. "Well, there you go. That's the one thing we've got."

I grinned. "So, is it time to head back to our home-sweet-home, the Walmart parking lot?"

"Not tonight. It's not polite to stay more than two nights in a row at the same Walmart, and that's one universal force I don't want to have to reckon with."

My eyebrow shot up. "So, what are we gonna do? Not another sleazy motel, please."

"No. Tonight we have an invitation to camp out."

"Where?"

"It's a surprise."

My nose crinkled. "I don't like surprises."

Grayson grinned like a fox. "Where's your sense of adventure?"

"I left it in my other jeans."

"But those cute pink ones make your breeding-stock hips look so hot."

I closed my eyes and blew out a breath. "Oh, geez. Please tell me we're not going back to Dreadmore."

Grayson laughed. I opened my eyes. He was grinning at me.

"We're not, are we?" I pleaded.

"Nope."

I blew out a breath. "Good. So where, then?"

Grayson motioned to the waitress for the check. "Someplace I know you're going to like even more."

Chapter Thirty

*T*ap. Tap. Tappity-tap.

I cracked open one eye the narrowest slit humanly possible, then scanned my surroundings.

I was in the RV.

Good.

My pink jeans were still on my breeding-stock hips.

Also good.

At least I had *those* two things going for me.

Tap. Tap.

Through the tiny slit, my eye searched the room for the source of the ear-splitting, brain-crunching sound. It was coming from Grayson. He was at the stove, tapping scoops of coffee into a filter. I closed my eye and prayed that I might lapse into a coma.

But instead, I farted.

"Good morning to *you*, too," Grayson replied.

I clamped my jaw shut.

Don't laugh, Bobbie. Don't laugh. I'm telling you, girl, don't you dare freaking laugh!

I laughed. Then I opened my eyes to half-mast. Grayson was grinning at me.

"Sorry," I croaked.

Grayson shrugged. "Farts happen. You up for a cup of coffee?"

"Depends. Do I have to actually be *up* to get one?"

"Rough night, cadet? Oh. Silly question." He shot me a smirk. "Remind me to never leave you unchaperoned with Jose Cuervo again.

Nice Mexican hat dance, by the way. If Pan was watching, I'm sure he was impressed."

I slowly peeled the side of my face off the vinyl couch. "Oh, crap. I thought I'd only dreamt that."

"You wish."

I shot Grayson a sheepish smile with the half of my face that was functioning. I sat up. A millisecond later, my brain followed my body's upward trajectory and slammed into my skull with a thud that ached all the way to my toenails.

Ouch.

I rubbed my forehead. Grayson handed me a mugful of coffee and studied me as I took a greedy gulp. The scalding heat of the bitter liquid on my tongue felt better than the jackhammer assaulting my brain. I groaned from both the pain and the relief.

Grayson shook his head and laughed softly. "Who knew you were such a party animal?"

I scowled. "What are you talking about?"

"You were the life of the campfire last night. Don't you remember?"

"Not exactly."

"I must say, that was the most unusual act I've ever seen performed with a corndog and a tequila bottle."

"Hardy har har." I looked over at ET, the intergalactic lighting fixture. He was bald. My hand went to my head. Nothing but stubble. "Where's my new wig?"

"If memory serves, you said, 'I don't need no stinkin' wig,' and threw it into the fire."

I felt my eyes pop halfway out of my skull. "I did not!"

Grayson grinned. "You did. And I'm sure most would agree it was the highlight of the evening."

I cringed. "*Most?* Who all was there?"

"Oh, pretty much everybody we've met since we blew into town. Plus an old friend."

"Huh?"

"Your cousin Earl. He showed up last night."

I'd have slapped my forehead if I thought I could survive the impact. "Ugh. Great."

The rumbling of a massive diesel engine rattled the RV windows. I knew the sound. It was Bessie, Earl's monster truck.

Grayson looked up. "That must be him now."

He padded over to the RV's side door and opened it. From the glimpse I caught of the rusted-out Buick chassis outside, I deduced we'd spent the night in the Wells brothers' junkyard compound.

Ugh. This just keeps getting better and better.

"Good morning, Earl," Grayson said. "Come on in."

Earl slowly stuck his shaggy head in the door like a cautious sloth. He winked at me, then turned to Grayson. "She had her coffee yet?"

Grayson laughed. "She's working on it."

"Whew! Good. Everybody knows she's just plain evil till she's had a cup."

I scowled at Earl as he squeezed the rest of his bear-like, six-foot-four frame into the RV's tiny main cabin.

"Howdy cuz," he said. "Nice floorshow last night. Or was it a dirt show? You know, on account a there wasn't no real floor?"

"Don't start," I groaned.

"I guess it's too early to argue semantics," Grayson said.

Earl nodded. "Yep. Grandma Selma always told us don't talk religion before breakfast. Speaking of which, look what I got." Earl opened a grocery sack and pulled out a box of donuts.

My eyes lit up. It was only the second time in my life I felt like kissing Earl Shankles on the mouth.

"Did you get me a banana crème?" I asked.

"'Course I did. And this little beauty, too. Thank the lord for twenty-four-hour Walmarts."

Earl pulled out what looked like a life-size Barbie scalp. He shook the platinum-blonde hooker wig at me and made googly eyes. It was only the millionth time in my life I felt like kicking Earl Shankles in the nuts.

"Put the wig on ET," I grumbled. "I still need to get a shower."

"ET?" Earl stared at me like I was crazy.

Garth poked his head inside the RV.

Awesome. It's a full-on party. Again, apparently.

"Morning!" Garth said. "I thought I smelled donuts. Got a spare to share?"

"Only glazed and crème filled," I answered sourly. "They were fresh out of spirulina-flavored."

"Spiro what?" Earl asked, staring at Garth's mullet as he reached for a donut. "You get that wig at Walmarts?"

Garth turned to face him. "Hey, have any of you seen Tooth?"

Earl blanched as his confusion grew. "You looking for a missing tooth?"

"Tooth's a canine," Grayson said.

Earl scratched his head. "Have I done had a stroke? ET and spirals and missing teeth. I don't understand a darn thing what's goin' on up in here."

I smirked and took a noisy slurp of coffee. "Welcome to the fun-house, cuz."

Chapter Thirty-One

I poured Earl another cup of coffee and topped off my mug. Then I set the empty carafe back on the burner and slid into the banquette opposite my burly cousin.

From the shower, Grayson's strangled-cat rendition of the Bee Gees' *Stayin' Alive* seemed a fitting background for Earl's and my equally off-key conversation.

Earl winced and tried to clean out his ear with his index finger. "Lordy! Somewhere a Gibb brother's gettin' a hernia operation."

I gave him half a smile. "I don't mean to sound ungrateful or anything, but what the hell are you doing here, Earl?"

"Checking up on you." He looked down at his coffee mug. "A feller can worry, can't he?"

"I've only been gone less than three days."

"I know." Earl locked eyes with me. "But we both know a lot can happen in a short time."

Like finding out your father's not your real father. And that your mother ran off with the guy who is. Or that you have the vestiges of a twin brother's nuts banging against your brainstem.

Or was that just the tequila?

"True enough," I said, and rubbed my aching head.

Earl laughed "You keep sowing your wild oats like you done last night and you're gonna run out of thread."

"Thanks for the life tip, coach." I blew out a breath. "So how're things going at the garage?"

147

Earl shrugged. "Slow, but okay, I guess. Since you took off, the only person left to talk to is Beth-Ann. And she don't even live in Point Paradise."

Oh, crap. I need to call Beth-Ann.

Earl slurped his coffee. "What with Artie shuttin' down the Stop & Shoppe for the weekend to fumigate for rats, I thought I'd take me a drive out to see you."

I cocked my head. It still thumped, but not as badly. "Is that your way of saying you miss me?"

Earl grinned. "Nah. But I *do* miss getting fired by you."

We laughed for a moment, then Earl's face grew somber.

"You really doing okay here with Grayson? He treatin' you okay and all?"

As I thought about Earl's question for a second, despite the hangover, an unexpected lightness of being took me by surprise. I smiled. "Yeah. I guess I've been too busy with our case to think about much of anything else. But, yeah, it's going okay."

Earl's eyes lit up. "You said on the phone you was investigatin' some feller that got hisself squashed, right?"

"Yeah. A guy named Lester Jenkins was found dead five days ago. Nearly every bone in his body was broken."

"Poor feller. What done it?"

"That's what we're still trying to figure out. We thought at first he'd stumbled onto a secret alien invasion. But that turned out to be a sky-wave transmission."

Earl's face crinkled in confusion. "Hold up a sec. You sayin' you think an alien's transmission fell out of the sky and flattened that feller?"

"No. It's ... ugh." I heaved a sigh. "Listen. The thing is, *how* Jenkins died isn't even the biggest mystery anymore."

Earl's left eyebrow flattened out. "Well, then what in the world is?"

"Where his body went. Jenkins was about to get embalmed when his body disappeared."

Earl sucked in a breath. "Alien abduction!"

"Of a corpse?" I snorted, sending a dull shockwave of pain pulsing through my skull.

"Hmmm," Earl said, his lips twisted to one side. His gaze shifted from the ceiling onto me. "I know! Bigfoot nabbed him!"

I shook my head. "No tracks."

"Then what's left?"

"Grayson thinks it may be some half-goat man named Pan."

"What would this Pan feller want with a dead guy?"

"No. Grayson thinks Pan may have *killed* Jenkins. But wait. You're right. What would *anyone* want with a dead guy?"

"That may be a moot point," Grayson said. He'd emerged from the bathroom wearing his signature black jeans and six-pack abs.

I tried not to stare. "What do you mean?"

"I just got off the phone with Officer Wells. Someone called in a report yesterday about a man sneaking out the back window of Mc-Greggor Funeral Parlor. According to the eyewitness description, it was Lester Jenkins himself."

I nearly dropped my coffee mug. "He's *alive?* How? And why are we just hearing about this now?"

Grayson slipped a black T-shirt on over his head. "The operator who took the call thought it was a prank and dismissed it. Then she saw the report in the newspaper this morning about the body going missing and—"

"Wait a minute," I said. "Come on! Jenkins was as dead as you can get. He couldn't have crawled out the window. It had to be someone else."

Grayson held up his hands as if proclaiming his innocence. "Look. All I know is that Wells told me the physical description fit Jenkins.

And when he ran the tag number in the report, it was a match to Jenkins' truck."

"But that don't make no sense," Earl said.

Grayson grinned. "I know." He shifted his attention to me. "So, you know what that means, right?"

My nose crinkled. "What?"

"We're back in the game."

Chapter Thirty-Two

Bessie's humongous tractor tires whined as we sped down the highway toward our date with a dead guy on the lam.

Either Lester Jenkins had come back to life and crawled out a funeral-home window, or, well, I didn't want to think about what the other options might be. Careening down the road in a pimped-out monster truck, I already had enough troubles on my mind.

To my left, in the driver's seat, sat my cousin, Earl. An unsophisticated, barrel-chested, straight-talking, country boy—he represented everything good *and* bad about my past. To my right sat my future. Grayson. A mysterious, wiry, enigmatic smooth talker who, at the moment, was chewing on a plastic straw like a deranged Pekingese.

It was times like these I wished I didn't think so much.

"Turn right here," Grayson yelled over the buzz of the tires. "Wells said he spotted Jenkins on Harney Road."

Earl yanked the steering wheel, sending me lurching sideways into an impromptu lap dance with Grayson. As I struggled to get back to the center of the seat, Grayson yelled. "That's them!"

Off to the side of the road ahead, a police car's lights flashed. As we drew nearer, the vehicle in front of it—an old red pickup truck—came into view.

Earl shifted into low gear and maneuvered Bessie into the grass behind Wells' patrol car. As soon as he hit the brakes, we opened the doors and tumbled from the monster truck like discarded beer cans.

Grayson and Earl took off toward the vehicles. Hindered by a blowout in my cheap flip flops, I was the last to arrive at the scene. When I did, I took my place in line beside Earl and Grayson, who were staring, open-mouthed, at Lester Jenkins. He was slumped behind the steering wheel of the red pickup like a sack of old potatoes.

I stood, dumbfounded, as Officer Wells questioned Jenkins through the driver's side window.

Earl elbowed me out of my stupor. "Pee-yew! That feller Jenkins might've come back to life like you said, Bobbie. But lord help. He brought the dead stank with him."

Grayson crinkled his nose. "Somebody needs to invent dead-guy cologne."

I was too stunned to even shake my head. "I don't understand," I mumbled. "How is Jenkins alive again?"

Officer Wells lowered his notepad and turned to face us. "He's not. This is Hank Chambers. Lester Jenkins' half-brother."

Chambers looked over at us and shrugged. "People say we look alike."

"What's that smell?" I asked.

Chambers' eyes narrowed, then his face went sheepish. "Oh. Sorry about that. My wife cooked up a pot of collard greens for me to take to Lester's wife, Arlene."

Earl whistled. "That'll do it, all right."

Wells adjusted his stance and glowered at us. "You three mind if I ask Mr. Chambers here a few more questions?"

Earl and I exchanged naughty-kid grimaces.

"Sorry, Officer," Grayson said. "Please. Proceed."

"Thank you." Wells turned back to Chambers. "Sir, when was the last time you talked to your brother, Lester?"

Chambers' mouth hitched up on one side. "Well, I guess that'd be the night he died. He buzzed me on the radio. Told me he was having wifey troubles again. I was supposed to meet him at Blarney's Bar, but he never showed."

Wells' right eyebrow shot up. "And you didn't think to go check on him?"

"Nah. You see, that wasn't the first time he's stood me up. Besides, he's a grown man. He can ... uh ... I mean, he *could* take care of himself, I thought." Chambers looked down. "Maybe I was wrong."

Wells scribbled on the notepad. "Why are you driving your brother's truck?"

"Mine's low on gas. Drove straight to Arlene's place when I got the news yesterday. Nearly didn't make it." He held up a five-gallon gas container. "I was just headed to the gas station to pick up some more go juice."

"Speaking of Mrs. Jenkins, do you know if she quarreled often with Lester?" Wells asked.

Chambers sighed. "Yessir."

Wells jotted a note. "How about you?"

"Me and Lester?" Chambers took off his ball cap and ran his hand through his unkempt, graying hair. "We had our share of brotherly squabbles. Nothing out of the ordinary."

Wells scribbled something on the notepad. "What about you and Arlene. Did you two get along?"

Chambers coughed. "Sure. Why? Did she say something?"

Wells shook his head. "No. But her doctor says she's been acting a little off since she came out of that bunker."

Chambers' face grew red. "Well, who wouldn't? Poor woman just lost her halibut."

"Halibut?" Wells asked.

"What?" Chambers said.

"You said she just lost her halibut."

"Clean out your ears, son. I said husband."

"My apologies," Wells said in a tone that negated his words. "There were reports that this vehicle was seen out at McGreggor Funeral Parlor yesterday."

Chambers' bulbous red nose twitched. "Well, I wouldn't know anything about that. I was with Arlene all day. Listen. Are we done here? I don't want to leave Arlene alone too long. Like that doctor said, she's mighty shook up."

"Uh ... sure," Wells said. "Thank you for your time. Here's my card."

Chambers took the card and tossed it onto the dashboard.

Wells took a step back from the truck. "We might need to examine this vehicle for evidence. I'll be in tou—"

Chambers hit the gas. The back tires spun gravel. Wells joined our gape-mouthed conga line.

"He sure was in a hurry," I said to Wells, then coughed at the dust.

He nodded. "There's definitely something off about him."

"Yeah," Earl said. "He got the haint stank."

"I'm going to tail him," Wells said, ignoring Earl. "Grayson, you're a private investigator. Could you drive over and keep an eye on Arlene Jenkins' place until I can get there?"

Grayson winced. "Well, we were going—"

"Oh! Oh! Can we? Can we?" Earl asked, jumping up and down like a kid.

Grayson shot me a look.

I shrugged. "Earl doesn't get out much."

Grayson sighed. "Sure, Officer Wells. We'd be happy to assist."

Chapter Thirty-Three

After a quick run through the Taco Bell drive-thru, we settled into a spot in front of Arlene Jenkins' place behind a huge hydrangea bush. Earl thought it made the perfect hide.

"You think that bush is gonna cover this huge truck?" I asked, taking a taco from the bag. "That's like trying to smuggle an elephant behind a paper church fan."

Earl sneered. "Well, you got any better ideas Miss Smarty Pants? I'm—"

"Can it, kids," Grayson said, and nodded toward a white Chevy pickup parked at the Jenkins' residence. "That must be Chambers' truck in the driveway. The good thing is, Arlene doesn't know Earl or his truck. We can use that to our advantage."

Earl was about to take a bite out of his burrito, but stopped. "Hold up. What do you mean 'to our advantage'?"

Grayson's lips curled upward slightly. "We need to get a better assessment of the situation. You know, get inside the house."

Earl frowned. "How we gonna do that?"

Grayson lifted an eyebrow. "What you mean is, how are *you* going to do that."

"Huh?"

Grayson grinned like a mad scientist. "You wanted to play investigator, Earl. Now's your big chance. Go up and ring the bell. Ask Arlene for a glass of water or something."

Earl cringed. "Can I finish my burrito first?"

"Time waits for no beans."

Geez. Grayson has absolutely no grasp for metaphors whatsoever.

"Yes, sir," Earl said. He stuck his burrito on the dashboard and climbed out of the truck.

I elbowed Grayson and whispered. "Shouldn't you give him some kind of instructions?"

He locked eyes with me and raised an eyebrow. "Did that ever work for you at the garage?"

My face went limp. "Good point." I smiled to myself and settled in for the show as Earl slinked down the driveway like a hunchbacked crab.

"Earl's the kind of guy better off winging it, anyway," Grayson said.

"Sure," I said. "You keep telling yourself that. Admit it. You get your jollies throwing newbies to the wolves, don't you?" I shoved the last bite of a taco into my mouth.

"Don't *you?*" Grayson grinned and nodded toward the house. "See? He's doing fine."

I looked past Grayson's shoulder at Earl. He was at the door talking to Arlene. She smiled and let him in.

I nearly choked. "Well, I'll be."

I took a sip of Dr Pepper to clear my throat, then scrounged around the bottom of the Taco Bell bag. I pulled out a taco, wadded the empty sack, and tossed it onto the floorboard.

I glanced over at Grayson coyly. "I wonder what Earl said to win Arlene's confidence."

Grayson eyed the empty bag. "You gonna eat the last taco?"

I unwrapped it, took a bite, and smiled up at Grayson. "Nah. She would've never fallen for that line."

Chapter Thirty-Four

I'd barely had time to regret my lunch choice when Earl came flying out of Jenkins' house as if he were being chased by a gun-toting madman.

Correction: mad*woman*.

Arlene Jenkins was hot on Earl's heels, a pistol in one hand, a hammer in the other. If she hadn't tripped on a garden gnome and fallen face-first into a planter bed made from an old tire, I think she might've done Earl harm.

"That woman's plum crazy!" Earl hollered as he yanked open the driver's door. He heaved himself up into the cab, twisted the keys in the ignition, and stomped on the gas.

The G-force of Bessie's 540-horsepower Hemi engine sent my cheap wig flying off my head. It flopped like a platinum squid onto Earl's horrified face.

"What the?" He grabbed a handful of it and flung it out the window.

The sharp blast of a gunshot sounded behind us. I looked back just in time to see Arlene fire again. My poor wig flew apart like a dandelion in a hurricane.

Grayson hollered across me at Earl. "What the hell happened in there?"

"Damned if I know!" Earl punched the gas again. "Everything was going fine and dandy until she found out I wasn't the life insurance guy."

"Did she say how much she was expecting to get?" Grayson asked.

"All of it, I reckon. Call me a prude if you want, but I don't go for recently widowed women. Especially those of the lunatical variety."

My eyebrows met my hairline. "What? Are you saying Arlene Jenkins *came on* to you?"

Earl bit his lip and glanced in the rearview mirror. "Yeppers."

My nose crinkled. "Then she really *must* be nuts."

I turned around and stared out the back window of the cab. Arlene was smaller now, but I could still see her waving the pistol in the air. Earl hooked a right and the bleach-blonde, would-be assassin disappeared from view.

"That's not what I meant," Grayson said. "I was talking about the insurance policy. How much was Arlene expecting for a payout?"

Earl eased up on the accelerator and shrugged. "Told me she had a couple policies. The biggest was Mutual of Malaprop for seventy-five grand."

Grayson sighed. "Were any of these life insurance policies actually *real?*"

Earl's lips pooched out as he thought. "Pretty sure, yeah. She had a calculator, and papers spread out all over the dining room table."

"Hmm." Grayson rubbed his chin. "Anything else suspicious?"

"Well, now that you mention it, her house smelled like Clorox and Pine-Sol. I had her figured for the slobbenly type."

"*Sloven*—ugh!" I said. "You think she did a murder-scene clean-up?"

Earl's eyebrow shot up. "Huh. Well, that's a thought. But I tell you what. That place didn't smell like no collard greens to me. If that Hank feller brought her a mess of collards, you sure wouldn't know it by the stink. Unless a course, she done ate 'em all."

"Wait a minute," I said. "If Chambers brought Arlene the collards from *his* place, wouldn't *his* truck be the one that smelled, not Jenkins'?"

"Good point," Grayson said.

I gave myself an imaginary pat on the back. "And if he lied about that, Chambers could've also lied about the gas can. Maybe he's planning on burning Jenkins' body with gasoline."

Grayson looked at me funny. "A brother barbeque? Sick idea. But okay, I'll bite. Why would he do that?"

"To hide the evidence that he killed him. What else?"

"Nice idea, cadet, but Jenkins body's already been autopsied. What would be the point in destroying it now?"

I slumped back in my seat. Earl picked up the debate.

"Well, what about to hide a suicide? Them life insurance policies don't pay jack crap if you do yourself in."

Grayson smirked. "So you're saying Jenkins beat himself to a pulp for fun and profit?"

"Nah," Earl said. "I'm saying maybe somebody *else* did, after they found him already deader'n a doornail. They figured they'd cover up the suicide and get 'em some insurance money for their troubles."

Grayson sighed. "Like I said, the body's already been autopsied. I saw the report."

"What was the cause of death?" I asked.

"Indeterminable."

Earl laughed. "An insurance company ain't gonna settle for that. Not for a big payout anyhoo. I watch *Forensic Files*. Them fellers would exhume the body. Burnin' it to cinders would take care of that option."

I turned to Grayson. "I think Earl's on to something. But Arlene couldn't have taken the body. Crum had her sedated. Could Chambers have done it?"

Grayson said nothing, but I could almost see the gears in his mind turning.

"Well, look who we got here," Earl said, and hit the brakes.

Officer Wells' patrol car was approaching in the opposite lane. He stopped alongside us and rolled down his window.

"Chambers seems legit," the young cop said. "I followed him. He picked up the gas like he said he was going to. Then he stopped at Walmart. I figured I'd get over here and interview Arlene while she's alone. Anything to report on your end?"

"No sir." Earl waggled his eyebrows. "We got her all warmed up for you, Officer."

Wells' face went slack. "What are you talking about?"

Grayson leaned across me and yelled out Earl's window. "You might want to get Dr. Prepper to give her another sedative before you go in there."

A vein on Wells' neck popped out. "Aww, nuts. What did you all do now?"

Chapter Thirty-Five

I was doing an encore of my sandwich performance, this time with Earl and Grayson the bench seat of Earl's monster truck. Officer Wells sat stewing in his patrol car beside us. We weren't exactly in what you'd call the cop's "good graces," but he didn't have much choice.

He needed us for what was about to go down.

The mission at hand was to capture and sedate a rather crazed and pissed off Arlene Jenkins. To that end, both vehicles were parked around the block from Arlene's place, waiting for the star of the show, Freddy Crum—aka Dr. Prepper—to arrive.

Earl was just about to get on my last nerve with his inane knock-knock jokes when finally, like manna from 1976, an orange Ford Fiesta sputtered into view. The driver, a pudgy guy wearing pink glasses and a green-and-orange pineapple shirt, waved at us as he drove by.

"That's him," I said.

Earl lifted an eyebrow. "Dr. Quack, M.D.?"

I jabbed him with my elbow. "It's a *cover*, okay?"

"Could a fooled me."

I rolled my eyes. "That's kind of the point."

Earl cranked the ignition on Bessie and we rolled in behind Wells' patrol car, forming a three-vehicle convoy with the Fiesta in the lead. We rounded the corner, then converged in front of Arlene Jenkins' house. Wells and Crum got out of their vehicles. We, like delinquent teenagers, were relegated to staying in the truck and awaiting further orders from Wells.

"It may take all of us to restrain her," Crum said, peering up at us from our high perch in the monster truck.

Wells frowned. "You sure we need them?"

"It pays to be on the safe side," Crum said.

Wells blew out a breath. "Okay. Here's the plan." His words were aimed at us, but his eyes stared at Jenkins' house as he spoke. "I'll ring the doorbell. You guys hide in the bushes by the house. You are *not to move* unless I tell you to."

"Got it," Grayson said.

Earl sucked his teeth. "If y'all don't mind, I think I'll wait this one out in the truck. I already done my round a hammer time with that crazy woman."

I winced. "Maybe I should wait with him."

Grayson shook his head. "Nothing doing, cadet. You want that P.I. license, you gotta learn to hang with the big boys."

I looked over at Earl. "You heard him."

My cousin grinned. "What? I never said nothin' about wanting to be no P.I."

"Come on," Grayson said, tugging my arm. "They're already almost to the front door."

I slid out of the seat, then Grayson and I ran across the front yard, skirting a virtual obstacle course of tire planters full of prickly-pear cacti. Crum lay in wait up against the wall beside the front door, a syringe full of happy juice at the ready. Grayson and I took position behind some overgrown hedges. Crum stuck out an arm and gave Wells the thumbs-up sign.

Wells nodded and rang the doorbell.

Nothing happened.

He rang it again.

As he reached over to make a third attempt, the door flew open. A wild-eyed, wild-haired Arlene Jenkins came barreling out, delivering an encore performance of her infamous Maxwell's Silver Hammer routine.

"Oh, crap!" Crum cried out.

Right before the hammer came down on Wells' head, he grabbed Arlene's striking arm. Crum seized the opportunity to jab her bicep with the syringe. He hit the plunger. A second later, Arlene dropped the hammer, then collapsed like a cardboard box in the middle of a monsoon.

"Help us get her inside!" Wells yelled at us.

Grayson and I scrambled to assist. Each of us grabbed an arm or a leg and hauled Arlene to the couch as she muttered crazily the whole way.

"Don't touch. Prickle people. Who are you?" she said as we carried her into the living room. Suddenly, Arlene's eyes flew open and she screamed. "Help! I'm gonna die in here!"

As we laid her on the sofa, Wells asked, "What's wrong with her, Freddy?"

"Post-traumatic hysteria," Crum said. "Here, this will help." Crum gave her another shot. "Arlene? It's me, Dr. Freddy."

She shot him a bleary glance. "Froggy?"

"Freddy." He smiled and reached toward her.

Arlene squirmed to avoid his touch, babbling like a sloppy drunk. "Stop prickling me, you fleak. Where shank. We die shank don't ... come bah." Her eyes rolled up in her head, then she passed out.

Crum shook his head. "I've been her doctor for years. This behavior—it's totally out of character. I've never known her to act so aggressively. She's definitely displaying signs of paranoia."

"Could she be ill? Poisoned, maybe?" Grayson asked.

Crum pursed his lips. "I suppose it's possible. I'll get some blood from her and run some tests."

"Hot in here," Arlene muttered, coming back to consciousness. "Kill you all." Her eyes closed again.

"That does it," Crum said. "I'm calling 9-1-1. Sorry, but it doesn't look like you're going to get any answers out of Arlene Jenkins today."

Chapter Thirty-Six

As the ambulance drove away with a wigged-out Arlene Jenkins in tow, we sat in Earl's truck and debated whether the weirdness going on in Plant City had a down-to-earth explanation, or it originated from somewhere off-planet.

Earl was still an ardent proponent of alien implants. I was torn between poisoning and early-onset dementia. Grayson, apparently giving up on his buddy Pan, was insisting the whole thing could be chalked up to your basic, garden-variety domestic homicide.

"The only way life can be a bed of roses," he philosophized, "is if you're buried under one."

I shot Grayson a dour look. "I had no idea you were such a romantic."

"Let's ask the law," Earl said, nodding toward the house.

Officer Wells was coming down the driveway with Dr. Crum. If I didn't know better, I'd have suspected the doctor himself was under arrest. His expression was textbook nerdy bewilderment.

As they got close, Wells took a quick glance at us, then studied the ground a foot in front of his shoes. "Thanks for the backup. Things could've gotten way out of hand."

Crum shook his head. "I don't know what's gotten into Arlene. But I'm going to find out."

I dragged my gaze up from the hula-dancing pineapples on the doctor's shirt and locked eyes with him. "Dr. Crum, if Arlene was poisoned, could the same thing have happened to her husband, Lester?"

Crum raised his open palms. "I guess. But why would anyone want either one of them dead?"

"Insurance money," Grayson said. "Lester and Arlene didn't have any kids. With Lester out of the way, Arlene would be the sole beneficiary of his policies."

"But it *couldn't* be Arlene," I argued. "She has an—excuse the pun—*airtight* alibi. She was locked in that bunker when Lester was killed."

"That's not provable," Grayson said, slapping on that know-it-all professor expression I was beginning to loathe. "If she was, *who* locked her in there?"

"Lester," I said.

Grayson cocked an eyebrow. "You sure about that?"

I frowned. "Who else could it be?"

"How about Hank Chambers?"

"What?" I nearly gasped. "You think *Chambers* locked Arlene in there?"

"Yes."

"Why? As part of some evil plan to kill Lester and split the insurance payout?"

Grayson winked. "Bingo, cadet. She's got the alibi. He's got the girl."

"Nah," Earl said, shaking his head. "I don't buy it. Hank wouldn't do that to Lester. Them two brothers was tight. I seen pictures of 'em baggin' game together from all over the county. They was good hunting buddies."

Grayson snorted. "Two hombres alone in the woods together with dueling *pistolas*. What could possibly go wrong?"

"Listen," Wells interrupted. "The whole insurance angle doesn't hold water. I checked. The only life insurance on Lester was for five grand. Barely enough to bury him."

Grayson's lips twisted. "Well, if it wasn't for money, then it had to be for love."

"Hold up a minute," Wells said. "You think *Hank's* having an affair with Arlene?"

"I'd say it's a distinct possibility," Grayson said. "And it could've been going on for a long time. This scheme of theirs took a little planning."

I grimaced. "But Chambers is married!"

Earl laughed. "Since when's that stopped anyone from foolin' around?"

"That's also not accurate," Wells said. "Chambers' background check showed he's divorced, as of last month. Not too amicable, I might add. His ex-wife threw him out of the house with nothing but a restraining order for company."

Grayson glanced at his cellphone. "Speaking of Chambers, where is he? Shouldn't he be back from Walmart by now?"

"You're right," Wells said.

Earl shrugged. "Well, it *is* the first of the month an' all."

Wells sighed. "I forgot about that."

The police radio on Wells' belt crackled. "Excuse me, I need to get this." He turned and walked away.

I glanced over at Dr. Crum. He was staring at the pavement, chewing his lip.

"What's wrong?" I asked.

Crum looked up, wide-eyed, as if I'd startled him. "Oh. Nothing. I just ... well, I'm kind of baffled by what's happening. First with Lester, and now Arlene."

"What do you mean, 'first with Lester'?"

"Well, I wasn't going to say anything because of patient confidentiality. But your question about poisoning got me to thinking. And, well, since he's dead, I guess Lester won't mind."

Crum looked at me in a way that made me think he was seeking my approval to continue. I gave it to him with a quick nod. "Right. Lester won't mind."

Crum shifted onto his other pink sneaker. "Lester came to see me a few weeks ago. He was having hot flashes and tingling in his hands. We'd made a joke out of it—that he was suffering from *men*opause."

He looked up at me. I gave him a weak smile.

"Anyway," Crum continued, "I didn't think that much of it until today. When I tried to touch Arlene. She told me to stop 'prickling' her."

"She was mumbling crazy talk," I said. "She could've been talking about the injections. Nobody likes needles."

Crum pursed his lips. "That's true. But she felt a bit warm to the touch, as if she had a slight fever."

"So you think instead of poisoning, she and Lester might've both contracted some kind of illness?"

Crum sighed. "Either one is possible. The flu's going around. And lots of things in the environment can cause adverse reactions. Food additives. Exposure to pesticides. Even the chemicals in cleaning products."

"You got any theories on which it might be?" Grayson asked.

Crum shook his head. "No. But I'll get on it as—"

"I'll catch you all later," Wells hollered, running by us and nearly bowling Crum over. "Got an emergency to get to," he yelled as he raced toward his patrol car.

"What's happening?" Grayson called after him.

Wells yanked open the car door. "Not sure yet, but I think we might've found Rexel."

"Where?" I yelled.

"Climbing the giant strawberry," he hollered, and took off with the lights flashing.

Chapter Thirty-Seven

"What the heck?" I asked. "Giant strawberry? Did I hear that right?"

Crum nodded, his face drawn with concern. "Wells must mean the city water tower. It's painted like a strawberry."

"I got to see me that," Earl said, and fired up Bessie's massive diesel engine. "How do we get there, Doc?"

Crum sighed. "Take I-4 to Park Street. Head south. Can't miss it. Believe me."

"Thanks," I said. "You coming?"

Crum shook his head. "No. I've seen enough crazy for one day. And I need to get to the lab."

"Let's go," Grayson said. "Keep us informed on what you find out, Dr. Crum."

Crum nodded, but his eyes were studying some faraway corner of the sky. I figured he was either deep in thought or was trying to avoid seeing his own shirt.

Grayson strapped on his seatbelt and said, "Punch it, Earl."

My cousin obliged. He mashed the pedal to the floor, and we took off like a tractor out of hell. I tumbled into the side of Grayson, causing him to grunt.

Earl laughed. "You two just can't keep your hands off each other, can you?"

My ears burned. When I pushed myself off Grayson, I saw his cheeks were pink, too.

"THE FUN NEVER ENDS around here," Grayson said as Earl took the corner of Wilder Road on two wheels. Straight ahead, the massive water tower loomed at us like the villain in a low-budget horror flick—*Attack of the Man-Eating Fruit Mutant.*

"Turn here, Earl," I said. "Onto Cherry Street."

Earl's face twisted into a lopsided grin. "Really? You sure we ain't looking for *Strawberry* Street?"

Grayson snorted and nodded toward the tower. "From the looks of it, we're already on *Sesame* Street."

Below the giant berry-shaped tower, a group of elementary-school-aged children were running wild, threading in and out of the growing throng of gawkers. Three patrol cars were already on the scene, their lights flashing. They looked like toys compared to the humongous strawberry.

"There!" Grayson said, pointing to an empty space on the side of the road.

Earl squeezed Bessie in between a faded blue church bus and an old ice cream truck. Grayson opened the door. The tune *It's a Small World* filled our ears as it crackled from the ice cream truck's audio system. The speakers sounded like they'd been shot since the early '70s.

"Somebody needs their xylophone tuned," Grayson said as we piled out of the truck.

"Hey, he's got creamsicles!" Earl hollered.

"No time." Grayson nodded toward the tower. "Look."

I stared up at the tower and blinked. I blinked again, thinking it might have been another twin-induced hallucination, but the view didn't change.

About a hundred feet up the stem of the colossal strawberry, a naked old white man was hollering and shaking his fist at the crowd like an angry maggot. Blue and red lights flashed alternately in my eyes. *It's a Small World* plinked at my ears like a toy piano hammered on by a chimpanzee.

This must be what it's like to have an acid flashback.

"You think that's Rexel?" Grayson asked.

I cringed. "Yeah. I recognize the liver spots on that shiny bald head even without my cheater glasses."

Earl elbowed me. "You sure that's *all* you recognize?"

I punched Earl in the gut. After a round of retaliatory sparing, we settled down and joined Grayson. He was staring up at an enormous yellow crane. It lurched in fits and starts toward the monstrous strawberry like a ten-story-tall praying mantis.

Mantris vs Strawzilla. It's got a nice ring to it.

Once the crane got within range, it extended a long, pendulous arm toward poor old Rexel, who was still flailing his fist like an angry, albino fruit-fly larva. Some guy dressed like a shortstop grabbed him by the torso, then yanked Rexel, kicking and screaming, into the basket of the cherry picker.

The crowd erupted into cheers, then half of them made a beeline for the ice cream truck.

"Well, I'll be," Earl said, succinctly summing up the event.

"Rexel was such a stickler for the rules," Grayson said. "What the hell's gotten into him?"

"Probably the same thing that got into Lester and Arlene," I said.

Earl's eyes grew wide. "You talkin' demon possession?"

I shot my cousin some side-eye. "Absolutely. And on a Sunday, no less."

Earl swallowed hard. "What do we do now?"

A man's voice sounded behind us. "I'd say dinner and a movie, but how're you ever gonna top *that* show?"

I turned to find Garth, the mullet-boy-wonder, grinning at us. "What are *you* doing here?" I asked.

"Same as you," he said. "Gawking. I heard about it on my ham radio." He laughed. "For us local operators, this is the event of the season. Maybe even the *decade*."

I frowned. "Why do you say that?"

Garth grinned. "Old T-Rexel, of course. The guy's always on our butts to follow protocol, then he gets naked and climbs the water tower like a geriatric King Kong. You can't make that kind of crap up."

"What you think got into the poor feller?" Earl asked.

Garth shrugged. "I dunno. But Rexel's definitely off his regular feed. Nobody's heard from him for days, and then last night he kerchunked my repeater."

Earl grimaced. "Listen here, Garth. It's better for ever'body if you keep your personal life to yourself."

"Wha—?" Garth gave everyone a good look at his buck teeth, then cringed. "Oh! No, man. It's not—ugh. Look, all I can say is, something's totally up with that old dude."

The flash of red and blue lights made us turn and stare. A police car drove slowly by. Rexel's face and palms were plastered to the rear side-window like a kid forced to leave the carnival too soon.

"There he goes," Earl said.

"Yep," Garth nodded. "Looks like the show's over. Where you guys crashing tonight?"

Grayson shrugged. "No particular plans."

Garth shot me a grin. "Well, you're welcome to camp at my place again. Pandora, your sombrero act last night put Rexel's puny deal here to shame."

I cringed inside. "Uh ... thanks, but—"

"We'd love to," Grayson butted in. He turned to me and winked a green eye. "But not too heavy on the booze tonight, honey. We've got a big day tomorrow."

Chapter Thirty-Eight

Against all my will and most of my better judgment, I'd ridden with Earl and Grayson back to Garth's chain-linked junkyard of a compound.

Earl was excited about the idea of camping out again with the guys in his monster truck. I, on the other hand, was trying my best to convince Grayson not to spend another night there.

"Come on, Grayson," I said as we climbed down out of Bessie. "We might as well head down the road and find a new case. There's nothing out of the ordinary going on here."

"You sure about that?" He studied me with those unreadable eyes of his. "It seems like only yesterday *you* were the one hell-bent on staying. Wait. It *was* yesterday."

My face flushed pink. I attempted to cover it with a white lie. "I changed my mind. You were right. This is just an ordinary case of domestic homicide."

Grayson's eyebrow ticked up a good inch. "I'm *right?*" He grinned and shook his head. "Come on, Drex. What's *really* going on here?"

Crap. It's like the guy can see right through me.

The truth was, at the moment, I didn't give a flip whether the folks around here were being driven wackadoodle by malaria-infested mosquitoes or sadistic, Southern-fried poltergeists.

I just wanted to get the hell out of Garth's compound.

If we stayed, I'd be facing a humiliating ribbing from the guys about last night. I could've probably handled the jokes if I'd known what to expect—but the fact was, I couldn't remember squat about what I'd done after that third shot of tequila.

I blew out an angry breath. "*Nothing's* going on."

It was a childish rebuttal, but the best I could come up with given the shaky state of my defense.

Grayson smirked. "So, what's the harm in staying another night then?" He turned to my cousin. "You in, Earl?"

Earl grinned. "You bet."

I scowled at my cousin. "What about the garage? Who's going to run it?"

Earl hooked his thumbs in his armpits and rocked back on his heels. "Seeing as how you can't fire me no more, I'm taking the liberty of a well-earned vacation day."

Grayson's lip curled up on one side. "Besides, we haven't entirely ruled out Pan as the perpetrator."

My molars clenched hard enough to crush rocks.

"Fine," I hissed. "We'll stay."

WITH MY ESCAPE PLAN foiled, I sat by the campfire and awaited my fate, armed with a marshmallow stabbed onto the end of a stick. I figured if anybody got me too riled, I could jab them in the eye with it.

I poked my jousting weapon into the flames and watched the marshmallow on the end swell, then begin to turn golden-brown on the edges.

"Nothing like cooking over an open fire," Earl said. He sat beside me and stuck a skewered hotdog over the flame.

Garth nodded. "It's probably the thing I look forward to the most when the apocalypse hits."

The most?

"I don't get it, Garth," I said. "Why are you a member of that Dreadmore camp when you've already got this place?"

Garth smiled, making me wonder how long it had been since I'd seen a dentist.

"Backup," he said. "Every smart prepper has a secondary bugout location. You know, in case the first one gets raided or blown off the map. Only a fool like Jenkins thinks they can survive alone in some old World War II bunker."

"He had the cabin as a secondary," I said.

Garth snorted derisively. "That rundown cabin wouldn't save him from a mosquito invasion."

"I *heard* that," Earl said, and swatted his forearm.

Garth shook his head. "The dude thought he could go it alone with his wife. But what if one of them gets sick or dies? No way, man. A real prepper knows there's safety in numbers. You need reinforcements in case you lose a crucial member. You know, like—"

"Rexel?" Earl asked.

Garth shrugged. "I was gonna say Tooth, but yeah, Rexel, too."

I cringed. "That lunatic's still missing?"

"Yeah."

Earl cocked his head. "But I thought they found him climbing that monstrositous strawberry."

I sighed. "I meant Tooth."

"Oh." Earl shifted his gaze across the small campfire toward Garth's brother, Jimmy. Dressed in jeans and a flannel shirt, the young cop could've been mistaken for a teenager at a Southern Baptist boot camp. Earl yelled to him across the blaze. "What's gonna happen to him, Officer Wells?"

Red flames reflected in Wells' eyes as he glanced up from his hotdog on a stick. "Tooth or Rexel?"

"Rexel!" I rolled my eyes in exasperation, and caught sight of my marshmallow. It had burst into flames and was dripping molten goo onto the red-hot coals. "Dang it!" I jerked my stick out of the fire, but it was too late. My marshmallow was nothing but charred remains.

"You never *could* cook worth a darn," Earl quipped.

"Shut it or this thing's going in your mouth." I looked over at Wells. "So, what about Rexel?"

Wells shrugged. "I don't know. He's at the hospital under twenty-four-hour observation. We're waiting on the psych evaluation to see if we can release him on his own recognizance."

"T-Rex's always been wound up pretty tight," Garth said. "It was just a matter of time before a spring broke."

I flicked the crispy black remains of my burnt marshmallow into the fire like I was casting a fishing rod. I stuck another one on the stick. "Any idea yet if what's going on with Rexel is related to the Jenkins' case?"

"If you ask me, I think their brains are being alterated by alien implants," Earl said, then shoved half a hotdog in his mouth.

I jabbed him with the marshmallow on the end of my stick. "I wasn't asking *you*. And would you can it already with the alien implants?"

Earl's back stiffened. He mumbled at me with a mouthful of wiener. "Geez, Bobbie. Open that mind a yours to the possibilities. You didn't believe in Mothman, neither. And look where that got you."

I shot my cousin a dirty look. "What are you implying?"

Earl smirked, then glanced up and nearly choked on his hotdog. I followed his line of sight across the fire pit. Crum was standing there wearing his donut shirt, pizza pants, and the kind of facial expression I'd only seen on soap opera doctors—usually after unsuccessful brain transplants.

Earl rose to his feet. "What's up, Doc?"

Grayson, who'd been working away feverishly on his laptop, glanced up and said, "Whatever it is, it doesn't look good."

Chapter Thirty-Nine

Inside Garth's prepper compound, all eyes switched from the camp-fire to Dr. Crum.

He cleared his throat as flop sweat poured from his temples and dripped onto his donut shirt.

"Let me start by saying that what I'm about to tell you is, at this point, purely hypothetical," Crum said, wobbling as if he might faint.

I waved my marshmallow-on-a-stick at him like a magic wand. "I think you should sit down, Doctor."

Crum nodded. "Yes. I think we all should."

Eyebrows ticked up around the campfire. Each of us grabbed a lawn chair and dragged it toward Crum. We formed a tight circle next to the fire pit, and waited expectantly for the doctor to speak.

Crum wiped his brow with a paper napkin. It was so quiet all I could hear was the fire crackling. As the doctor nervously cleared his throat again, I shot a glance at Grayson. His eyes were shining like a kid let loose in a candy-store free-for-all. I could almost envision his hands rubbing together maniacally.

That weirdo lives for this stuff.

"I spoke to a friend of mine at the CDC," Crum coughed out like a confession. "According to Dr. Easterly, a new form of transmissible spongiform encephalopathy is affecting free-ranging deer, elk, and moose."

"Transpo *what?*" Earl asked.

Crum shot him a worried glance. "Trans—never mind. In layman's terms, it's called chronic wasting disease, or CWD for short. Anyway, the disease causes abnormal proteins to collect in brain and spinal cord tissues. They eventually burst and cause microscopic empty spaces, basically turning the animal's normal brain tissue into a sponge-like material."

"You mean like Spongebob Squarepants?" Earl looked around and laughed at his own joke. No one laughed back. He pouted and sat back in his lawn chair.

Crum chewed his lip. "No. I'm afraid this is no joke. The infected animals really suffer."

"What happens to them?" Grayson asked.

"It's subtle at first. Weight loss, drooling, droopy ears. Then a general wasting away of their health. So far, the disease has only been reported in western states."

"How many?" Grayson asked.

"Twenty-four."

Grayson whistled.

"I ain't followin' y'all," Earl said. "What's a sponge-headed deer got to do with anything?"

"I'm *getting* to that," Crum said. "You see, in the final stages of CWD, these animals lose their fear of people, and can get aggressive."

"Are you saying you think an infected deer attacked Lester Jenkins?" Grayson asked.

"Possibly. But it could be worse than that. A lot worse." Crum took a deep breath and steadied himself. "Lester and Arlene Jenkins—and perhaps even Rexel—could have contracted CWD themselves."

Garth flew up out of his chair, knocking it over. "Are you saying this CWD crap is *contagious?*"

Crum cleared his throat. "Yes. I mean, no. Not contagious like you might think. And right now, like I said, this is just a theory. As far as we know, the disease is only affecting deer. But according to Easterly, it's likely that human cases *will* show up."

"But if it's not contagious, how do humans get it?" Garth asked.

Crum locked eyes with Garth. "From eating the meat of contaminated animals."

Garth's mouth dropped open. "You're kidding me."

Crum shook his head. "I wish I were. The disease has already proven to be transmittable to other animals, including primates, our closest relatives. Easterly thinks it's not a matter of *if*, but *when* CWD will transfer to humans."

I cringed. "Geez! If it does, would the symptoms be like what happened to Arlene and Rexel?"

Crum shook his head. "We can only speculate at this point. But they would probably be very similar to Mad Cow Disease. First, a tingling and burning sensation in the face and extremities. In later stages, most likely dementia and psychotic behavior."

"That would certainly explain a few things," Grayson said.

Crum nodded. "That's what I was thinking. The symptoms Arlene is displaying would fit the profile to a T."

"If you're right, what will happen to her now?" I asked.

Crum shook his head. "Nothing good. This isn't nicknamed zombie deer disease for nothing."

"It turns deer into zombies?" Earl asked. "If people eat the zombie deer, do they turn into zombies too?"

Crum blew out an exhausted breath. "Basically, yes."

Grayson whistled long and low. "How many people are we talking about here, Doc?"

"Who knows? Easterly told me around fifteen thousand infected animals get eaten every year in the US. If a diseased animal got into a meat processing plant ... well, I'd hate to think about the consequences."

Wells rubbed his chin. "You said this disease is only affecting deer out West. If that's true, how'd Lester Jenkins get infected?"

"Oh! Oh! I think I know that one!" Earl said, bouncing up and down in his lawn chair.

I could almost hear a collective groan.

"And what would that be?" Wells asked tiredly.

Earl beamed. "I seen pictures of him and his brother, Hank huntin' out West. They must've brought some infected deer meat back with 'em."

"Huh. That actually makes sense," Wells said. "But what about Rexel? He didn't go out west, and he wasn't a hunter."

Garth shrugged. "He's old. He could've just gone off his rocker naturally."

"Or Rexel could've taken some infected meat from Jenkins' cabin," I offered. "It's just a short walk from his house."

"All he'd need was a nibble," Crum said.

I shot Grayson an "I told you so" stare. From the expression on his face, I didn't need to remind him how I'd slapped that hunk of deer meat from his hand a millisecond before he'd taken a bite.

"Awe, crap!" Garth said, and let out a groan so loud we all turned and stared at him.

"What's wrong?" I asked.

Garth cringed. "Rexel was in charge of alternative food procurement. He might've bartered with Jenkins for venison. If he did, he could've infected everybody at Dreadmore!"

I blanched. "You mean we could be looking at a whole army of zombies out there?"

"Not just zombies," Grayson said. "*Prepper* zombies."

We all stared at Garth. He shrunk back in his lawn chair. "Don't look at *me*. Except for chicken wings, I'm a vegetarian!"

Suddenly, an unearthly howl rang out from the darkness beyond the campfire.

The hair on the back of my neck stood on end. I joined the circle of anxious eyes darting back and forth, exchanging panicked glances.

In the dumbstruck silence came the sound of footsteps ...

fast and furious ...

crashing through the bushes toward us.

I shot a glance at my cousin. Earl's eyes were as big as boiled eggs.

He jerked his body to standing and bellowed.

"Run everybody! It's the zombie apocalypse!"

Chapter Forty

I knew I'd never be able to haul my breeder hips up into Earl's monster truck in time to save them, so I scrambled for the RV instead. Grayson was hot on my heels.

"What the hell's going on?" I yelled as we crashed into each other in front of the RV's side door.

"You think *I* know?" Grayson yelled. "Get in!"

I yanked open the door and scrambled inside, assisted by a less-than-helpful push from behind. Grayson climbed in nearly on top of me, slammed the door behind him, and set the lock.

I cringed. "I hope Earl's all right."

Grayson grimaced. "I hope he's all *wrong*. I'm not ready for a freaking zombie apocalypse."

I chewed my lip anxiously. "I'm gonna go turn on the headlights and see what's going on."

Grayson grabbed my arm. "I don't think that's a good idea. The lights may set them off."

I locked eyes with Grayson. "Then what are we gonna do?"

His green eyes flickered a shade darker. "Ride it out, I guess."

A sickening thought hit me. "Are the cab doors locked?"

Grayson's eyes locked onto mine. "Crap!"

"Out of my way!" I yelled.

We both bolted for the front of the RV. Our heads collided, then our bodies crammed together in the narrow passage leading to the driver's cab. Neither of us was going anywhere unless one of us budged.

Grayson grunted, tried to squeeze past me, then his chest went limp against mine. "Look," he said. "You do the passenger seat, I'll get the driver's side."

"Deal."

He stepped back enough for me to break free. I burst into the cab and nearly ran headlong into the windshield. I caught myself with both hands on the dashboard.

Through the glass, I saw something flit by in the darkness.

Panic shot through me afresh. I dove for the passenger seat. My hand flew up, ready to slam down on the door lock. But right before I made contact, I heard the sickening click of the door handle.

The door swung open.

"Grayson!" I screamed, and jumped a foot when his arms wrapped around me from behind. He held me tight as I stared out the open door, straining to see what I didn't want to see.

Two inhuman red eyes bore down on us from the darkness. A low, menacing howl pierced the night again. White fangs flashed in the moonlight.

With no better option coming to my scared-witless mind, I closed my eyes and screamed bloody murder.

Chapter Forty-One

As I waited for the zombies to eat my brain, I heard Grayson exhale a nervous laugh.

I opened my eyes.

Garth was standing outside the open passenger door, staring at me with a sheepish grin. "Look who came home for supper. Must've smelled the hotdogs." He glanced down at his furry, black companion. "Tooth, you're a bad doggy."

Grayson gave me a bear-hug squeeze and burst out laughing. I wriggled free from his arms and shot him a glance that made him nearly swallow his tongue.

I turned my anxious rage on Garth. "Your dog scared the bejeebers out of us!"

Garth grimaced. "Sorry, Miss Pandora." He patted Tooth's huge head. The dog whimpered. "He didn't mean any harm."

"Argh!" I bit down and took a deep breath to regain my composure. The two men looked at me expectantly. What they were expecting, I had no idea. I took another deep breath and said, "Well, at least he's okay. We're *all* okay, right?"

"Except for Crum," Garth said. "His favorite pizza pants got ruined."

I winced. "Did Tooth bite Doc in the butt?"

Garth rubbed Tooth's head. "Nah. Don't tell anybody, but Tooth here's a wimp. He just talks a big game."

Earl came lumbering up. "Y'all okay in there?"

"Yeah," I said, relieved to see him. "But what happened to Crum?"

"Ol' Doc?" Earl laughed. "He'll be all right. He's just cleaning up a little special sauce he let loose in his pizza pants."

Chapter Forty-Two

After doing a quick headcount, it was confirmed that we'd all survived the zombie-free Tooth apocalypse. Granted, some of us a little better than others.

"Come with me," Wells said to Crum. "I think I've got a clean pair of sweats that'll fit you."

Too wired for sleep, the rest of us followed the men into the Wells brothers' trailer. Jimmy led Crum to the bathroom. Garth lured Tooth into his crate with a bone smeared with peanut butter and CBD oil—some kind of cannabis-based sedative, according to Garth.

"You want a squirt?" he asked me, holding the eyedropper.

"No. But I wouldn't mind a cup of coffee."

"Make that two," Grayson said.

"Coming right up." Garth put the coffee on, then reached into the cupboard and pulled out dainty china cups and saucers adorned with a delicate pink rose pattern.

"Nice dishes," I said. "Family heirloom?"

"No," Garth said. "I just like 'em. Have a seat."

I looked around and grimaced. From the state of the place, the maid hadn't been here since our last visit. I tried not to think about it, and joined Earl and Grayson on the couch. A moment later, Wells came back down the hall and sat down in a chair across from us.

Maybe it was the adrenaline crash, the dreadful deer disease, or the shock of still being alive, but none of us seemed to have much to say. Garth handed each of us a cup, and we drank our coffee in silence, waiting on Crum to finish wiping up his pizza sauce.

It took longer than any of us had anticipated.

It was Earl who finally broke the silence. He nodded at the crate, then addressed Garth. "You don't think that there hound of yours is going zombie, do you?"

Garth shook his head. "No. Tooth just suffers from separation anxiety. He's been like that since he was a pup. Jimmy's got the scars to prove it."

Wells nodded and touched his neck absently.

"So, where do we go from here, Mr. Gray?" Garth asked.

Grayson set down his china cup. "Good question. Let's see. So far, we've got one dead guy—"

"*Missing* dead guy," I said.

Grayson eyed me. "One *missing* dead guy, presumably murdered, and two people who appear to have lost their marbles eating zombie deer meat. Not exactly the storyline for a Hallmark movie."

"We don't know for sure it's zombie deer disease," Wells said, shooting Grayson a perturbed look. "There's no point in getting everybody all worked up about that. I think Arlene Jenkins is most likely suffering from hysteria brought on by Lester's death and being locked in that bunker."

"But what about Lester and Rexel?" I asked. "They don't have those excuses. Whether this deer disease thing turns out to be real or not, I'm thinking the cases still have to be related somehow."

"I agree," Grayson said. "When you look at it, Rexel and Jenkins shared several commonalities. They both were preppers. And ham radio enthusiasts." He turned to Wells. "Was Jenkins ever in the military?"

Wells shook his head. "I don't recall that from his background check. But they were both transplants to Florida."

Earl laughed. "Who ain't?"

Wells pursed his lips. "Jenkins' cabin was close to Rexel's house. There could be some environmental factor at play there."

"You mean besides the sponge-brain thing?" Earl asked.

Wells sighed. "Yes. It could be some toxin in the soil or water, or—"

"That still wouldn't explain his crushed bones," Grayson said. "Or the slimy substance you said was on his head."

"Halibut," Earl said.

We all turned and stared at my cousin.

Earl chewed the side of his cheek. "That Hank Chambers guy. He said halibut instead of husband."

"Are you saying you think he might be infected, too?" I asked.

Earl grinned. "All I'm saying is there's something mighty *fishy* going on. Get it?"

Wells shot Earl some side-eye. "I don't think—"

"Excuse me," Crum interrupted. He'd emerged from the bathroom wearing dark-blue sweatpants. They coordinated well with his donut shirt, which, unfortunately, appeared no worse for wear. "Sorry that took so long."

"Dr. Crum," I said. "You told us this chronic wasting disease can make animals lose their fear of humans and get aggressive. Do you think a deer is capable of crushing Jenkins' bones like the autopsy report showed?"

The doctor shrugged. "I guess it's possible."

"That would be some major overkill," Wells said. "I don't see why a deer would waste the energy."

"What about Rexel's bizarre behavior?" I asked. "Could chronic wasting disease make a man strip naked and climb a water tower?"

Crum thought about my question for a moment. "Yes, I suppose. But here's the thing. He and the others would've had to have eaten infected meat four or five months ago, maybe longer."

"Why's that?" I asked.

"Assuming it's like Mad Cow Disease, that's how long it took for advanced psychotic behavior to begin to manifest."

Earl opened his mouth to speak. Wells gave him a glare that would shut a normal person down. Earl, of course, didn't pay him any mind.

"Them hunting pictures I saw at their house. Looked to me like Lester and Hank bagged 'em a deer out West in spring or early summer. The grass was fresh and green."

Wells' hard expression softened. He shifted his attention from Earl to Crum. "If they *are* infected, how can we prove it?"

Crum chewed his lip. "I'll need to take another look at Jenkins' brain biopsy."

"What do I tell the folks at Dreadmore?" Garth asked.

"Nothing, for now," Crum said. "There's no point in stirring up hysteria until—" Crum stopped midsentence. "I need to get samples of that deer meat for testing. Where can we get some?"

"There may still be some in Jenkins' cabin," I said.

"Or in the bunker behind their house," Grayson said.

"Or Dreadmore," Garth said.

"That's a lot of places," Crum said, grimacing softly.

I winced. "If this does turn out to be CWD, can it be treated?"

Crum shook his head. "I'm afraid not. If it's anything like Mad Cow Disease, every victim will be dead within a year."

"Oh."

Crum sighed. "Seeing as it's nearly midnight, I suggest we all get some sleep and get cracking on this first thing in the morning."

"Right," Wells said. "I'll check out the Jenkins' bunker at daybreak. Should I take any special precautions when handling the meat?"

"Absolutely," Crum said. "If I were you, I'd wear thick gloves and put the samples in evidence bags. If you have a cut or scrape on your skin, well, I don't know if that would be enough to transmit the disease or not."

"Thanks," Wells said. "Okay, everybody, you heard the doctor. Let's reconvene in the morning."

AS WE HEADED BACK TO the RV, I turned to Grayson. "Do you still think this is just another domestic homicide?"

"No."

"What changed your mind?"

"The pieces don't fit. A deer—even a crazed one—wouldn't stomp a man until every major bone in his body was broken. Wells is right. Animals don't waste energy on revenge."

"What would, then?"

Grayson kicked a stone out of the path. "Someone playing a game."

"Pan?" I scoffed.

"Maybe. Or one of his friends."

I opened the RV door. "What are you talking about?"

"Lester Jenkins was less than what you might consider a stellar representative of the human race."

I climbed the first step. "Yeah. So?"

"Maybe the folks upstairs decided to crush Jenkins for his own repugnance."

I turned and looked Grayson in the eye. "That's pretty brutal."

He shrugged. "No worse than you stepping on a cockroach."

Huh. I guess he had me there.

Chapter Forty-Three

I was in Dreadmore Village.
    And they were after me.

Hordes of rigor-mortis-faced zombies with earthworms and green goo dripping from their mouths.

Struggling for breath, I stumbled as I ran from their eerie, Frankenstein shuffling. Frantic, I scanned the falling-down hovels for a refuge. My eyes fell upon a familiar one. I ducked inside the tin-roofed shack. My eyes darted around at the glowing green tanks of spirulina.

In a dark corner to my left, something moved. My knees knocked together audibly. To my horror, old man T-Rex lunged at me, naked. He jabbed a tablespoon of green slime at my face. I bolted past him through the dirty plastic flaps and into the compost area.

I climbed inside one of the wooden boxes to hide. As I sank into the dark, crumbly dirt, worms began to wriggle up and down my body. I wanted to scream, but the gurgling, snore-like breaths of nearby zombies made me hold my breath instead.

I closed my eyes and prepared to die.

Something tapped me on the shoulder. I turned and saw Grandma Selma. She was inside the box with me, stirring a pot of black goo. She lifted a spoon from the pot and offered me a taste. It looked and smelled like sh—"

"You okay there, Drex?"

I blinked. I was sitting in the RV banquette, a mug of coffee in front of me. "Uh ... yeah."

"Where were you? Didn't you feel me tapping you on the shoulder?"

"I ... oh. Yeah. I felt it. I guess I was just having a daydream."

"About what?"

I cringed. "Dreadmore. Everyone there was a zombie."

"I hope it was a dream and not a premonition," Grayson said as he sat down across from me. "I hate to say it, but this zombie deer disease is a real powder keg. If it goes ...." He shook his head. "We could be looking at the tip of the iceberg, Drex—at a whole new ball game."

"What do you mean?"

"These preppers. They're waiting on the apocalypse, right?"

"Yeah."

"But what if they *are* the apocalypse?"

Grayson sat back and laughed bitterly. "It all fits. I should've seen it before. It's a classic ploy from the universe's twisted mind."

I stared at Grayson. "What are you talking about?"

He blew out a breath. "The universe has a history of turning goons with guns into mindless assassins."

"Okay."

"While you were toasting marshmallows last night, I did some research. Do you know that *sixty-eight million* Americans own survival gear?" He shook his head. "There are over four million hardcore preppers out there, Drex. All sitting around waiting in fear of the total collapse of society. But what if it's a self-fulfilling prophecy? What if, by preparing for the end of the world as we know it, they bring it on themselves?"

I swallowed hard. "You mean by becoming zombies?"

Grayson smiled wryly. "You have to admit, it would be the ultimate irony. And you know how the universe loves irony."

"But what about—"

A knock sounded on the side door. I sprung from my seat to answer it, glad for the distraction.

Officer Wells was at the door. "I just came back from checking the bunker at Jenkins' house. If there was any deer meat in there, it's long gone now. Somebody left the bunker door open."

I sighed. "Great. So, now we might be looking at an army of zombie raccoons and possums, too. Come on in."

Wells grimaced at the prospect and stepped inside.

"I'd say at the moment, that's the least of our worries," Grayson said. "So, where next? Jenkins' cabin?"

"I was just heading over there," Wells said. "You guys mind giving me some backup?"

"Be happy to," Earl's voice sounded from the open door.

Wells' boyish face drooped like a soggy piñata. "Great."

AS WE DROVE PAST REXEL'S house on the way to Jenkins' cabin, I noticed his military-precision lawn had gone to pot like the rest of the abandoned subdivision.

"I hope the poor guy doesn't have mad deer disease," I said.

"Maybe he's just off his meds," Earl said. "Which way?"

"Follow Wells," Grayson said.

"Can't. He stopped back yonder."

I glanced in the rearview mirror. Wells' patrol car was pulled to the side of the road in front of one of the dozens of vacant lots. He was waving for us to go on ahead.

"It's just straight up there at the end of the road," I said to Earl. "We'll stop there and wait for him."

Earl pulled Bessie up to where the abandoned road disappeared abruptly into swampy pine forest and palmettos. The three of us climbed out of the monster truck and fed a few mosquitoes while we waited for Wells to catch up.

"How far back in them woods is it?" Earl asked, swatting the back of his neck.

I envisioned the zigzagging trail and wondered if its erratic design was intentional, or if it was a sign that Lester Jenkins had been losing his mind for some time now.

"As the crow flies, I'd say a tenth of a mile," I said. "As the possum trots, a good half mile, minimum."

Grayson shot me an amused grin. "Possum trots?"

"Here he comes," Earl said.

Wells pulled his patrol car alongside us and climbed out slowly. His face was as pale as talcum powder.

"What's happened?" Grayson asked.

"You're not going to believe this," Wells said. He shook his head. "*I* don't believe this."

"What?" I asked.

"I just got a call from dispatch. Someone reported finding a pile of coffins dumped along the road to Dreadmore."

"That's weird," I said.

"That's not the weird part," Wells said. "According to dispatch, the person who called in the report said that two of the coffins contained dead bodies."

"Well, they *are* coffins," Grayson said.

Wells shook his head. "That's not the weird part, either. The dispatcher said he was on the line with the caller when the guy screamed, 'They're coming back to life!' Then the connection went dead."

Chapter Forty-Four

The search for infected deer meat in Jenkins' cabin would have to wait. If Wells' police report about people in coffins coming back to life was true, that meant Earl had been right, too. A zombie apocalypse was well underway—and ground zero was Dreadmore Village.

"Climb in, Officer Wells," Earl hollered. "From what Bobbie told me, that puny little patrol car of yours'll never make it down the road to Dreadmore."

Wells took half a second to concede Earl's point and yelled back, "I call shotgun."

We scrambled up into Earl's monster truck and wedged ourselves in for the ride. Grayson and I were the ham and cheese between two slices of American white bread—one at the wheel and the other barking directions out the window.

"Take a left," Wells said. "Then a straight shot down SR39."

Earl hit the gas, then eased off. "Hold up. You think this might be a trick?"

"A trick?" I asked as we coasted down the road.

"You know. By all them zombies. Think they're just trying to lure us out to Dreadmore so's they can eat our brains out?"

"The one that got you would starve to death," I said. "You think maybe we should stop by Walmart and pick up some torches and pitchforks?"

Earl shook his head. "Some monster hunter you are, Bobbie. Everybody knows you got to shoot a zombie in the noggin to kill it."

I glanced over at Wells. Good thing he was by the window. He looked as green as a dill pickle. "Let's get going," he said. "I'm the only cop responding."

"Why?" Grayson asked.

The tendons in Wells' neck tightened. "Thanks to my brother and you guys, I'm the department's official 'Monster Boy.'"

Grayson stifled a grin. "In that case, better step on it, Earl. If lore is correct, you're right. The only way to stop a zombie is with a bullet to the head."

My mind flashed back to my daydream, premonition—whatever it was—of zombies run amok in Dreadmore. I'd said I'd wanted to be at ground zero when the apocalypse happened. God had finally answered one of my prayers.

Gee. Thanks, God.

I grabbed my purse and scrounged for my Glock. I found the pink carrying case under a stack of coupons for Glade air freshener, which I kept forgetting to buy. I pulled out the gun case and yelled, "If this is it, I hope everybody's packing plenty of ammo!"

"THAT'S IT, COMING UP on the left," Wells said.

He pointed to a road that wasn't much more than two orange clay strips worn into the knee-high grass of an abandoned cattle pasture. "Turn here, and try to stay in the ruts."

Earl hooked a left and Bessie's fat tractor tires started mowing down grass on either side of the overgrown road. The first quarter mile wasn't too bad. But when the pasture gave way to palmettos and the ground turned marshy, even Bessie began to struggle.

"Last night's rain didn't help matters," Wells said. "We may have to get out and push."

"Bessie don't like people touching her rear end," Earl said, and punched the gas.

After flinging enough red mud to plaster a Zeppelin, Bessie maneuvered through an acre of swamp glop all the way to the base of a small hill. Earl shifted to low gear, stuck his tongue out for assistance, and steered the monster truck toward the top of the mound.

"Woohoo! Thank heaven for Bessie!" he hollered as we reached the top.

We all sighed with relief—until we rounded a corner and another patch of pasture came into view.

Earl slammed on the brakes. But this time, the terrain wasn't the problem.

A black pickup truck was angled sideways across the lane. Behind it, scattered along the side of the road, lay a jumble of cheap wooden coffins, most of them broken open. Amongst them, three men were busy beating the life out of one another.

A fourth man was already face down on the ground.

"I'm confused," Earl said. "Are they fighting to get *inside* them coffins, or out of 'em?"

I cringed. "What the hell's going on?"

"Zombies," Grayson muttered.

"Which ones?" I asked.

Given that all four men had bloody faces, torn clothes and stunk to high heaven, it was a fair question.

"Only one way to find out," Grayson said.

"How?" Wells asked.

Grayson answered his question, but I wasn't listening.

I didn't want to know.

Chapter Forty-Five

"You know how to drive this thing?" Grayson asked me. I tore my eyes away from the wrestling zombies. "Bessie? Yes."

"Good. You stay here. Keep the engine idling. We may need to make a quick getaway."

Wells and Earl were already out of the truck and getting a feel for their weapons. Earl had his trusty Mossberg shotgun aimed at the zombies. Wells had his service revolver aimed at the ground.

"You got your Glock?" I asked Grayson.

He gave a quick nod. "Always."

"Be careful," I said, and scooted into the driver's seat. I watched through the windshield as the three men took cautious steps toward the brawling trio.

"Break it up!" Wells yelled.

The three zombies looked up, surprised at the intrusion. I recognized one of the brawlers as Jake, the hard-faced survivalist who thought bugs and field mice were perfect dinnertime snacks. Another one was Lester Jenkins' half-brother, Hank Chambers. The third guy I'd never seen before.

"What's going on here?" Wells demanded.

"He did it!" Chambers yelled.

"I did not!" Jake yelled back.

"Did too!" the third man screamed.

The three men went at each other again like bullies in a graveyard playground.

Men. Even when they're zombies, nothing changes.

197

"Hold it right there," Wells said, "or I'll shoot all your kneecaps out."

The zombie-men stopped strangling and punching each other, and slowly turned toward Wells. Their faces, bruised and bloody, appeared, for lack of a better word, *hungry*.

I swallowed hard. *Now what?*

"Any of you armed?" Wells asked.

"Only if you count treachery," Chambers said.

"Takes one to know one, Judas!" Jake hissed.

"Shut up!" Wells said. "Which one of you called this in?"

The unknown man took a step forward. Wells, Grayson, and Earl trained their guns on him like a vigilante firing squad.

"Don't shoot!" the man said. "I'm the one who called!"

"What's your name?" Wells barked.

"Samuel Simpson."

Wells grunted. "Come forward. *Slowly*."

Jake and Chambers took a step forward along with Simpson. Earl and Grayson shifted their weapons in their direction, stopping the two men in their tracks.

Wells nodded at Simpson. "Just you."

Simpson resumed his slow shuffle toward Wells. When he got within six feet, the young officer held up his hand.

"Hold it right there," Wells demanded. "Show me some I.D."

"I'm truly sorry about all of this," Simpson said, fishing a hand in his back pocket. He pulled out a wallet and held up a driver's license.

Wells took it. "What's going on here?"

"You won't believe it if I told you," Simpson said.

"I *might*." Wells glanced over at Grayson. "I've recently been working on expanding my belief system."

Simpson shot Wells a confused look. Wells tossed him back his wallet.

"All right, Mr. Simpson. Why don't we start with you telling me whose body that is over there taking a dirt nap?"

"It's Lester Jenkins, Officer."

While Earl held Chambers and mouse-munching Jake under armed guard with his Mossberg, Grayson made his way toward the coffins. He toed the dead guy's head and called out, "Yeah. It's Lester Jenkins."

Wells eyed Simpson. "So, you weren't lying about *that*."

"No, sir."

Wells escorted Simpson up to the passenger-side window of Earl's monster truck. "Here," he said to me, and reached through the window.

I leaned across the bench seat and took what he handed me. It was the tiny tape player Lester Jenkins had used to record the skywave transmission of *War of the Worlds*.

"I want you to get this on tape," Wells said.

My brow furrowed. "What about—"

"Just do it."

"Yes, sir."

I scooted across the seat to the passenger window, hit the record button, and positioned the device on the window's edge to document the men's conversation. For the record, I wasn't too keen on the idea. I was worried we would tape over crucial evidence that no one in their right mind would believe without hearing it for themselves.

But as it turned out, it was worth it.

The story Samuel Simpson spilled was so bizarre it made the whole zombie apocalypse thing sound like a children's nursery rhyme.

Chapter Forty-Six

"Look, Officer, I'm just a lowly coffin delivery guy," was the line Simpson opened with.

I bit back against innate revulsion.

Simpson definitely had the right look for his profession. Pasty. Sweaty. Bony. Insectoid features topped with a greasy gray comb-over not even a mother could love. With any luck, the gash Simpson got on his chin during his scuffle with the other non-zombies would leave a scar. Then his face might have a feature worth remembering.

"That's my vehicle over there." Simpson pointed toward the battered black pickup. "It's not my usual delivery vehicle, but the road here is rough. And I was working ... sort of ... *off the books.*"

Wells' eyes flashed. "Explain 'off the books.'"

"I work for a company called Ash 200." Simpson paused and grinned like a coffin salesman. "Perhaps you've heard of it?"

Wells ground his teeth. "Not that I recall."

"No? Well, we help those of modest means with their *transition.*"

"You sell cheap coffins to poor people," I translated.

Simpson shot me some side-eye. "That's an uncharitable interpretation, Miss. But, yes."

"So you were transporting coffins to Dreadmore," Wells said.

"Yes."

"Why?"

"You see, Officer, occasionally, we have damaged or defective coffins that don't meet our high standards for customer quality. I have an ... uh ... arrangement with Dreadmore. They purchase them."

"What for?" Wells asked.

One of Simpson's thin, gray eyebrows shot up. "I never asked."

Wells' eyes narrowed at Simpson. "And the dead bodies? Did Dreadmore 'purchase' them, too?"

Simpson's eyes bulged. "No, sir! You must believe me. I knew nothing about them. That is, not until the accident. It was terrible, I tell you. I hit a pothole and the tailgate unlatched. The coffins ... well, you can see for yourself what happened."

Wells glanced over at the splintered coffins strewn along the road. He turned back to Simpson. "How could you not be aware there were bodies in the coffins?"

"I didn't load them. Just transported them."

"Who did, then?"

"Load them? Why, my assistant of course."

"Your assistant?"

"Yes. He works part-time for me and my brother, Jeremiah Simpson. You might know Jeremiah? He's the director at McGreggor Funeral Parlor." Simpson smiled broadly and reached for a card. "Perhaps you've heard of it?"

Wells sighed. "I've heard of it."

"Excellent! My brother and I like to keep the death business all in the family."

My nose crinkled. *I bet your family reunions are a real blast.*

Wells cleared his throat. "So, Mr. Simpson, do you have any idea how Lester Jenkins' body ended up in one of your defective coffins, and why your assistant loaded him in the back of your truck?"

"I'm afraid you'll have to ask *him* that. I was as surprised as you were when I found Jenkins' body lying in the dirt. And then to hear that banging."

"Banging?"

"Yes. From inside one of the coffins."

Wells' eyes grew wide along with mine. "From *inside*?"

Simpson cocked his head at Wells. "Well, yes. That's why I called the police, of course. You know. Because I found that man over there alive inside one of the coffins."

Simpson pointed toward the men being guarded by Grayson and Earl.

"Which one?" Wells asked.

Simpson sneered. "The unattractive older gentleman with the distended belly."

Wells blanched. "Hank Chambers?"

Simpson shrugged. "I don't know his name. All I know is when I got the lid off, he came at me like a crazy man. He's the one who started this whole unfortunate fracas."

"Wait a minute," I said. "You say you don't know Hank Chambers, but you knew who his brother Lester Jenkins was?"

Simpson's pasty features scrunched together, making me think of Templeton the rat. "Well, of course."

"How? From the funeral home?" I asked.

His face relaxed a notch. "Yes. That's it."

"So, how do we get in touch with this assistant of yours?" Wells asked.

Simpson's lips curled upward, but I wouldn't call it a smile.

"Easy," he said. "He's standing right next to your Mr. Chambers. His name is Jake Hinson."

Chapter Forty-Seven

"Hit record again," Wells said to me.

His interview with Samuel Simpson was over. Simpson's assistant, Dreadmore's very own "Emeril of insects," Jake Hinson, was next in the hot seat. With no lips and a skeletal face, Jake looked like Fire Marshal Bill after a particularly nasty arson case.

"I know my rights," Jake hissed through his slit of a mouth. "I don't have to answer your questions without my attorney."

Wells' face registered surprise. "You have an *attorney*, Jake?"

"No."

"Then why bust my—" Wells glanced over at the recorder, then back to his fellow Dreadmore member. "I just have a couple of quick questions. Okay, Jake?"

Jake gave a quick nod and grunted his consent.

"You're a member of Dreadmore, correct?" Wells asked.

"You know I am, Jimmy. Why you wasting my time?"

"It's for the *record*," Wells said. "Do you really work part-time with Mr. Simpson at McGreggor?"

"Yeah."

Wells' nose crinkled. "That's kind of gross, even for you."

Jake sneered. "I just started a couple a months ago. Just to pick up some extra cash during the winter rush. Snowbirds don't always outlast the snow, you know."

What a sentimental sweetheart.

Wells nodded. "Okay. So Simpson says you loaded the coffins onto his truck. Is that right?"

"Yeah."

"Why?"

Jake scowled. "Because they told me to."

"Did you know what was in them?"

"No. Only thing they told me was that your brother ordered 'em."

Wells nearly choked. "*Gary* ordered the coffins?"

"Yeah. For the worm farm. Simpson told me he has some kind of deal going with old man Rexel to drop off defective coffins." Jake laughed. "But turns out this time Rexel was too busy doing a strip tease on the water tower, so your brother took the delivery. Or, at least he was supposed to."

A vein pulsed on Wells' neck. "But when you loaded the coffins, you'd have to have noticed two of them were pretty heavy."

Jake's tanned-leather face twisted into a sour sneer. "Listen, I don't want nobody snooping in my business, and I return the favor by doing likewise."

Wells sighed. "I get that, Jake. But I'm trying to help you out here. Who had access to the coffins before you loaded them?"

Jake shrugged. "Just about anybody, Jimmy. They were in a heap out in back of the funeral home."

"Okay," Wells said. "So you had no idea what was in the coffins?"

"I figured they were stiffs. But at least they were going to a good cause."

"What do you mean?"

"For the *ALF* program. Hey, we all end up as worm food in the end."

I cringed and almost ALF-ed.

"Okay, Jake. You're free to go for now. But stick around."

Jake nodded. "Much obliged, man."

The two men shook hands. Jake turned to leave. Wells called after him. "Oh, and Jake?"

Jake turned around. "Yeah?"

"Do you guys have any *deer* meat in the ALF program?"

Jake shook his head. "Like I told you, Jimmy. Deer ain't sustainable."

Wells nodded. "Good. I mean, no. Deer isn't sustainable. So do me a favor. If you run across any, don't eat it."

Jake eyed him suspiciously. "Why?"

"Just a friendly heads up. You mind your business, I'll mind mine."

Jake nodded. "As it should be."

Jake headed on foot back toward Dreadmore. I clicked off the recorder and shook my head. "Now what, Officer Wells?"

"Time to figure out who's lying."

Wells nodded over at Hank Chambers, who was busy trying to stay out of the sights of Earl's shotgun.

"I'm thinking Chambers should have the answer. If he doesn't know who nailed him into that coffin, then we may have a real twister of an investigation on our hands."

Chapter Forty-Eight

"All I know is, I fell asleep on Arlene's couch and woke up in a coffin," Hank Chambers said. He pointed over at Samuel Simpson. "That ghoul over there was standing over me. I freaked and came out swinging. I mean, what else was I supposed to do? Look at his face! I thought I'd died and gone to Hell."

Wells and I glanced over at Simpson, then at each other. We could see Chambers' point.

"Why do you stink to high heaven?" Wells asked. "And don't say collard greens."

Chambers grimaced and brushed dirt off his sleeves. "I think the coffin was used."

Wells cringed, but not as much as I did.

"What were you doing at Arlene's?" he asked.

"You *know* what, Wells. You called me yourself when you found Arlene in that bunker. I was watching over her place while she was ... you know ... in the hospital recovering."

"Right," Wells said. "Do you know anything about that guy?"

"Who?"

"The ghoul," I said.

Wells shot me a dirty look. "Samuel Simpson."

Chambers glanced at Simpson. His face twisted with disgust. "No."

Wells glanced over at me. "Hit stop."

I mashed the button on the recorder.

Wells sighed. "Okay, Mr. Chambers, you're free to go for now."

Chambers nodded, took a step to leave, and stopped. He eyed both of us. "How the hell am I supposed to get home?"

"SO LET ME GET THIS straight," Earl said from the driver's seat of his truck. "*None* of those fellers was zombies?"

"For the last time, *no*," Wells said. "And please, do me a favor and drive slower. We don't want to tip our cargo."

Earl shifted gears, and I flinched as his humongous elbow came at my face like a side of beef. The four of us were wedged into the cab like human sardines, rocking and swaying in unison as Earl pivoted his muddy black monster truck forward, then backward, four times until he'd turned the massive vehicle around on the rutted old country road.

Compared to Bessie, Simpson's battered black pickup looked like the loser in a bar fight as it wobbled down the road in the opposite direction, carrying its load of empty, damaged coffins to Dreadmore Village.

I, personally, was overjoyed at the prospect of not having to see Dreadmore again. Or Simpson, for that matter. As far as I was concerned, the guy was up to no good.

"I can't believe you let Simpson go," I said to Wells.

"Being creepy isn't a crime," he replied.

Grayson eyed me playfully and pressed his palms together as if in prayer. "And for that, I am truly thankful."

I smirked and elbowed Grayson in the ribs. Then I shot a glance in the rearview mirror at Bessie's payload.

Hank Chambers sat in the back left corner of the truck bed, his longish gray hair flapping in the breeze. His weathered face was tilted toward the sun, and his arms rested atop the truck bed's side and tailgate.

On the other side of the truck bed lay a broken coffin containing the pulverized remains of Lester Jenkins. Seeing as how both men smelled like "eau de dead guy," we'd voted unanimously for them to make the trip together alfresco.

"What's going to happen to poor old Lester?" Earl asked. "He can't seem to get no rest."

"I guess that'll be up to Arlene," Wells said.

"I say ixnay on an open casket," Grayson quipped.

Earl, Wells, and I groaned in unison.

Distracted, Earl hit a pothole so deep it sent our butts rising off the bench seat.

"Watch it!" Chambers called out from the back.

Earl rolled down the window. "Sorry 'bout that."

All four of our faces puckered.

"Whoo-wee!" Earl hollered, rolling up the window. "Smells like polecat stew!"

"And weed," Wells said. "Anybody else smell pot?"

Grayson and I exchanged quick glances, then we knocked heads trying to catch a glimpse through the rearview mirror. Grayson reached up and adjusted the mirror to his advantage. He took a peek and laughed. I grabbed the mirror and angled it for a peek of my own.

Chambers was sitting on Jenkins' coffin—smoking a fat number.

"Maybe it's medicinal," Grayson said to Wells.

The young cop blew out a sigh. "At this point, I honestly don't give a rat's ass."

Grayson grinned. "So what do you think's going on with this whole 'coffin-whack-a-mole' business?"

"I have no idea," Wells said. "I just hope things don't get any weirder."

"Hate to break it to you, Officer," Earl said. "But I think they just did."

He nodded toward the back of the truck. We all turned and stared.

Chambers was yammering away, a joint in one hand, and Lester Jenkins' rotting skull in the other.

I nearly swallowed my tongue and then puked it back up.

"Alas, poor Yorick," Grayson said.

I stared at him, incredulous.

He shot me a snobby look. "What? Not a Hamlet fan?"

Chapter Forty-Nine

"I told you he was acting fishy," Earl said, winking at me. "You ought to listen to me more, Bobbie. Just for the halibut."

"We need to get him to a hospital," Wells said.

"Exactly what I was thinking," I said, glaring at Earl.

Earl's grin melted. He blew out a breath and climbed out of the truck. We all piled out after him and scurried to the back to get a better look at Chambers. He was still in the truck bed, engrossed in a riveting conversation with his half-brother's rotting head.

"Chambers? You okay, buddy?" Wells asked.

Chambers' wild, dilated eyes darted from his brother's skull to us. His expression was one of a man who'd never seen us before, and wasn't sure he liked what he saw.

"Go away. I don't want any!" he growled.

Grayson elbowed me. "Either that was some killer ganja, or he's been bogarting the venison."

"Chambers, we need to get you to a hospital," Wells said.

"Hospital?" Chambers asked. His gaze returned to his brother's rotting head. "I thought we were going to the Poconos."

"I think we'd better hurry," I said. "He doesn't look too good."

Earl opened his mouth, but I shut it with a dirty look.

"You're right," Wells said. "Earl, once we get to the highway, step on it. I'll call Freddy—uh, Dr. Crum, and have him meet us at County Memorial."

Chapter Fifty

Dr. Crum was standing outside the ER when we arrived. Dressed in blue scrubs and a white coat, I almost didn't recognize him.

He scurried over to the truck, took a gander at Hank Chambers' Shakespearean sonata, and went as pale as his lab coat.

"Holy mother of pearl," he muttered.

"What's wrong with him, Doc?" Earl asked.

"Looks like advanced stages of Mad Cow," Crum said. "I'm still waiting on Arlene's results before I call the CDC, but Chambers here pretty much confirms my worst fears."

"What should we do with him?" Wells asked.

"I already called for a stretcher," Crum said. "I'm going to admit him, then run some tests."

Earl crinkled his nose. "Might want to hose him off, first."

Crum ignored him. "Jimmy, did you get the samples of deer meat I asked for?"

"Not yet," Wells said. "So far, we've checked the Jenkins' bunker, but came up with nothing. We've still got Jenkins' cabin and Dreadmore to search."

Crum nodded, his brow furrowed. "Well, I suggest you get on it. And hurry."

"Dr. Crum!" a woman's voice shrieked.

We turned to see a nurse running toward us. She grabbed Crum by the shoulders, nearly slamming into him. "Dr. Crum!" she panted. "Arlene Jenkins ... she's missing from her room!"

Crum's face went slack. "Oh, crap."

"It's an angel!" Chambers hollered at the nurse. He dropped Lester's skull. It rolled down the pavement and came to rest at the nurse's feet. She took one look at it and collapsed in a heap.

"Oh, crap," Crum repeated absently.

"What should we do?" I asked.

Grayson cleared his throat. "First, might I suggest—"

"Shut it. I'll take it from here," Wells said, his jaw set like a vice.

A couple of orderlies arrived with a stretcher. "You, men," Wells barked at them. "Help me load this man, then get a wheelchair for the nurse."

The orderlies looked over at Crum. He nodded. "You heard the man."

Wells turned to Grayson, Earl, and me. "I'm going to search the hospital for Arlene. You guys go back to Jenkins' cabin and see if you can find any of that contaminated venison. The sooner we get a sample, the sooner we'll have some answers."

"Yes, sir," Earl said, and saluted.

"What should we do with the rest of Lester?" Grayson asked.

"I'll call for a body bag," Crum said.

Earl sniffed the air and winced. "Better double bag him, Doc."

For once in my life, I thought Earl had a valid point.

Chapter Fifty-One

"So here we are, back at the scene of the crime," Grayson said. Earl shifted into park. The three of us stared through the truck's windshield into the ocean of palmettos and pines that stood between us and Lester Jenkins' cabin.

An eerie feeling came over me. I felt as if the woods had been waiting for this moment all along, patiently biding its time. Something told me that the second we stepped off the crumbling asphalt, we'd be crossing into enemy territory.

Mother Nature's declaration of war.

I swallowed hard. "You got the baggies?"

Grayson nodded. "Right here in the trusty Walmart bag."

"Barbeque tongs?" I asked.

"Roger." Grayson pulled out the tongs and clapped their ends together like a pair of castanets.

"What? No sauce?" Earl quipped.

I shot my cousin a sour look. "All right, guys. Remember, nobody touch anything that even *looks* like meat. And that means you, too, Earl."

Earl laughed and opened the door. But as he climbed down out of the truck, his demeanor changed. "I hope we don't run across no zombie deers out here."

I touched Grayson's arm. "I hope we don't run across any zombie *anything.*"

WE WERE ABOUT HALFWAY down the switchback trail. Earl had the machete and was in the lead, chopping at the palmettos, which seemed hell-bent on scratching raw every inch of exposed skin they could reach.

Suddenly, Earl stopped short. I nearly ran into the back of him.

"What?" I asked impatiently.

"Look at that."

Earl pointed to a scraggly vine with hairy, serrated leaves. A half-dozen yellow fruits hung from it, each roughly the size and shape of a small egg. Bands of tiny spikes, about half an inch apart, ran lengthwise down the odd fruits. One of the pods had split open, revealing a stash of shiny, pea-sized seeds, each bright red with a black spot in the center.

"What is that?" Earl asked. "Looks like Seymour ate a bunch'a eyeballs."

"Momordica charantia," Grayson said. "Genus Cucurbitaceae. Class one invasive."

"Huh?" Earl asked, touching one of the fruits.

"It's some kind of cucumber, and it's not native," I translated.

Grayson eyed me. "Pretty close. It's also known as bitter melon, bitter pear, and balsam apple."

"Can you eat it?" Earl asked.

"Sure," Grayson said.

Earl plucked the fruit and opened his mouth.

"But only when it's green and cooked," Grayson said. "Ripe like that, it can cause you to rapidly lose fluids out both ends, and quite possibly expire."

"Huh?" Earl glanced over at me, the fruit almost on his tongue.

I reached over and swatted it out of his hand.

"It's poisonous!" I hissed. "Geez, Grayson. You've got to dumb things down in situations involving imminent death!"

"Pardon me," Grayson said. "Earl, for future reference, red and yellow are nature's warning colors. Didn't Ronald McDonald teach you anything?"

Earl took a sideways look at the thorny, poisonous fruits, then smiled at me. "Thanks for having my back, Bobbie."

"Yeah. Okay. Now get going, already!"

We trudged on through a dozen more zigs and zags in the trail. I was about to get seasick when we finally spotted the small clearing in front of Jenkins' cabin.

The broken front door was half ajar. On the weathered posts holding up the front porch, a second strand of yellow police tape, torn like the first, fluttered below it in the light breeze.

"It seems nobody bothers to heed the rules out here," I said.

Earl sucked his teeth. "Now what?"

"Let's go collect some zombie meat," Grayson said. "Some for Dr. Crum, and some for me."

I eyed Grayson. "What do *you* want with it?"

His right eyebrow raised an inch. "Have I taught you *nothing?*"

I winced. "Sorry. Of course. What was I thinking?" I ambled forward, but truth be told, I didn't have a clue what Grayson was talking about.

Rain had pooled in depressions in the camouflage tarp that covered the cabin's broken-down roof. I climbed the damp, rickety stairs and crossed the front porch. Earl took hold of the doorknob and forced the warped door open, nearly taking it off its hinges.

Inside the ramshackle dwelling, the section of tarp covering the large hole in the roof had filled with rainwater like a balloon. It sagged down between the joists like a washtub-sized hernia.

"Who's the Jenkins' new designer?" Grayson quipped. "Andy Warthog?"

"Earl, don't touch that!" I shouted.

My cousin was reaching for a ragged hunk of deer meat still cling-ing to the clothesline. He pulled his hand back as if he'd touched a hot stove.

"Geez, Earl! Use the tongs!"

"Actually, let me do it," Grayson said. "I prefer to collect my own specimens."

Earl grimaced at the moldy meat. "Knock yourself out, Mr. G."

While Grayson whipped out the baggies and went to work, Earl and I quickly surveyed the rest of the one-room cabin. The radio equip-ment was gone. However, the empty wrappers from the prepper meals were still strewn about the place.

On the floor by the window, I spied the white brick Grayson and I had discovered on our first visit. Though the deer meat showed signs of being gnawed on, nothing had touched the ugly, square-shaped lump.

"What *is* that thing, Earl?" I asked, pointing to it. "Grayson thought it was a fire log. I'm thinking it's a fruitcake."

Earl scrunched his face as he studied the thing. "Well, nothing's touched it, so I'm thinking fruitcake."

I shot him half a smile. "What's with the white stuff?"

"Lemme see." Earl leaned over and picked up the bumpy, ashy brick. He grinned and shook his head. "Maybe old Jenkins was into pottery."

I snorted. "If he was, that's one butt-ugly ashtray."

Earl held the lumpy brick up to the broken out window for a better look. He took a sniff. "Whew! Kinda pungent, even for a—"

Suddenly, an arm wielding a board shot through the window and whacked Earl over the head with it. My big, bear of a cousin keeled over onto the floorboards like a felled redneck pine tree.

Chapter Fifty-Two

"What the hell?" Grayson yelled and dropped one of his baggies.

"Someone's out there!" I squealed. I knelt by Earl's side. He had a nasty gash above his right eye, but he was still breathing.

Grayson dropped his other baggie and reached for his Glock, but he didn't make it. A man burst through the open cabin door and aimed a rifle at his head.

"Put your hands up!" the guy demanded.

Hidden behind a full beard, moustache, sunglasses, and a cowboy hat, it was impossible to make out the man's face.

"What do you want?" I hissed.

"You!" a woman's voice shrieked.

For a second, I thought the voice had come from the gunman. Then I caught a movement in the doorway behind him.

"I *knew* you were cheating with my Lester!"

I stared into the wild eyes of a wigged-out Arlene Jenkins.

She might've been going slowly insane, but she still had the presence of mind to get herself to a hairdresser. Her platinum blonde hairdo looked fabulous. Her AK-47, not so much.

"Tie 'em up," she barked at the man.

"Hold on," Grayson said. "We just came to collect samples. See?" He started to reach for a baggie on the floor.

"Hands behind your back or your head comes off," the man said.

Grayson obliged. The man searched around for something to tie us up with. He spied the bloody clothesline drooping with deer meat. He cut it down and stripped the dried venison from it.

"Please, not that," I said.

"Shut up!" Arlene hissed. "Make it good and tight."

From the grunts Grayson was making, the man knew how to follow orders. He finished with Grayson and looked over at me. I started to stand.

"Stay down," he demanded. He knelt beside me. I put my hands behind my back and felt the jagged specks of dried meat on the twine saw into my wrists.

Not good.

"What about *him?*" the man asked Arlene. He stood up and toed Earl's body with his boot.

"He's dying," I said. "Look, this is all some kind of misunderstanding. All we wanted was—"

"Liars!" Arlene yelled. "You came to steal Lester's gold!"

"Gold?" Grayson and I asked.

"Don't play dumb with me, tramp," Arlene hissed. "Lester told you all about his secret stash, didn't he? Two-timing jerk! Well, where is it?"

I locked eyes with Grayson, looking for a clue. His face read, "Play along."

I blew out a breath. "Okay. You got me, Arlene. Untie Grayson and he'll show you where the gold is."

"You think we're idiots?" the man asked.

You really want to know the answer to that?

"Of course not. You see, it's just that you have to walk the site off in *paces*," I said, winging it.

"*Man*-size paces," Grayson said, picking up my lead. "I've got the treasure map. Untie me and I'll show you."

"They're lying," Arlene said, and raised her AK-47. "I say we put some bullets in both of 'em."

"Hold on!" the man said. "Without the gold, we don't have enough money to get to Georgia, much less the Poconos."

"I said let's kill 'em!" Arlene shrieked.

She aimed her gun at Grayson and pulled the trigger. My mouth fell open in horror as the AK-47 blasted out ... a round of hollow clicks.

"What the hell?" Arlene screamed.

The man snatched the AK-47 from her hand. "You really think I'd trust you with a loaded gun?"

Arlene grabbed for the man's rifle. "Now you listen to me, you two-bit coffin stealer!"

"Why should I? You three-timing, dime-store floozy!"

Arlene screeched and jumped onto the man's back. As she dug her red nails into his face, he collapsed to his knees, discharging his gun as he fell.

A spray of yellow water squirted from the herniated tarp as the bullet pierced it. A second later, it ripped open and a deluge of rancid rainwater sloshed down over the pair. The unexpected cold shower halted their wrestling match for half a second, then they went right back at it, yanking hair and throwing punches.

Amidst the chaos, I heard Earl snort. I tapped him with my foot. "You okay?"

He didn't answer.

I glanced over at Grayson. He was struggling with the rope that had him tied to a post.

"What do we do now?" I whispered.

He yanked on the twine around his wrists. "Hope the man wins." He gave me a hopeful glance, then his eyes darted up and past me.

His mouth fell open.

I was tied up facing the opposite direction. I couldn't see what Grayson was looking at. But something told me things were about to get a whole lot worse.

Chapter Fifty-Three

"What is it, Grayson?" I whimpered, not wanting to know. He didn't answer. He just stared, mouth agape, at something moving behind me. I winced, set my jaw to determined, and craned my head slowly to the right.

A mere three feet away stood the most hideous creature I'd ever seen. Its eyes bobbled and pulsed in its toad-spotted skull.

It was old man Rexel.

High as a kite.

And naked.

Again.

"Where be the fine wench?" he asked, drool dripping from his leering mouth.

A thin strip of leather crossed his boney, hairless chest. It supported a quiver of arrows, their pointy heads poking up from behind his back. In his right hand was an archery bow.

"Rexel!" I yelled.

He looked my way, his eyes spinning like whirligigs.

"Hurry! Untie us!" I nodded toward the soggy pair still wrangling around amongst the foil wrappers and filth littering the floor. "They think we know where Jenkins kept his gold. Help us before they kill us!"

Rexel's eyebrow shot up, along with something else I wish I hadn't seen.

"Do ye now?" Rexel said.

"Yes, m' lord," Grayson answered.

I turned toward Grayson. His face was dead serious. He shot me a subtle wink and nodded toward Rexel. I turned my head back toward the naked avenger, just in time to see him bend over and pick up the rifle.

Ugh. Shoot me now.

Rexel aimed the gun at Arlene and the mystery man. I closed my eyes, for a myriad of reasons.

"Enough of your tomfoolery," I heard Rexel say. "Untie them, you scoundrels!"

I opened my eyes. Arlene and her accomplice were sitting on the floor, arms crossed, glaring at each other like pissed-off brats. Arlene's hairdo was in ruins. So was the man's disguise. Minus his sunglasses and false beard, I recognized him right away. It was rat-faced Samuel Simpson, the coffin peddler with the black pickup truck.

"Hold it right there," a man's groggy voice sounded. Earl had come to. He had the AK-47 trained on Rexel.

Rexel laughed like a deranged schoolgirl. He thrust out his boney, bare chest and said, "Go ahead, ye puny human! Take your best shot. You can't kill me. I'm immortal!"

Rexel swiveled the shotgun toward Earl. Earl ducked, then squeezed the trigger on the AK-47. A series of rapid, hollow clicks rattled through the cabin.

Earl's eyes doubled. "Good golly! You really *are* immortal!"

"See?" Rexel laughed maniacally. "Told you!"

He dropped his bow and danced around like a frog on a hot stove. During his performance, a gold coin fell from somewhere on his person. I didn't want to know where. It hit the floor with a *plink* and rolled to my feet.

"Well, now," Rexel said, "I'm really sorry you all had to go and see that."

"What? The dancing or the coin?" Grayson asked.

He nodded over at Earl. "You. Chewbacca. Tie up those two."

"Why?" Earl asked.

"'Cause I *said* so. You've seen my lucky coin. I can't have you knowing the secret to my charms! Nope. Looks like you're gonna have to go on a little rampage and eliminate the witnesses! Then commit suicide. Now get busy."

Rexel kept the rifle aimed at Earl as my cousin tied up an endlessly babbling Arlene Jenkins and her creepy, comb-over sidekick, Samuel Simpson.

"Why are you doing this?" I asked.

Rexel's face registered sanity for a moment. "You ever try to live on Social Security?"

"I thought you had a military pension," Grayson said.

Good one, Grayson. As if that might bring Rexel to his senses.

"War don't pay like it used to," Rexel said, scratching his naked butt cheek as his eyes glazed over again.

"Now *you*," Rexel said to Earl. "Get over there by the stove. One false move out of you and I'll fire my gun into that propane canister. Send the bulk of us to Timbuktu."

Rexel laughed as if he'd made a joke, then he tied Earl to the stove. He stripped off his quiver and walked over to the cabin door. Using the rifle for support, he bent over and reached for something.

I shook my head.

Rexel's scrawny butt is the last thing I'll ever see. Good one, universe.

"Looky what I found." Rexel straightened up and turned to face us. He grinned and waved a loaded AK-47 clip.

We all stared, slack-jawed. But it wasn't the scrawny, naked man who'd made our jaws drop. It was the creature behind him.

The one lurking in the doorway.

It struck like a blur of lightning.

Rexel fired the rifle, but by then it was already a pointless gesture.

He didn't stand a chance.

Chapter Fifty-Four

We watched in horror as, in one quick strike, Rexel's leathery bald head was entirely engulfed in the mouth of the biggest damned snake I'd ever laid eyes on.

Tied to the cabin's posts with bloody twine, we were a captive audience to the grotesque drama playing out before us. With Rexel's head firmly in its jaws, the snake slowly wound its thick, thigh-sized body around Rexel's scrawny torso.

Rexel's body twitched at first, then gave up. The sickening crunch of his bones as they crushed made me nearly lose my lunch.

Arlene screamed. I closed my eyes and turned away. Unfortunately, Earl kept me up to date with a blow-by-blow account, right up until the snake had swallowed Rexel whole and slithered off into the woods.

"How's that possible?" Earl asked.

"Rexel was a small man," Grayson said. "There've been reports—"

"No," Earl said, shaking his head. "That man was immortal. That's why I didn't fight back. So how is it that snake was able to kill him?"

My face went slack. Good thing my hands were tied, or I'd have throttled Earl to death myself.

Grayson stared out the cabin door. "I hope somebody finds us before that thing comes back for dessert."

"Dessert!" Earl said. "The fruitcake!"

I cringed. "How can you think about food at a time like this?"

Grayson sneered. "Especially *fruitcake*."

"Nah!" Earl said. "That log thing on the floor over there." He nodded toward the ashy brick. "That ain't no fruitcake."

"What is it, then?" I asked.

"It's *snake* poop! I got a friend who's a herpes a'tologist. You wouldn't think it, but when them big old snakes take a dump, it can come out all square like a brick."

"Well, that solves that mystery," I said.

"It certainly does," Grayson said. "I always wondered where fruit-cakes came from."

Chapter Fifty-Five

It was nearly dusk when we heard Officer Wells and his brother, Gary, aka Operative Garth, calling our names.

"Mr. Gray! Pandora!"

"In here!" Grayson yelled back.

The brothers' silhouettes appeared in the doorway of the cabin.

"You're okay!" Garth said with a happy, buck-toothed grin.

His brother didn't look quite so cheerful. Pale and sweaty, it appeared as if Jimmy Wells might faint. "Thank goodness," he whispered breathlessly.

The brothers looked us over for a moment. "Sheesh. Who all's in here?" Wells asked. "Is everybody all right?"

"Yes. Pardon us if we don't give you a hug," Grayson said.

Wells blanched. "Oh. Sorry. Gary, don't just stand there. Help me untie them." He nodded over at Arlene and Simpson. "But save those two for last."

"Use gloves if you've got them," Grayson said. "The twine is covered in deer blood. It might be infected."

Wells glanced at Grayson's raw wrists. "Crap." He handed his brother some rubber gloves. Garth attended to Grayson. Wells knelt by my side.

"Can you explain to me how *all* of you ended up tied to posts?" he asked.

"It's a long story," I said. "But it all ends with Rexel."

Wells' eyebrow shot up. "You found Rexel? Where is he?"

"In the belly of the beast," Grayson said.

"A ginormous snake came and swallowed him up whole," Earl said, filling in the details.

Wells shook his head. "Not again."

"*Again?*" we said in unison.

Wells pursed his lips. "Well, nothing's been confirmed yet, but more than a few free-ranging pets have gone missing around the area. And animal control just caught an eighteen-foot python in a sewer drain yesterday."

I cringed. "You mean there's more than one of those things slithering around?"

Grayson sighed. "Invasive species are called *invasive* for a reason, Drex."

OUR SEVEN-PERSON CHAIN gang wound its way through Jenkins' crazy maze of a trail, hopefully for the last time. Garth was in the lead, followed by Simpson, Earl, Arlene, and me, with Grayson and Officer Wells bringing up the rear.

"Keep your eye out for snakes," Wells called to Garth.

"Roger that," Garth called back. He squinted through his thick lenses and swung a machete at a palmetto leaf.

"I don't get it," I said to Grayson. "Why did the snake eat Rexel, but not Lester Jenkins?"

"Maybe it got disturbed," Grayson said. "When stressed, snakes have been known to regurgitate their food. But I think he may have just been too big to swallow."

"Swallow *this*," Arlene whined, and stuck out her butt. "I'm hungry!"

Hands cuffed behind her back, Arlene's mouth was open wide as she bobbed for a pendulous yellow fruit hanging from a hairy-leaved vine.

"Stop!" I yelled, and slapped the side of her head. Hard.

She glared at me, her eyes still wild. "You! You're after my Lester, you two-timing—"

"Yadda, yadda, yadda," I said. "Save it for your statement."

"Get going up there, Jenkins," Wells barked. Arlene scowled, turned back around, and trudged down the trail.

Grayson grabbed my arm and whispered in my ear. "You're no hero. You just wanted to slap her, didn't you?"

I didn't dignify his query with an answer. But damned, it was uncanny how well that man could see right into my soul.

Chapter Fifty-Six

I was showering in the RV, getting ready for a farewell meeting with the preppers at Blarney's Bar, when I noticed the small cuts on my wrists. They were red and swollen.

The bar of soap I'd been holding landed in the shower pan with a thud.

"You okay in there?" Grayson called through the door.

"I don't know. I need to show you something."

Grayson opened the bathroom door and was at the shower curtain before I could even yell, "stop."

"I didn't mean this second!" I said.

"Oh. Sorry." Grayson turned to go.

"Wait. Look at this." I stuck my arm out from behind the shower curtain. "Do you think I got infected by the deer zombie disease?"

Grayson's hand wormed its way into the shower. His wrist had the same swollen cuts.

"If you did, so did I."

All of a sudden, I felt punched in the gut. My knees buckled, and I let out a cry. Grayson stepped into the shower, clothes and all. He wrapped his arms around me.

"Are we gonna die, Grayson?"

"I don't know. But look on the bright side, Drex. Worst case scenario, we can be zombie buds together."

Chapter Fifty-Seven

I stared at the mountain of Blarney's chicken wings, but somehow they'd lost their appeal. I wasn't the only one. Grayson eyed them with disgust and sipped his beer instead. Earl, however, dug right in.

I supposed ignorance truly *was* bliss.

I figured I'd let my cousin stay uninformed of the possibility he'd been infected with mad deer disease. Ignorance suited him. Besides, there was nothing we could do to change the fact that we could, quite possibly, be dead within the year.

"Officer Wells," Grayson said, greeting the young man walking toward our booth.

"Howdy, Officer," Earl said. "Sit down and help me out with these wings. Them two love birds are off their chicken feed."

Wells studied our faces. "Why's that?"

Earl shrugged and grabbed another wing off the pile. "Beats me."

"So, what've you found out?" Grayson asked.

"We'll know more when Freddy—Dr. Crum gets here. But for now, I think I've figured out the motive."

"For Lester's murder?" Earl asked.

Wells brow furrowed. "No. I think the snake solved that. What I'm talking about is why his corpse was taken."

"Right. The old disappearing corpse act," Grayson said. "Do tell. Was it love or money?"

"As it turns out, a bit of both."

Garth joined us. "Oh goody," he said. "Pandora, you wore those pink jeans again."

I rolled my eyes and scooted over for him to join me in the booth.

"Did Jimmy tell you yet?" Garth asked. "It was a love triangle."

"More like a love *quadrangle*," Wells said.

Earl sneered. "Can't you fellers see I'm trying to eat? Keep that kinky sex talk for after dinner."

I blew out a breath. "Okay, so what are we talking about here?"

Garth started to speak, but Wells stopped him. He answered my question himself. "Long story short, it turns out that Hank Chambers, Jake Hinson, and both Jeramiah and Samuel Simpson were all after the same woman."

"Arlene Jenkins?" I asked, incredulous.

"Yeah," Wells said.

My upper lip snarled. "Why?"

Garth's grin made me want to go take another shower. "You should know why, Pandora. They were all after her sexy breeding hips."

My nose crinkled. "I thought they wanted Lester's gold."

"Gold?" Wells asked.

"Yeah. I gave you the coin that fell out of his ... uh ... that Rexel had, you know, somewhere on his person."

Wells cocked his head. "That thing? It was a commemorative coin from last year's Strawberry Festival. Worth exactly squat."

"Then why was Rexel ready to kill for it?" I asked.

Earl laughed. "Why'd he think he was Cupid? That's what *I* wanna know."

Wells stifled an eye roll at Earl. "I ran some background on him. Turns out Rexel was discharged from the military for failing a psychiatric evaluation back in 1978."

"Okay, so that's Rexel covered," Grayson said. "He was one brick shy of a load. But what about the whole body-in-a-coffin shell game?"

Wells nodded. "From what I could piece together, after Lester Jenkins died Arlene found out he'd let all his life insurance policies lapse except for one—the five thousand dollars to bury him. I think we could all agree that could righteously piss a woman off."

We all nodded.

Wells chewed his cheek. "I think Arlene decided not to waste the money burying Lester. She and Hank Chambers decided to get rid of his body on the cheap. The trouble was, he'd already been delivered to McGreggor Funeral Parlor. So Chambers had to bust him out."

"It's a dirty job, but somebody's got to do it," Earl quipped.

Wells shook his head. "So Chambers is pulling Lester out the window at McGreggor's when he gets caught by one or more of Arlene's other suitors. Either Jeremiah or Samuel Simpson, or both. Maybe even Jake Hinson, their assistant."

"That's when the crap really hit the fan," Grayson said.

"Exactly how I see it," Wells said. "Chambers tries to explain the predicament—that he and Arlene needed the money to run off to the Poconos to get married—and the jig is up because Arlene had promised *every one of those guys* the same thing."

I snorted. "And she said *I* was the two-timing floozy!"

"So how did Chambers end up in a coffin?" Grayson asked.

"That part's still not totally clear," Wells said. "I think the three spurned lovers—Jake and the Simpsons—conspired together to get rid of their main rival. They had the motive and means to seal Chambers in a coffin and haul him out to Dreadmore with his brother, Lester."

"Dispose of both of them in the back forty of a prepper compound," Grayson said. "That's two birdbrains buried with one stone."

"Right," Wells said. "But Samuel's accident with the truck foiled those plans. When the coffins dumped and broke apart, he and Jake weren't able to subdue Chambers. He came out of the box swinging. Chambers was beating those two to a pulp. That's why Samuel called the police for help."

"But Chambers said the last thing he remembered was being at Arlene's," I argued.

"And them three scrawny old men would a had a heck of a time gettin' Hank Chambers to go willingly into a pine box," Earl said.

"Arlene had to be involved," Grayson said. "I think she saved a sedative syringe from Dr. Crum and pumped it into Chambers when he wasn't looking."

I chewed my lip. "Why?"

"Chambers had just divorced," Wells said. "He was actually planning on marrying Arlene. He'd already changed the beneficiary on his life insurance policy to her."

"That meant Chambers had to die for her to collect," I said.

"Right." Wells took a sip of water and continued. "Arlene met Samuel Simpson when she called around for cheap ways to bury Lester's body. Samuel and she worked out some kind of deal, for love, money, whatever. But then Jake got involved and wanted his cut. Again, for love or money, I'm not sure at this point."

My nose crinkled. "But back at the cabin, Arlene was arguing with Samuel Simpson as if she hated him."

Grayson snorted. "Maybe because she figured he would end up being just like Lester, only with worse breath."

"Maybe," I said. "Or maybe she just wanted to break free of the whole prepper scene."

"Why?" Wells asked.

I shrugged. "Think about it from Arlene's perspective. What would be the use of surviving in a world with no gel nails or peroxide?"

"Or cosmetic procedures," Crum said, walking up to the table.

"What's up, Doc?" Earl said. "Thanks for the staples." He lifted his bangs to reveal his Frankenstein starter set.

Crum was eyeing me and Grayson. The look on his face made my gut flop. He didn't appear to be the bearer of good news.

"What have you been able to find out?" I asked as he took a seat in the chair at the end of the booth. I could barely see him over the mountain of chicken bones on the table.

A waitress came over. "One more order of wings," Dr. Crum said, "and a beer. A *big* beer."

I glanced over at Grayson. His eyes met mine. He pursed his lips.

"Let me start with the good news first," Crum said. "Jenkins' brain biopsy showed no signs of transmissible spongiform encephalopathy." He glanced over at Earl. "That means no zombie deer disease."

I shot Grayson a small, hopeful smile.

"But it's too soon to tell about Arlene," Crum said.

"It's got to be zombie deer disease," Garth said. "What else could make those dingbats start living the *la vida loca?*"

"You of all people should know the answer to that," Crum said, staring at him sourly.

Garth frowned. "What are you talking about, Doc?"

"You smoke weed," Crum said. "Hank Chambers came to the hospital higher than a kite on Mars."

Garth blanched. "I've been known to inhale, sure. But I never stripped naked and climbed a water tower."

"I know," Crum said. "And that got me to thinking, what would make someone do that?"

"Zombie deer meat," Earl said.

"Thanks for that suggestion," Crum said tiredly. "However, I may have another explanation."

"What?" I asked.

"Embalming fluid."

"What?" I asked again, nearly choking on my iced tea.

Crum blew out a breath. "You see, when Chambers' blood tested positive for marijuana, I searched his clothes and tested the stub I found in his pocket. It came back positive for methanol, formaldehyde, and ethanol. Embalming fluid."

"So?" I asked.

"Those are the same basic ingredients in the street drug, PCP."

"Would that explain his crazy behavior?" Wells asked. "The man was talking to a *skull*."

"Yes, it would," Crum said. "Typical effects include both visual and auditory hallucinations. So, more than likely, in Chambers' mind, Lester's severed head was talking back to him."

"I'd loved to have heard *that* conversation," Grayson said.

"What about climbing a water tower?" Wells asked.

"Actually, it makes perfect sense, now that I think about it," Crum said. "People under the influence of PCP report feelings of invincibility, euphoria, and an overwhelming desire to disrobe."

"What about archery?" Earl asked.

Crum ignored him and turned to Garth. "It also gives some people a strong distaste for meat. Didn't you say you're a vegetarian?"

Garth nearly choked on his beer. "Sometimes. But you just saw me eat a chicken wing!" He shot a glance at his brother. "I swear, Jimmy. I've got nothing to do with this. I didn't even sell them a brownie!"

Wells frowned. "I believe you. And I guess we can all think of a few people who might be able to get their hands on some embalming fluid."

Chapter Fifty-Eight

It was Tuesday morning, and we'd survived another night at the Wells' friendly neighborhood doomsday compound.

"You know, I think I'm going to miss all this junk," Grayson said.

I peered out the window of the RV at the rusted hull of a harvest-gold washing machine. A small tree had sprouted in its drum.

My eyebrows furrowed to a point. "Why would you miss camping in a junkyard?"

Grayson set his coffee mug on the counter. "Think about it. It's the perfect camouflage."

Given the condition of the RV's exterior, Grayson's statement was one of the few that had made real sense in the past couple of days.

A knock on the door saved me from having to reply. I opened it to find Officer Wells nodding at me.

"Morning. Coffee?" I asked.

Wells shot me a grateful smile. "Sure. I could drink a cup."

"Come in. Have a seat," Grayson called out.

Wells ambled inside and slid into the banquette. I handed him a steaming cup of coffee.

"What's up?" I asked.

The young cop shifted in his seat. "Before you two left, I wanted to let you know that Crum called me. The meat from Jenkins' cabin tested negative for chronic wasting disease."

I gasped. "So ... we're in the clear?"

"Looks like," Wells said.

"That's great!" I patted Wells on the shoulder and smiled at Grayson. He winked and gave me a subtle nod.

"From what I've been able to gather, Samuel Simpson and Arlene are the masterminds of this whole mess," Wells said.

"What's going to happen to them?" I asked.

"Simpson confessed to tripping out Arlene with embalming fluid-laced joints. But we're still not sure whose idea it was to bury Hank Chambers alive."

"Maybe you can get that snake to squeeze the truth out of 'em," Earl said, emerging from the bathroom.

Wells shook his head. "Since Chambers is still alive, and you three decided not to press charges for false imprisonment, Arlene might get to take that trip to the Poconos after all—with Chambers, one of the Simpsons, or whoever."

I shook my head. *Now that's what you call spoiled for choice. Not.*

Wells' police radio crackled.

"I better take this," he said and got up from the table. He shook hands with Grayson and me. "It's been weird, but I have to say, it's still been a pleasure meeting you all."

"We feel the same," Grayson said. "Take care and be safe."

"You, too." Wells smiled, then disappeared out the door.

"I guess I better be takin' off directly myself," Earl said. He turned to Grayson. "Before I do, can you answer me something, EB?"

Grayson shot him a look. "EB? You think I'm an extraterrestrial being?"

"Huh?" Earl's eyebrows converging below his staple line. "Well, there's a thought. But nah. I meant Encyclopedia Britannica. On account a you got all that crazy knowledge up in your brain."

"Oh." Grayson's enigmatic smile faded a notch. "What do you want to know?"

"All these prepper fellers we got tangled up with. They called themselves mercenaries. But as far as I could tell, there weren't 'nary a mercy among 'em. Would you say that's ironical or apropos?"

Grayson's right eyebrow shot up. He gave me a weird glance, then stood up and patted Earl on the shoulder. "Some questions just don't have any clear-cut answers, Earl." He nodded toward the restroom. "You done in there?"

"Yeah."

"Take care. Hope to see you soon, as far as you know."

Earl smiled. "You, too."

I looked up at my bear of a cousin. "Thanks for coming. You really helped us out."

"I dunno about that, Bobbie. I think I might a just got in the way. You had to save my hide more'n once."

I grinned. "You saved mine back."

Earl smiled. "Bobbie, I think you might a found where you belong."

I frowned. "You mean with Grayson? For the umpteenth time, Earl, we're just friends."

"That's not what Grandma Selma said."

My eyes bulged. "Don't tell me you're seeing ghosts!"

"Nah. I'm talking about that dream you told me about. You know, where she was in the coffin with you, stirring that pot of poop."

"Are you saying I'm stirring up crap?"

Earl blanched. "What? Heck, no!"

"What then?"

"In your dream, Granny offered you a spoonful, didn't she?"

"Yeah."

"I think she's tellin' you not to poop where you eat."

My jaw flexed. "Ugh! Earl, Grayson and I are just business partners!"

Earl nodded at me skeptically. "Well, it might be good to keep it that way. 'Cause, like I said, I think you're damned good."

I cringed and stared at the floor. "At messing things up? Yeah, I'm good at that all right."

"No, Bobbie." Earl took my chin in his huge hand and gently tugged my face upward until my eyes met his. "You're good at being an investigator. It's your calling. I can just feel it."

"Really?" My eyes filled with tears. "Like yours is to be a mechanic?"

Earl shrugged. "Yeah. For now. But life don't stay the same forever. You know that, cuz"

I smiled. "I know. Keep the garage afloat for me, will you?"

Earl nodded. "You know I will."

I thought Earl would turn and go. But he just stood there, staring at me expectantly. Finally, he winked and said, "Come on. Say it."

"Say what?"

He grinned. "You know what."

I laughed. "Earl, you're fired."

He snorted. "Ahh, now *that's* what I been missin'."

I smiled. "Speaking of missing, I want to give you back Lucky Red."

Earl frowned. "You sure?"

"Yeah." I grabbed the ball cap from atop the ugly alien lamp. "My hair's growing in, and ET doesn't like being affiliated with the tobacco industry."

Earl shot me a look. "Ok. Whatever that means. You take care now, Bobbie."

"You, too, Earl."

As he stepped out the door, Earl turned and waved to the little green lizard in the terrarium. "Bye, Gizzard." He winked at me, then squeezed his big frame out the door. Right before he closed it, I heard him say, "Bye, Garth!"

A moment later, the door opened again. A beaver with a blond mullet stuck his head in and grinned at me.

"Just came by to say goodbye," Garth said. "It's been a pleasure, Pandora. Where's Mr. Gray?"

I nodded toward the bathroom. "Indisposed."

Garth smiled and shook his head wistfully. "They say even the great ones do it. Tell him goodbye for me, will you?"

"Sure."

"I'll miss you most of all," Garth said, looking down at my breeding-stock hips.

"Right," I said, and closed the door.

With Grayson in the shower, I finally had a moment to text Beth-Ann. I picked up my cell phone and looked at the date. I smiled. I'd survived beyond the expiration date she'd predicted. I tapped a message into the phone.

It's Tuesday and I'm still alive.

A few seconds later, my phone chirped with her reply.

Glad to hear it. Now call me today or I'm going to track you down and kill you myself.

I grinned and gave her a call.

Chapter Fifty-Nine

"Breeder hips," I said to Grayson as he came out of the bathroom. "All of this craze about breeder hips. I just don't understand preppers."

"You and Arlene have that in common. Embrace your similarities."

I gave Grayson a dirty look. "I've got nothing in common with Arlene Jenkins or *any* of those other guys."

"I wouldn't be so sure. From the stories I heard, you and Lester appeared to have shared a certain propensity for getting drunk and—"

I slapped a hand over Grayson's mouth. "If what you're about to say has anything to do with that night at the campfire, please don't tell me."

Grayson grinned. "Have it your way. What say we have one more cup of coffee and hit the road. You ready?"

"Am I *ever*."

THE CHAIN LINK GATE swung open with a high-pitched *squeal*. "Thank you for your hospitality, Operative Garth," Grayson said into the intercom. "We'll be in touch."

"That would be awesome cool," Garth's voice crackled over the speaker.

Grayson hit the gas, and we sputtered down the dirt driveway in reverse. As he maneuvered the RV onto the paved road, I looked over at him and grinned mischievously.

"What?" he asked, shifting into first gear.

I stifled a smirk. "Sorry your theory about a half-goat, half-man didn't *pan* out."

Grayson shook his head and groaned.

I laughed. "Come on, Grayson. You *had* to have seen that one coming."

Grayson sighed. "I wasn't expecting a sneak attack from my own partner."

Partner. I like the sound of that.

I sat back and watched through the window as the occasional trailer peeked out from amongst the palmettos and pine trees. We rode on in silence until the sign for the interstate loomed ahead.

"So, where to now?" I asked.

Grayson grinned and waggled his eyebrows. "Well, seeing as how we're both still practically bald, it would be the perfect time to join the Hari Krishnas."

I laughed. "You're aware that I now know how to kill you with a Tootsie Pop, right?"

He smirked. "You got any left?"

I fished in my purse and handed him a green sucker. I unwrapped a blue one, stuck it in my mouth, and tossed the wrapper onto the floorboard. Grayson neatly folded his wrapper and tucked it in the ashtray.

OCD freak.

Grayson shifted the Tootsie Pop to his left cheek. "Okay, now I've got something for you."

"What?"

Grayson reached into his shirt pocket and pulled out a silver badge. "Here," he said, handing it to me. "I think you've earned it."

I grinned and grabbed the badge. My smile faded. "This says *Official Donut V.I.P.*"

Grayson shrugged. "Hey, you've got to start somewhere."

I blew out a sigh. Becoming a private eye was a lot harder than I thought it would be. But it had its perks. According the badge, I was now an official V.I.P.

"You ready for your next assignment?" Grayson asked.

"Sure. What is it?" I asked, pinning the badge to my purse.

"Your pick. At the moment, I've got reports about vanishing vets in New Port Richey, or a killer tomato in Ruskin."

I looked up at the fluffy clouds in the sky for an answer.

Hey. You up there. I need a sign.

In the distant blue horizon loomed a behemoth strawberry—Plant City's world-famous water tower. I smiled and turned to Grayson.

"Is a tomato a fruit or a vegetable?"

Grayson shot me a curious glance. "A fruit. Why?"

"I've dealt with enough fruits for the time being. Let's go find some missing vets."

"East it is," Grayson said, and turned right toward I-275.

The End

Ready for more Freaky Florida Investigations?
Check out the next episode, Oral Robbers!
https://www.amazon.com/dp/B081VS4S77

I HOPE YOU ENJOYED Dr. Prepper. If you did, it would be freaking fantastic if you would post a review on Amazon, Goodreads and/or Book-Bub. You'll be helping me keep the series going! Thanks in advance for being so awesome!

https://www.amazon.com/dp/194998902X#customerReviews

Get a Free Gift!

Don't miss another sneak preview, sale, or new release of *Freaky Florida Investigations!* Sign up for my newsletter for insider tips. I'll send you a free copy of the *Chronicles of Florida Woman* as a welcome gift!

https://dl.bookfunnel.com/ikfes8er75

For more laughs and discussions with fellow fans, follow me on Facebook, Amazon and BookBub:

Facebook:

https://www.facebook.com/valandpalspage/

Amazon:

https://www.amazon.com/-/e/B06XKJ3YD8

BookBub:

https://www.bookbub.com/search/authors?search=margaret%20lashley

Where do Drex and Grayson go from here?
Find out in Oral Robbers!

https://www.amazon.com/dp/B081VS4S77

I HOPE YOU ENJOY THE following excerpt from:
Oral Robbers: Freaky Florida Investigations Book 3

Oral Robbers Excerpt:

Chapter One

"Hold still, Drex. And take that Tootsie Pop out of your mouth."

"Why?"

I glared into the eyes of Nick Grayson. He was my boss, private-eye instructor, and current owner of the world's cheesiest moustache.

We were in a sleazy motel off US 19, just outside New Port Richey. I was in bed, propped up on mysteriously lumpy pillows. Grayson, a physicist turned conspiracy-theory nut, was hovering over me, pasting electrodes onto my scalp.

His eyes gleamed maniacally as he hooked me up to his electroencephalogram machine. His plan was to scare whatever miniscule amount of wits I had left right out of my half-shaved noggin.

Fun times.

The last time Grayson strapped me to his EEG contraption, he'd shocked me to the core with a video of gray-skinned aliens being ambushed by military-style Rambos. After the mysterious militia freed three kids from glass holding tubes, they'd freed the aliens of their oversized heads.

Not pretty. Not pretty at all.

As I lay there, I still had no idea whether that bizarre video was real or not. I wasn't sure Grayson knew, either. And, for the time being, it didn't matter. Half an hour ago, I'd experienced something that had scared the bejeebers out of me even more—and it hadn't come from Grayson's test program.

I sat up in bed and frowned at Grayson. "Why can't I keep the Tootsie Pop?"

Grayson glanced up from fiddling with a knob on the EEG monitor. "You might choke on it. Besides, it's a crutch, Drex."

I scowled. "A crutch?"

Grayson locked his mesmerizing green eyes on mine. Dressed all in black, the wiry, fortyish man with the washboard abs had a mysterious hold on me. At times, I wanted to kiss him. Other times, I wanted to run from him—screaming. But most times, I felt compelled to follow his lead, glued to his side by my own twisted curiosity.

"An oral fixation," he said, studying me like I was his favorite new lab rat. "Like smoking. Or chewing gum. Typically brought on by insufficient breastfeeding during infancy."

My eyes narrowed. "Are you saying I have *mommy* issues?"

He smirked. "If the sucker fits ...."

I shot Grayson some side-eye. "That's rich coming from a guy with two navels. As far as *I* know, *you* came out of a test tube."

Grayson's eyebrows wagged below his stubble-covered head, which was usually covered by a black fedora. "An excellent argument for why I *don't* have mommy issues, I'd say. Now lose the Tootsie Pop and lay down."

I plucked the sucker from my mouth and put it in an ashtray on the nightstand. Cringing with disgust, I cautiously laid back onto the mystery-stain pillows. "Satisfied?"

"Yes." Grayson glanced at the used red Tootsie Pop. "But if *you* were, you wouldn't need *that* thing."

I scowled. "Just fire up your gross-out program before I change my mind."

Grayson's right cheek dimpled, a sure sign that a deviant smile lurked beneath his bushy black moustache. He snatched my Tootsie Pop from the ashtray and stuck it in his mouth.

Gross.

His right cheek bulged as he clicked a key on his laptop computer, then handed it to me. The screen blinked to life in my hands. On it, a yellow emoji face grinned above the words, "Welcome to My World!"

The ludicrous cliché was so on target I nearly laughed out loud. Grayson certainly lived in another world, all right. And, like some sort of pseudo-Stockholm Syndrome victim, I was slowly becoming part of it.

I'd just finished the first two weeks of my internship with Grayson. It had been a crazy ride—akin to costarring in a low-budget remake of *The X-Files*.

In redneck Florida.

In a rundown RV.

Let's just say, I wasn't expecting a call from Hollywood anytime soon.

"Okay. Here we go," Grayson said.

I glanced over at him. Something about his expression triggered my fight-or-flight response.

But it was way too late to make a run for it now.

Besides, it wasn't exactly like my life was brimming with other possibilities. Who else but Grayson would've taken on a reluctant, wet-behind-the-ears private-eye wannabe like me?

I'd been under the influence of vodka when I'd ordered a detective correspondence course from a late-night infomercial. And I'd been so angry I couldn't see straight when I'd handed over my family's auto repair business to my cousin Earl.

Suffice it to say, at 37, I was a tad behind schedule on my plan to retire at 45. Broke, angry, and recovering from being shot in the head, I'd been headed for a meltdown.

Instead, a meltdown found me.

Grayson's arrival at my auto-repair shop in his busted Winnebago had been the catalyst that had spawned the perfect storm—a tornado of emotions powerful enough to blow the remnants of my old life to smithereens. When he'd offered to provide the two years of training I needed to become a real private investigator, I'd jumped at the chance—and into his RV.

And now, here I was, in a sleazy hotel room, my shaved scalp glued by electrodes to a mind-altering machine invented by, quite possibly, a madman.

But, in all honesty, nobody had forced me to drink Grayson's crazy Kool-Aid. I'd made my very own pitcherful, spiked it with vodka, and willingly downed every last drop.

I blew out a sigh, slapped on a determined face, and gave Grayson a thumb's up. He nodded, then turned his attention back to the display panel on the EEG machine.

I glanced down at the computer in my lap and braced for impact. My job was to observe the macabre images that would soon be popping up on its screen. Grayson's task was to monitor my alpha brainwave activity during the test. The more alpha waves I produced, the more relaxed my nervous system was.

The concept behind Grayson's self-designed program was to help him—and now *me*—gain control over the physical reactions any sane person instinctively experienced when encountering the weird, the freaky, and the blatantly bizarre.

As Grayson had so artfully enumerated, "Screaming, pissing one's pants, fainting, and/or running for one's life aren't particularly helpful tactics when it comes to investigating unexplained phenomena."

He was right. Thanks to his tutelage, I'd already gained first-hand experience with all of the above. As a result, I was now eager to up my game.

"I'm ready," I said. "Let her rip."

Grayson nodded. "Okay. Here we go."

The screen on the laptop blinked. The yellow smiley face disappeared. In its place came the image of a cute, golden-haired little girl prancing in a field of daisies.

"Good. The baseline's set," Grayson said.

The next image appeared. It was the little girl again. This time, her mouth morphed into an evil grin, complete with a set of blood-dripping Dracula fangs.

My pulse quickened. I glanced up at Grayson.

He was staring at the monitor. His eye ticked like he was experiencing the early stages of Turrets.

My alpha waves must've taken a hit.

I took a deep breath to calm myself. A moment later, the screen changed to a vintage, black-and-white video clip of *Nosferatu,* rising straight up from his coffin like the world's creepiest post-mortem erection.

Geez. Nosferatu doesn't mean "hideously ugly vampire" for nothing.

My heart skipped a beat. I breathed through it.

"Good," Grayson said, his eyes glued to the EEG display.

The image on the screen switched back to full color. A green-skinned, yellow-eyed vampire lunged toward me, snapping his bloody fangs at me like a ravenous piranha.

Breathe deep. It isn't real.

"You're not telling yourself it isn't real again, are you?" Grayson asked.

I flinched. "Why would you say that?"

"Because your alpha waves are remaining unusually high. Either you're mastering this, or you're still in denial."

I bit my lip. "What's so wrong with denial?"

Grayson eyed me. "Well, for one thing, in the case of a *real* encounter, it could get you killed."

I rolled my eyes at the ceiling. "I mean *besides* that."

Grayson frowned. "Don't you value your life?"

Maybe I would if I actually had *one.*

I shrugged. "Sure."

"Humph," Grayson grunted, and turned back to the EEG monitor.

In a way, I envied Grayson. The man had a distinct mission in life. He was absolutely certain that unknown creatures were hiding out in the nooks and crannies of rural Florida, and that, one day, we would be the ones to prove it.

In the past two weeks, we'd definitely shared some undeniably odd experiences. But whether what we'd encountered had been real or merely hoaxes, hallucinations, or the residual effects of brain damage, was still up for debate as far as I was concerned.

I'd yet to come across anything I could, with absolute certainty, say was "the real deal."

But then again, my life to date had presented me with very few "real deals." Instead, I'd honed my cynical chops on dead-end jobs, cheating boyfriends, and a mother who'd scammed me out of knowing my real father.

And now, here I was, hitching my wagon to a man who got his jollies searching for freaks of nature.

The irony made me nearly laugh out loud.

Was *I* Grayson's latest freak, or was *he* mine?

Get Oral Robbers Now!
https://www.amazon.com/dp/B081VS4S77
Follow me on Amazon to be notified of all my new releases:
https://www.amazon.com/-/e/B06XKJ3YD8
Thank you!

More Freaky Florida Investigations

by Margaret Lashley
Moth Busters
Dr. Prepper
Oral Robbers
Ape Shift
Scatman Dues
Smoked Mullet
Half Crocked

"I want to believe, but I mean ... really?"

Bobbie Drex